UNFORESEEN

A Green Bayou Novel Book Four

Rhonda R. Dennis

UNFORESEEN
A GREEN BAYOU NOVEL
BOOK FOUR

Cover Photo/Cover Design: Brandi Money Photography

ISBN: 1478387491
ISBN-13:   978-1478387497

ACKNOWLEDGMENTS

As usual, big thanks to the Preview Squad! Big thanks to Cheryl at Fairfax Plantation for making our cover shoot overnighter so special! To my editor: you'll never know how honored I am to have you on this journey with me. Much love!

Crystal, this one is dedicated to you. Thank you for being a fan, cheerleader, sounding board, and most of all—a friend. May you forever rest in peace.

1

Panic gripped me like a vice. Each shallow, ragged breath was a struggle. Thirty seconds prior, Armageddon struck Bienville, but now, the sudden silence was overwhelming. *Why is it so quiet? I died. That has to be it. My luck has finally run out.* Reigning in the fear, I forced one eye open. No bright lights or pearly gates, just the faint glow from an IV pump across the room. Opening the other eye, I unfurled from the tight ball I'd contorted myself into. My body trembled uncontrollably.

"Colin?" I softly called with an unsteady voice.

"I'm here," he said, pushing away the stretcher that had rolled between us so he could stand.

"Are we okay?" I ran my hands over my body, assessing for damage.

"I'm pretty sure we're okay. Do you see anyone else?" he asked.

"Chuck! Chuck, are you okay? Where are you?" I yelled, my eyes still trying process the devastation.

"I think so. I'm over here," Chuck, my paramedic partner, said while dusting himself off. "Wow! Now Emily Boudreaux gets to add natural disasters to her repertoire."

"Shut it, Chuck!" I warned, accepting Colin's extended hand. "This isn't the time or place to pick on me."

"Awww, come on! We're alive!" Chuck closed the gap between us to squeeze me in a tremendous bear hug.

He slowly rocked from side to side. "Oh, sweet lovin', we're alive!"

"Doctor Richardson, everyone's fine over here, but I really need to see you for a moment, please," one of the nurses yelled from across the room.

"Are you sure you're both okay?" Colin asked.

"Don't worry, we're fine. Go check the others," I mumbled, still trying to wiggle out of Chuck's tight embrace.

"I saw you with your cell phone earlier. Were you able to call out? Do you have a signal? I need to check on Bridget and Samantha," Chuck said, releasing me to hold his phone high in the air.

"Wait! I had one right before the tornado hit! Maybe I still have one," I said excitedly. The excitement was short lived. "Damn, it's gone now," I answered with a frown. I wondered if my text message made it before the cell phone towers went down.

"My signal's gone, too. We should try to get out of here. There's no telling how bad things are out there. I'm sure they need our help." He tugged on the large, wooden door of the x-ray room we were trapped in.

"Wait, Chuck. If you're having that much trouble opening it, something's probably wedged against the latch. You're gonna wear yourself out trying to pull it open. Why don't we wait for Colin, then the three of us can try to open it?" I suggested.

"No, it's okay. I think it's starting to move," Chuck said, once again jiggling the handle.

"I still think you should wait," I warned.

"The damn thing's just jammed, Emily! I bet I can get it open." He raised his leg, giving the door a series of swift kicks. Loud moaning and groaning emanated from somewhere above us.

"Would you stop kicking and listen!" I anxiously pointed upwards.

"What the... Watch out!" Chuck yelled.

I froze. Chuck shoved me and I went reeling to the floor just as a massive oak tree thundered through the roof. Leaves, mud, branches, and debris showered down.

Once again struggling to catch my breath, I couldn't help but wonder what I'd done to deserve all the close calls I'd had lately. I had been kidnapped, held hostage, stalked, tortured, nearly raped, and lost two loves since returning home to Green Bayou. The natural disaster should've seemed inevitable.

Stories of my misfortune spread very quickly throughout Atchafalaya Parish. Word was many side bets were being wagered at fishing camps, barrooms, and back porches about when and where the next big incident starring Emily Boudreaux would occur. I wondered who'd be profiting off this tornado.

Though I experienced a lot of tragedy and despair, things weren't *all* bad. There was Holden Dautry, the Sheriff of Atchafalaya Parish, and possibly the most gorgeous man to walk the face of the Earth. He was a man's man with wonderfully broad shoulders and a tall, strapping physique. His dark hair had the slightest sprinkling of gray at the temples and his intense, sapphire-colored eyes made me tingle whenever he looked my way. I was supposed to marry Holden, but the engagement ended after a series of regrettable misunderstandings. Our relationship was now strained and complicated, to say the least.

Holden's best friend, Jackson Sonnier, was fairly new to town. When Holden was pressured to recruit a new Chief Deputy, Jackson's experience in the Army and the FBI made him a logical choice. Though he was as broad as Holden, at six feet tall, he was a couple inches shorter. His skin was fair, his hair strawberry-blonde, and his eyes a unique, bluish-green color. It took a while for me to trust him because his deceased brother, who was once a Sheriff's deputy, had kidnapped and tortured me.

After proving that he was the polar opposite of his brother, Jackson and I grew closer. In a moment of revenge-fueled bad judgment, I slept with him. Holden found out and gave me an ultimatum: two weeks to fully commit or we were done. As much as I loved Holden, there was some doubt. *Could we be as great as we once were?* Holden wasn't the type to simply forgive and forget. Atonement I could handle, but eternal penance wasn't what I wanted in a relationship.

The quandary—do I take a chance with Holden or start fresh with Jackson? Kind, thoughtful, and handsome Jackson was the type of man I'd long for if Holden hadn't come into my life. Right before the tornado struck, I asked for a sign to show me which man I should be with, Mother Nature provided in a big way!

A simple, flashing neon that said "Pick Holden" or "Jackson's the One" would've worked. The monstrous tornado that ripped through the area that late September afternoon was overkill. Intense fear and impending doom were great motivators. My decision was a no-brainer. The loud beeping coming from one of the machines pulled me from my thoughts.

"Chuck! Colin! Anyone!" I yelled between coughing spells. Even though the bulk of the tree had missed me, my face and upper body bore cuts, scratches, and gouges. I wiped the blood trickling down my forehead on my sleeve before pawing through the wreckage. The beeping stopped and though it was muffled, Colin yelled that he was safe on other side of the room. Chuck didn't answer. I quickly dug through the thick layers of branches, leaves, and rubble. My heart sank when I saw Chuck's boots jutting from underneath a hunk of ceiling tile. I couldn't bear to lose another partner!

"No! Chuck!" I cried, stumbling to get to him. "Talk to me! Please be okay!"

"Don't freak. I'm okay, but my leg is caught," Chuck said, his voice riddled with pain. I was slinging the rubble off of him as fast as I could. Sure enough, a large tree limb kept him pinned.

"I need to get Colin. You stay right here."

"And just where do you think I'll be going?" he said, wincing.

"Hey, I'm supposed to be the smart ass. Cut it out." I softly patted his chest.

Holding on to some of the branches to keep my balance, I started the climb to the other side of the room. A voice called my name from up above. I stopped mid-climb and looked up—nothing but a gaping hole and gray sky. *Oh geez, hearing things couldn't be a good sign!*

"Emily! Where are you, Emily!"

"Jackson?" I yelled toward the voice that was now coming from the other side of the door. "Is that you?"

"Yes, are you hurt?"

"I'm okay, but I'm not sure about everyone else, yet."

"Stay there! You're not going to be able to get out this way. There's some kind of machine blocking the door. Give me a minute and I'll come and get you!" he said.

"Okay, be careful, Jackson! Colin, where are you?" I yelled.

"I'm trapped back here, but we're all fine!" I heard him answer from behind a pile of rubble. "What about you? Are you okay? It might take me a while to dig past this wall of debris."

"I'm okay. Chuck's pinned by a tree limb, though."

"Hang in there. I'll try to get through to you as fast as I can," he assured. I carefully started making my way back to Chuck.

"Emily! Heads up!" Jackson called through the opening in the roof.

"What in the hell are you doing up there? That roof can't be stable!" I fussed.

"I told you that I was coming to get you." He tossed down the slack from the rope he held in his hand. I had to admit, it was a pleasant sight to behold when he turned backwards to start a slow descent down the trunk of the tree. I held my breath until both of his feet were firmly on the ground.

"Jackson! What's wrong with you? Are you crazy? You could've killed yourself coming in like that! Never mind that, I'm so glad you're here!" I cried, holding him tightly.

"I was worried about you. You're full of blood, Emily. Where's it coming from?" he asked, anxiously pulling away to get a better look at my injuries.

"I'm fine. The tree branches scratched me. Chuck needs help." I pushed his hands away from my face to point. Jackson moved towards Chuck.

"It's pretty big, but I think I might be able to lift it high enough for you to slide out. Are you ready for me to try?" he asked.

"Anything to stop this pain." Chuck grimaced.

"You'll have to pull him out once I get the limb up. Are you up to it, Emily?"

"I think so. I'll do my best," I answered.

"I might be able to help with my good leg," Chuck said.

"Okay, everyone ready? On three," Jackson said, squatting into position. "One, two, THREE!" Between my tugging, Chuck's scooting, and Jackson's brute strength, he was freed. Seconds afterward, Colin broke through the debris pile. He immediately went to work assessing Chuck's injury. I moved Jackson to the side for a private conversation.

"How bad is it out there?" I whispered.

"It's pretty bad, Em," he answered. My lips were pursed together tightly in an effort to keep the profanity-laden rant running through my head from seeping out of my mouth.

"I need to get out there. There's so much I need to do! I have to check on Bert, Connie, and Andre. What about Holden? Have you heard anything from him?" I rambled.

"Slow down and take a deep breath. DeSoto bore the brunt of the storm. Green Bayou had minimal damage and here in Bienville, it appears as though this area was the only one struck. I heard from Bert. He and his family are fine. Our radios are still working, but our headquarters in DeSoto was heavily damaged. They know that Holden was inside when the tornado hit, but they haven't found him yet. The prison was also damaged. The injured inmates are being transferred to a hospital in a neighboring parish, and the others are being transferred to holding cells at the Green Bayou substation. There have been no fatalities reported so far. I'm still waiting on a final headcount," he explained.

"Can you get me to your headquarters? I might be able to help out," I said.

"I'll do what I can, but are you sure you want to go? Your partner might need you."

"Colin's got Chuck and all of the other injuries are minor. I'll be more helpful out there than in here," I reasoned. Jackson nodded and began fashioning a harness out of rope. I stepped into the loops, and once he was satisfied the harness would hold my weight, he began to climb the fallen tree.

"You're sure you want to do this?" he repeated.

"I'm sure I want to help, it's the getting out of here that worries me. All I'm doing is climbing a tree, right?" I asked, seeking encouragement to face my fear of heights.

"Just stay right behind me and you'll be fine," Jackson assured.

"Colin, I'll be sure to send help," I said, grasping onto a branch and starting the ascent.

"You be careful out there," Colin said, ripping away Chuck's shredded pant leg. Though Chuck remained silent, I could tell that he was fighting tremendous pain. My heart hurt for him.

I may have had confidence when starting the climb, but the higher I got, the shakier I became. My legs quivered like jelly so I stopped and drew in a deep breath.

"Hey, you," Jackson said with a reassuring smile. "Look up at me, don't look down. I've got you. You won't fall. I promise."

I mustered a half-smile before continuing up the tree. Relief flooded through me when I finally stood on the roof. It was premature. Shock and disbelief quickly took its place. The tornado had left a clearly defined path of devastation that extended as far as the eye could see. Miles of matted down cane showed the exact route of the twister. The Bienville station was gone. All that was left was the concrete slab, yet the ambulance and our cars were still there, seemingly unscathed. The same couldn't be said for the cars in the hospital parking lot. They were scattered around like toys.

My mouth fell open when I saw the gaping hole a fallen oak tree had left at the far corner of the parking lot. Half the hospital was gone. Not destroyed—gone. I choked back tears of gratitude. Thank God we'd made it to the x-ray department! As appreciative as I was, there was no more time for reflecting, it was time to get to work.

"Colin, I'm sorry, but I can't get you any supplies right now. You're going to have to work with what you've got," I yelled down once I was sure that my voice was steady.

"I'll manage just fine. Don't worry about Chuck; he's going to be okay. Please be extra careful out there, okay?"

"I promise that I will!" I yelled to Colin. "I'm ready to do this, Jackson. How do we get down from here?" I shrugged.

"Not a problem; follow me." He moved to the far edge of the building.

"So that's what happened to the roof of the ESMR station." I fought off vertigo while gingerly peering over the edge to see the roof of our station flush with the hospital wall.

"It's still intact and structurally sound. All you have to do is hop down and slide to the ground."

"Oh, that's all? Great!" I said sarcastically.

Jackson smiled. "I'll help you. Watch me." He vaulted the few feet down to the peak then held out his arms to steady himself. Once he was confident that his footing was solid, he stretched his arms toward me. "See? It's nothing. Jump and I'll catch you."

"Uh, what if I don't want to?" I asked, nervously tugging at my lower lip.

"Come on, you'll be fine," Jackson encouraged.

"Couldn't I just dangle over the edge until my feet touch?"

"You'll tear up your stomach that way. What's wrong? Don't you don't trust me?" he asked.

"I trust you, it's me. You know my track record isn't the best."

"I wouldn't let you try it if I wasn't sure you'd be okay. Have some confidence, Em," he insisted.

I nodded, took a deep breath, and after four false starts, finally went for it. Ecstatic that I didn't go tumbling down the roof, I tightly wrapped my arms around Jackson's neck, joyously bouncing up and down. "I did it! You saw that, right? I made it!"

"Yes, I'm glad you did it, but you're choking me, Em." He coughed.

"I'm so sorry!" I quickly released my hold on him.

He gave me a strange look while rubbing his neck, but quickly shook it off to show me the best way to slide down the roof. Once we were on solid ground, I gave him a much gentler embrace.

"Thank you for coming to rescue me," I said softly.

"It's not the first time, and I'm pretty sure it won't be the last. I'm glad to do it." He reached up to tuck a stray lock of hair behind my ear. "You look so beaten up. Are you sure you're not hurting?"

"I'm fine. Let's get out of here. Where's your unit parked?" I asked, scanning the area.

He nodded his head in the general direction, and we carefully made our way over the piles of debris to get to it.

"Where were you when the tornado hit?" I asked once we were on our way to DeSoto.

"On the highway between Green Bayou and Bienville."

"Did you see it?" I asked, opening a package of disposable wipes I found in the glove compartment.

"Yeah." He shuddered at the recollection.

I pulled the visor down to use the mirror and gasped at my reflection. No wonder Jackson was so concerned! I could've easily been an extra in a slasher film. Wiping away the dried blood was probably a mistake, because that's when the pain finally came.

"Are you sure you're okay?" Jackson asked, glancing my way.

"I'm sure. It looks worse than it is," I said, doing my best to ignore the stinging. "Do you know if your phone kept its service during the storm? Were you able to get text messages?"

"I'm not really sure. Why?" he asked.

"Just curious," I answered, examining my injuries.

He gave me a funny look and pulled the phone from his shirt pocket. "I'm guessing I kept my service. It's showing that I have some unread messages. Would you mind checking them for me?" He passed me the phone. Each time I tried, an error message came across the screen.

"I can't retrieve them. The system must be overloaded." I quickly passed the phone back to him.

"It's okay. I'll try later. Oh, man. That looks bad," Jackson said when we entered the outskirts of DeSoto.

The city may have had minimal damage, but the sheriff's department, which happened to be situated in a fairly remote area just outside of town, was destroyed. The closer we got to headquarters, the more debris we had to maneuver around. We slowly rode past the jail where I noticed a patrol car sitting in a gaping hole left in the prison wall. Heavily armed guards, some with K9's, patrolled the perimeter while deputies loaded prisoners into reinforced passenger vans. Jackson flipped through the channels on his radio.

"Charlie, this is Chief Deputy Sonnier. Are you guys okay?" he asked. One of the guards waved when he spotted Jackson's SUV and reached for the microphone that was clipped to his shoulder.

"10-4, Chief. As of now we have five unaccounted for, but we're still searching through the rubble. I'll update you as soon as new information becomes available," he responded.

"Thanks, Charlie. Keep up the good work."

"10-4, sir. Any word on the Sheriff yet?" Charlie asked.

"Negative. Heading that way now."

"10-4," Charlie said, throwing a quick salute before continuing his patrol. Jackson inched down the road. Cars from the department motor pool were tossed into the surrounding fields. The more devastation I saw, the straighter I sat in my seat. Somewhere along the way, I started picking at my nails.

"Oh, Jackson," I breathed when I finally saw where the main offices of the department used to stand. My hand flew to my mouth and tears threatened to spill from the corners of my eyes. I worked to choke them back. Fire trucks surrounded the rubble and several men and women could be seen sorting through the debris. Seeing the devastation up close made me fear the worst.

Jackson hadn't come to a complete stop when I flew from the SUV. He tried calling after me, but I was already running toward the scene. Grant, my extra-wide, extra-tall mentor and supervisor, used his body to block my path.

"Hold up there, kiddo!" he said with his deep, gravelly voice. His gigantic hand hooked me by the waist. "Those people are trained to do that, we're not. You're not going anywhere near that scene until we know it's safe."

Soon as he released me, I crossed my arms over my chest and stared him down. As usual, his hair was slicked straight back with gobs of gel. Obviously, not even a tornado could outmuscle Grant's hair products.

"I know we're not trained to do that stuff, but I can help find Holden. Don't try to stop me, Grant," I firmly insisted while trying to push past him.

He grasped my shoulder and spun me around. "No, *they're* going to find Holden. The only place you're going is to my truck so I can clean you up. And quit looking at me like that. You know your dirty looks don't intimidate me," he snapped, pointing to his SUV.

"I'm fine. I don't need patching up," I said defiantly.

"Emily, don't think that I'm above using brute force on you," he warned.

"Brute force." I laughed. "You wouldn't hurt a fly, Grant Johnson! You know it and I know it."

"It appears as though you know me too well, kiddo." He squinted his eyes. "So how about this? As your supervisor, I *order* you to come with me, and if you don't, I'll put you on immediate and indefinite suspension." His eyebrows shot high in the air and his hands rested on his hips.

I sighed. "Yes, you would do that, wouldn't you? Fine, you win. Where are you parked?" I begrudgingly asked.

"Right this way." He put his hand on the small of my back and led me to his SUV, then opened the back doors so I could sit in one of the rear-facing seats.

"Emily, some of these cuts are pretty deep," he said when he cleaned my face and neck. "What do you have on under that shirt?"

"A tank top," I answered.

"Good," he said, cutting away the polo shirt I wore as a uniform.

"Hey! What are you doing?" I fussed, pushing his hands away. Grant gave me a pair of eyes and I quickly quieted down.

"Damn, Emily," Jackson said when he joined us. Following his gaze, I turned to look at my arm and shoulder. Not only were they covered with jagged, little cuts, but the faint shadows of what would later become deep bruises were beginning to appear.

"A doctor should probably look at some of these lacerations," Grant remarked. As soon as he saw me opening my mouth to protest, he stopped me. "But, I know how obstinate you are. I'll use skin glue on your stubborn butt," he said, reaching in his bag for supplies. I couldn't help but smile.

"I love you, Grant," I said like a kid who'd gotten one over on a parent.

"Yeah, yeah, save it," he grumbled. He patched my wounds and was placing a bandage over a cut near my elbow when Jackson's radio went off.

"Chief, we need you at the main office," a voice urgently requested.

"10-4, I'm on my way," Jackson answered, starting to jog towards the debris pile.

"I'm going with you!" I yelled, trying to jump from Grant's SUV.

"Let him finish bandaging you up before you come," Jackson called over his shoulder.

"Chief, is that ESMR medic, Grant, still with you?" the voice said over the radio again.

"10-4," Jackson answered.

"Tell him we need him, too," the voice suggested.

No one could stop me at that point. I was in a full run and had passed Jackson before he or Grant had time to protest. Jackson easily caught up with me, snagging me around the waist.

"Jackson, put me down!" I yelled, my legs still pumping.

"Emily, you heard Grant. You can't go charging in there!" Jackson hands were on my shoulders after he placed me back onto the ground.

"Please promise me you'll let me know what's going on!" I panted, trying to catch my breath.

"I promise. Stay with Grant!" he said, quickly kissing my forehead before rushing off.

Grant walked up beside me, two medic bags slung across his shoulders and a long, rigid spine board in his hand.

"Wait! Let me help you with that." I took one of the bags from him and we made our way to a spot just outside the debris pile.

16

Jackson stood on the mound of rubble that used to be headquarters, his eyes locked on the area below him. He squatted for a moment to talk to one of the firefighters deep in the crater, before coming to update us.

"They've dug a hole, but it isn't large enough for any of them to fit into. There's a male trapped down there, but we're not sure who he is or what condition he's in," Jackson explained.

"Let me try," I volunteered. Initially, Jackson shook his head, but after a few moments of mulling it over, he reconsidered.

"I wish there were another way, but you are a lot smaller than those guys. What do you think, Grant? Should we let her try?"

"I think she's a damn good medic. If it's safe enough, let her go."

"I can do it. Please let me try. I promise I won't take any unnecessary risks," I encouraged.

"Okay, follow me and step exactly where I step. No crazy acts of heroism. Understand?" he said, taking the medic bag from me.

"I understand and you have my word."

The closer we got to the rubble pile, the more my stomach tightened with apprehension. I peered into the hole, and it took a second for my brain to register that I was seeing a bloody torso. With Jackson's help, I gently wiggled my way into the opening. Since most of the victim's body was buried in debris, I followed the anatomy of his arm to slowly run my hands up his chest and neck. Though I couldn't see his face, there was no doubt it was Holden. I'd know that chest anywhere. My breath caught.

17

Carefully moving a piece of wood aside with my fingertips, I felt for a pulse, but couldn't find one. Time stood still. I prayed to feel even the faintest beat. At first I wasn't sure if it was just wishful thinking, but I felt something. His pulse was extremely weak, but it was definitely there!

"Get me some oxygen and have my IV set ups ready to go!" I yelled out of the hole. An oxygen mask was lowered down to me as I continued to carefully remove rubble from his face. I desperately fought the urge to cry.

"Holden! Holden, I'm here. It's Emily. We're working on getting you out of here and to the hospital so the doctors can fix you up. Stay with me, Holden," I said as I went to work. After placing the mask over Holden's bloody and battered face, I moved enough debris for one of the smaller firefighters to join me. We packaged Holden for transport and carefully lifted him to the waiting hands above.

Once Holden was in the back of the Medical Response's SUV, Grant insisted that I drive. I pleaded with him to let me continue with Holden's care, but he would hear none of it.

"I got this one, kiddo. Take a deep breath and drive carefully, you hear?" he asked.

I conceded without bickering. Time spent arguing with Grant was precious time that Holden would lose getting the treatment he needed. I gently closed the back doors and ran around to the driver's seat.

We arrived at DeSoto General Hospital within ten minutes, but all of the training in the world couldn't have prepared me for what was at the hospital.

"Jesus, Grant. Where do I go?" I asked.

Grant peeked out the back. Lines of ambulances, with wide-open doors, filled the ER ramp. Walking, wounded patients were everywhere. Some were screaming and yelling for help, while others moved around in zombie-like trances. Children clutched their blankets and dolls, searching for their parents.

"He'll never get treatment here, Grant," I said, backing down the drive. "I'll try Bayou Side Regional."

"Do it," Grant said, digging through the medic bag for more supplies. Bayou Side was worse than DeSoto General.

"Shit! Shit! Shit!" I yelled, slamming my fists into the steering wheel. "Does this radio have the Sheriff's department frequency?"

"Channel sixteen," Grant answered, shaking his head as he looked at the sight before us.

"ESMR medic Emily Boudreaux to Chief Deputy Sonnier," I said into the microphone.

"Sonnier here," he answered.

"I need you to pick up Dr. Richardson from Bienville. We're trying to find a hospital to accept the Sheriff, but they're overtaxed. I need a doctor, pronto. Standby for a drop-off location."

"I'm on it," Jackson said.

"How long do we have, Grant?"

"I'm not sure, kiddo. The sooner the better," he answered.

"Hold on," I warned, quickly turning the SUV around to head back to DeSoto General. "Chief, once you have Dr. Richardson, get him to Desoto General. Don't use the emergency entrance. Go the back way to the cafeteria side. I'll be near the bay doors where they accept deliveries."

"10-4, I'm coming into Bienville right now," he advised.

"Damn, he must be flying," Grant murmured. "What's the plan, Emily?"

"The ER's packed because people need a doctor. I'm providing a doctor to treat Holden, so all we need are some supplies and I'm going to take care of that right now. I won't be long." After backing the vehicle up the deserted ramp, I tried to lift the large, rolling bay door. It wouldn't budge. All of the other doors I tried were locked, so I ran to the front of the hospital. Taking advantage of the chaos, I easily wove my way through the crowds, snatching supplies as I ran through.

On my way to unlock the door, I noticed that the CEO's office was nearby and no light shined from inside. I jiggled the knob and was surprised when it turned. Sure enough, the office was empty. In an instant, I swiped everything off the desk and onto the floor. Draped sheets over the top made an impromptu hospital bed. I sprinted to the delivery door and was relieved to see that the only thing keeping it closed was a simple latch. I pulled the chain to open it then jumped from the loading dock onto the pavement.

"What's his status?" I breathlessly asked Grant as I threw open the back doors of the SUV. Holden had obviously taken a turn for the worse, and the shock of seeing him that way made my knees buckle. He had a tube in his throat to assist with breathing; his face and body were swollen to the point that he was nearly unrecognizable. I grasped the door for support, and then slid into the back of the truck so I could peek at the monitors.

"Don't you dare think of giving up, Holden! I'll drag a damn doctor out here if I have to, Grant! Don't you let him give up!" I yelled, dashing a tear from my eye and scrambling back outside. "Keep working on him. I'll be right back!"

I was about to leap onto the loading dock, but the sound of screeching wheels stopped me. Jackson's unit skidded in. They jumped out and Colin immediately went to work assessing Holden's injuries.

"I don't have privileges at this hospital, Emily. I don't know how much they'll let me do here," Colin remarked from the back of the SUV. He took the stethoscope from around his neck to listen to Holden's chest.

"Are you kidding me? Now's not the time to worry about protocol! Tell me what you need and I'll get it. Put all of the blame on me. Tell them I forced you to do it at gunpoint. I don't care! Just help him, Colin," I desperately pleaded.

"Of course I'll help, but I need an exam room, CAT scan, access to the lab, medical supplies, and there's a good chance he may need surgery, so I'll need a surgeon, and that's just to start," Colin said.

"Stop! Just follow me. I'll find a way to make it happen," I said, rushing through the door.

I showed them to the office and left to make another mad dash to the emergency room. A young, blonde man wearing a white lab coat was inside of the supply closet I was about to raid.

21

"Are you a doctor at this hospital?" I asked anxiously.

"Yes, and this is a restricted area. You need to go outside and get in line where you'll be triaged and treated according to the severity of your injuries," he said, giving me a quick, unsure once over.

"No, you don't understand. I'm Emily Boudreaux, a paramedic for ESMR," I quickly spouted.

"Do you need a quick patch up so you can get back out there? I'll be happy to look at your wounds just as soon as I finish casting my patient's leg."

"Are you an ortho doc?"

"No, I'm a pediatrician helping out in the ER. I'm surprised that our paths haven't crossed before now. Do you normally work in this area?"

"No time for chit chat, Doc. The nearly dead Sheriff trumps your broken leg. You're coming with me," I said, knocking the supplies from his hands so I could take hold of his arm.

"What are you doing?" he fussed when I practically dragged him down the hallway. "You know, you're a lot stronger than you look!"

"The Sheriff of Atchafalaya Parish is in really bad shape and we couldn't get him into the hospital through the ER entrance," I said, shoving him into the CEO's office. Colin, analyzing a strip from the heart monitor, looked up when he heard the commotion.

"Doctor Colin Richardson, this is Doctor Pediatrician. I found him in a supply closet."

"Will Verrett," he corrected as he walked over to Holden. "He needs to be in a trauma room. I'll clear one out. Follow me."

Grant and Jackson carried Holden while Colin used a bag-valve mask to force air into his lungs. I stayed by Holden's side, carrying the IV's. Once we reached the frenzied emergency room, Dr. Verrett asked us to give him a few seconds. He'd barely ducked into one of the trauma rooms when a mob of medical professionals came rushing toward us. A nurse took the IV bags from me, another took over ventilations. Two more helped situate Holden on a stretcher before they brought him into the trauma room. I tried to follow but was stopped short.

"Dr. Richardson, your assistance would be greatly appreciated, but I'm sorry, Miss, you'll need to wait out here. The room's full enough as it is," Dr. Verrett said quite sternly.

"But he's…" I started before I was interrupted.

"Out here!" he insisted, pointing his finger for emphasis.

I sighed loudly, giving him a look that showed my disappointment. It didn't faze him. The door slowly closed behind him, affording me one last peek at Holden. There were so many people around him; so many wires, tubes, and machines. I flashed back to the day that Pete was killed and that same sinking feeling came over me. I slowly slid down the wall and put my forehead to my knees. I began to pray.

"You did real good today, kiddo," Grant said, gently rubbing my back when he squatted next to me.

"Thanks, Grant, but I'm not so sure about that. It doesn't look very promising for him, does it?" I said, finally looking his way. I broke down.

"You know as well as I do that anything's possible. You gotta keep the faith," Grant said.

Jackson, who took a seat next to me, reached over and pulled me to him. My head rested on his shoulder and he slowly stroked my hair to soothe me.

"It's been a hell of a day," Jackson said, kissing the top of my head. "Things will get better. I'm sure he'll be fine."

"I sure hope so," I said in between hiccups.

"He's in the best hospital he could be in. Think about it. People from all around come to DeSoto General because it's one of the best hospitals in the state," Grant said, patting my knee.

"True," I agreed. Grant walked over to the nurses' station for a box of tissues. Smiling my thanks to him, I accepted them as my hiccups turned into shaky sniffles.

"I hate being on this side of the door," I complained.

"About eighty-five percent of that's just because you're plain, old nosey. You want to know exactly what's going on and who's doing it," Grant observed.

"Uh, that's uncalled for!" I snapped.

"I didn't hear a denial," Grant said, making me smile. "That's better. Let me know what you find out and remember that I'm here if you need me. I gotta go check in with headquarters to see where they need me. How's Chuck? How's the Bienville station? With all the commotion I forgot to ask."

"Chuck hurt his leg, but he's fine. Grant, there's no easy way to say this—the station's gone."

"Gone?"

"Gone. No more. Disintegrated," I said.

"Shit," he mumbled under his breath. "Gone? Nothing left?"

"Just the slab, but the ambulance made it," I said.

"The ambulance made it. That's good to know. The station's gone?" he asked one last time.

After I nodded, he turned away, mumbling to himself while scratching his head. His entire scalp moved as one solid unit when he rubbed his finger up and down. I really wanted to laugh out loud, but managed to keep it inside. I elbowed Jackson to point out what I was seeing. We watched as Grant, who was still talking to himself, walked down the hall, threw his hands into the air, and turned the corner to leave the hospital.

"He's funny. You two must go way back," Jackson said.

"Grant's known me since I was a high schooler. Pete and I were on our way home from a date one night when we came across a motorcycle accident. Grant was one of the responding medics. I helped him with the patient and he encouraged me to pursue a career in EMS," I answered.

"I often wondered why you decided on a job in EMS," he said.

"Why? Do I not look the part?" I pondered aloud.

"Not really."

"So what do I look like I should be doing? And, if you say grinding a pole, I will knock you senseless," I warned. Jackson smiled.

"I wasn't going to say that, but now you've got me thinking about it. Damn it, I hate when you do that! I was going to say that you look like a teacher or maybe a veterinarian."

"There's a reason I have no pets, Jackson."

"You're not a pet person?"

"I don't really have time for them. I had fish for a while, but I went away for a long weekend and they were all floating upside-down when I got back. Bert and Connie have the tank now."

"Speaking of Bertrand Hebert," Jackson said, standing.

"Bert! I was so worried about you guys!" I yelled when I saw him coming down the hallway. I jumped up and threw my arms around his neck. The tears started again.

"Hey, there. No need for that, girlie. We're all fine," he said, pulling me off so he could look at me. "You on the other hand…"

"It's just a few scratches and bruises. I'm used to those by now," I said, plucking a fresh tissue from the box and dotting my eyes with it. "Where are Connie and Andre?"

Connie, Bert's petite, red-headed wife was my best friend and their two-year-old son, Andre, was my incredibly spoiled godchild. Bert, a Captain with Atchafalaya Parish Sheriff's Department, was like a brother to me.

"They're at home. Connie wanted to come with me, but with all the pandemonium, I thought it best that she stay home. I wish that this was purely a social call, but unfortunately, we need you Chief. Since you're acting Sheriff while Holden's out, I was sent to fill you in, sir. Things are starting to unravel out there," Bert explained in his big, booming voice.

"I wish I didn't have to leave you here, but I have to go," Jackson said to me.

"I'll be fine. Go do what you need to do. Colin's here if I need anything, and I promise that I'll let you know how things are going, okay?"

"Take this in case you need to reach me. I've got extras in my truck," he said, removing the portable radio from his belt. I nodded. He kissed me softly on the forehead and I hugged him in return.

"Both of you be careful out there, okay?"

"You know I will. I've got my radio, too, if you need me," Bert said.

I watched as they walked down the hall, Bert in his dark brown APSO uniform and Jackson in his tactical pants and blood-stained polo shirt. I let out a heavy sigh as I looked down at myself. I was in a torn tank top and shredded tactical pants, my left arm looked horrible, and I dreaded seeing my face; I could only imagine what it looked like now that it had time to swell.

The supply closet was still open. I rummaged through it, found a pair of disposable scrubs, and very gently pulled the shirt on over my tank top. The door to the trauma room opened.

"They're going to take him to surgery soon. He's bleeding internally and his right leg's crushed. We're waiting for an orthopedist to get here. There are other issues, but those are the two we're going to focus on right now," Colin said. The nurses wheeled Holden out of the room.

"Could I have one very quick moment?" I asked Dr. Verrett.

"Very quick," he said.

"Holden, I don't know if you can hear me. It's Emily. I'll be waiting for you," I said, lightly kissing his puffy, swollen cheek.

"Let's go," Dr. Verrett said. "You can follow us up. I'll show you to the waiting room."

"Thank you, I'd appreciate that," I said sincerely.

We snaked down several hallways before we got to a waiting room overflowing with people. Dr. Verrett looked sympathetic.

"Dr. Richardson, if you continue down this hall to the left you'll see a Doctor's Lounge. The access code is 61792. You and Emily are welcome to wait in there until he's out of surgery."

"Thank you, Dr. Verrett," Colin said.

I gave Holden's hand one last squeeze before they wheeled him through the doors that led to the surgical suite. Colin put his arm around my waist and led me down the hallway. My head rested on his shoulder until he opened the door to the deserted room.

The lounge was large and furnished with several recliners, sofas, and a few table and chair sets. Rows of book shelves lined one wall, while another held a large, flat-screen TV. I could see how the room-darkening blinds and the subdued lighting helped to make it a relaxing place for exhausted doctors to recharge.

"Do you need to get back to Bienville? Are there lots of casualties?" I asked.

"No, but I should go down and offer my help to the ER staff. You gonna be okay if I leave you?" Colin asked, turning on the TV. He opened the stainless steel refrigerator that was in a small kitchen area. "Want some water?"

"I smell coffee. Is there a pot over there?" I asked, yawning.

"Yep," he said. "You take it extra-sweet, extra-creamy, right? I don't know how you drink it like that," he remarked, carrying the cup over.

"I don't know how you drink it like *that*," I said, nodding my head toward his cup filled with black coffee.

"Touché. I'll be back as soon as I can. I'm sure the hospital operator can page me if you need me," he said, tossing his empty cup into the garbage. I smiled my appreciation to him and he walked out of the door.

I wanted to watch the news coverage of the event, but my mind refused to focus. I clicked the TV off and thumbed through a magazine, but quickly tossed it aside. I found a blanket in a closet, wrapped it around myself, and let my thoughts drift. It was hard to keep my eyes open, but each time I fell asleep, I'd jerk awake. My body refused to relax. I sighed heavily and gave the magazine another try. I still couldn't concentrate enough to read, so I paced the room.

Colin came in a couple of hours later. "They've got it under control downstairs. It's your turn to be the patient. Let me have a look at you," he requested.

It hurt to raise my arm when I tried to take the disposable scrub shirt off, so Colin ripped it down the middle and carefully slid it down my arm. He thoroughly inspected each wound.

"Colin, do you regret meeting me on the beach that day?" I asked.

"No," he said, adjusting his gaze from the cut above my elbow so he could look me in the eye. "That came out of nowhere. Why do you ask?"

"Have you noticed how many men have been mortally or near-mortally wounded after they got to know me?"

"What's your point?" he asked, pressing on my upper back. I winced. "How bad does it hurt?"

"On a scale of one to ten, three and a half or four. It's mostly tender. Sitting around here waiting for news reminds me of Pete and I'm feeling guilty because I introduced you to Georgia. What if you hadn't left town when you did? What if she had killed you, too?"

He stopped his examination to take a seat across from me and reached for my hand. "We've already talked about that. Let it go. Holden's here because of a tornado, not some deranged murderer. Emily, I'm happy to have you in my life, even if it's just as a friend. Now, I'm going downstairs to get something to clean this up with," he said. "That glue job didn't hold very well. When I come back, it's going be with a suture kit, so be forewarned."

"For real?" I asked. Colin raised his eyebrow. I sighed.

"I'll be right back," he said with a smile.

I leaned back in the soft, cushy recliner. It didn't take long for me to find a sweet spot. I tried to stifle a yawn, but was unsuccessful. After stretching my aching muscles until it became uncomfortable, I yawned some more. Colin walked into the room with an armload of supplies. He rolled a stool up next to me and began to clean my wounds. Exhaustion finally took its toll; I don't even remember falling asleep.

2

"Obviously, the coffee didn't work," Colin said when I opened my eyes.

"What time is it?" I asked, wiping drool from the corner of my mouth.

"Nine o'clock."

I jerked upwards in a panic. "Is he still in surgery?"

"They're finishing up now. He did really well, considering."

"That's great news," I said, breathing a sigh of relief.

"Okay, time for stitches," Colin said.

"What? Too late, you should have done it while I was sleeping." I flipped around and covered myself with the blanket.

"I don't think so. It doesn't work like that and you know it." He pulled the blanket from me, popped the little plastic cap off of a vial, and pulled some the liquid into a syringe. "Come on. Let's get this done."

"Fine," I conceded.

Colin was finishing up the last of the bandages when a thin, gray-haired doctor pushed the door open. He was absolutely stone-faced so I had no clue if the news he was about to give would be good or bad.

"Ms. Boudreaux?" he asked.

"Yes, sir." My legs felt like jelly when I rose from the recliner. Taking notice, Colin laced his arm through mine to help support me.

"I'm Doctor Brown. The Sheriff came through the surgery fine. However, he'll need to stay in ICU for some time. I'm sure you realize that his injuries were quite extensive; he's a very lucky man. We managed to stop the bleeding, but it's questionable if he'll regain use of his leg. It was crushed pretty badly and he's not out of the woods yet. The next twenty-four to forty-eight hours will tell a lot."

Once I was sure I could stand on my own two feet, I moved away from Colin. "May I see him, please?"

"He's heavily sedated and technically, you're supposed to wait until visiting hours, but I suppose you can go in. No longer than five minutes, though" he said.

"I understand and I'm very grateful for any amount of time," I said, fighting off the urge to hug the man.

"I'll be right here," Colin said. I nodded and reached out to squeeze his hand.

"If you'll follow me, Ms. Boudreaux," Dr. Brown requested.

I nervously rubbed my uninjured arm as we walked down the hallway. Dr. Brown asked how I was feeling.

"I'm sore. I guess I got pretty banged up, but I'll be fine, thank you," I timidly remarked. I stopped walking and

Doctor Brown turned to face me. "Doctor, if I were to ask you to give me a percentage…"

He held up his hand to stop my question. "I really don't like to give percentages, but if I had to, as of tonight, sixty-forty. Every hour that goes by, his chances get better. I'll level with you, Ms. Boudreaux…"

"Please, call me Emily," I insisted.

"Emily, I wasn't sure he'd make it through the surgery, but he did. That speaks volumes," he said with a reassuring smile.

"Thank you, Doctor." I continued through the door that he held open for me.

"The Sheriff is right over there in Room Four. I'm going to let the nurse know that I gave you permission to be here." Dr. Brown retreated to the nurses' station.

I stood outside the glass wall for a few seconds before finally getting the courage to look in. My heart shattered when I saw Holden. His face was incredibly swollen, and wires and tubes were everywhere. Machines hummed, and the rhythmic sound of the ventilator clicking and hissing filled the room. Most of his exposed skin was bruised or scabbed over, but the parts that were intact were extremely pale. It hurt me to see him that way. Slowly making my way to the bed, I took his hand in mine. He didn't need to know how upset I was, so I mustered up the strongest, most optimistic voice I could manage.

"Holden, it's Emily. Your surgery went fine. The doctor said he thinks you'll make a full recovery. It's important for you to rest so your body can heal. They won't let me stay with you tonight, but I'll be here in the morning for visiting hours. You know I'd be here if I could," I said, moving to kiss the top of his head. I gave his hand one last squeeze when the nurse motioned that it was time for me to leave. As I walked out, she handed me a plastic bag with Holden's belongings. I thanked her and went back to the Doctor's Lounge where I found Colin having a conversation with Jackson.

"How is he?" Jackson asked.

I took the blanket from the recliner and pulled it tightly around my body. "He's holding his own. His vitals are stable. They're keeping him sedated for now," I said, trying to be stoic. It didn't work; I sank into the recliner and started to sob. "He's pale, swollen, and banged up beyond recognition. He's got tubes everywhere and they don't know if he'll have use of his leg."

Jackson lowered his head and walked away, but Colin came to sit next to me. "Emily, I know you don't want to see him that way, but it's part of the healing process. It's how the body fixes things. You've been injured enough times to know that as horrible as an injury may look, with some time, it can heal as though it never happened."

I sniffled, accepting the tissue box he held out to me. "Colin, you've been so wonderful today. I want to thank you for staying with me and for coming to help Holden."

"Anytime, Emily. I'll always be here for you," he said with a smile. He reassuringly tapped my knee then stood. "Jackson said he'd bring us home and I think we should take him up on the offer. Are you ready?"

"Yes, let's go. I left my number with the nursing staff in case anything changes with Holden. I'm beyond exhausted. I can't wait to take a shower so I can climb into bed," I said.

I fell asleep in the SUV and didn't wake until the vehicle stopped. I anxiously looked around, trying to get my bearings. We were at Colin's. The light of day might reveal a different story, but the house looked like it survived the storm well enough. Once Colin was safely inside, Jackson drove the quarter mile to my house. He parked near the front porch of Greenleaf, yawned, and rubbed his eyes.

"Would you like me to check the house out before you go inside?" he asked.

"You don't have to do that, Jackson. I'm sure everything's fine here. Thanks for offering, though." I was about to step out of the SUV, but I stopped myself. "I never asked, how did things go after you left the hospital? Is the damage really bad out there?"

"Some places were hit worse than others. The outskirts of DeSoto, the ESMR station, and the hospital in Bienville bore the brunt of it. Overall, Green Bayou had minor damage; except for a few places."

"Really? What places?"

"The car wash and the strip mall next to it, the awning from Jerry's Gas and More, and my apartment complex," Jackson answered.

"Oh, Jackson! Is it livable?"

"Not really, it's pretty much in the same condition as your station," he said.

"That's terrible! You lost everything?" I said, using my hand to cover my agape mouth.

"It's okay. A lot of my personal things are still in storage, so the damage was limited to items that can be easily replaced. I'm going to stay at the Green Bayou substation until I can find a new place."

"As if! It's just me in this huge house. You're more than welcome to stay here," I said.

"I don't know, Emily. I didn't tell you about my place being destroyed to get an invitation out of you," Jackson said quietly.

"I know you didn't. You can't live at the substation, though. Come inside and I'll get you a key," I said, opening the door.

He hesitated for a bit before finally following me inside. "Are you sure?"

"I wouldn't have asked if I wasn't. Do you have any clothes? I may have something here that you can wear."

"I have what's in my gym bag and the uniform hanging in the back of my unit. I'll get some new stuff later."

"Well, if you're hungry, feel free to dig around in the fridge and help yourself to whatever you'd like. If you need anything else, just let me know." I went straight to the junk drawer in the kitchen to get him a key to the house.

"Thanks, Emily. I really appreciate this." He smiled and slid it onto his key ring.

"No problem. I'm glad to help. I'm going to visit Holden in the morning. Would you like to come with me?"

"It's probably better that I don't. We never resolved things and I don't want to risk upsetting him right now. And, since I'm acting Sheriff, I need to stay on top of things at the department. I've got a temporary building being delivered tomorrow. We'll use it until a new station can be built. Communications have been a nightmare. Our main dispatch center was in DeSoto. Luckily, Green Bayou was set up to be a backup for emergencies. Plus, I have to deal with injured personnel and five unaccounted prisoners, so I'll be leaving really early."

"That's terrible! Who else was hurt and how bad were the injuries?"

"Marla was cut up pretty badly. I stopped in after she was discharged from the hospital and she was resting comfortably," he answered. I knew Marla the dispatcher fairly well, so I was glad to hear that she was okay. "Nothing too serious with anyone else—mostly minor bumps, bruises, and cuts. Although I was told that the new dispatcher, Alphonse, was swept up and deposited in a tree. He's complaining of a bruised tailbone."

"What? I've got to hear this one before I go to bed! Let's sit."

Alphonse, the ex-Sheriff's thin and gangly nephew, was a well-intentioned idiot who always seemed to come through when he was most needed. He used to work as a patrol deputy, but when Holden became Sheriff, he fired him. Alphonse only recently started back with the department as a dispatcher.

Jackson began telling the story. "It's the damndest thing I've ever heard, Emily. According to some of the deputies, Alphonse showed up at the Green Bayou substation when the weather rolled in. They told him to go home because he wasn't needed, but to be on standby just

in case. The sergeant who talked to Alphonse assumed
he'd gone home as ordered, but he didn't. Instead, he went
into the parking lot and started pulling all kinds of stuff
from his pickup truck. They had no clue what he was
doing. They watched from the building as Alphonse put on
a diver's belt and strapped on a set of ankle weights. He
was trying to secure sandbags to his legs when the wind
suddenly picked up. Alphonse struggled to remain upright,
and they were about to run outside to get him, but a gust of
wind picked him up, flinging him into the big oak tree
outside the station. After the tornado passed, they ran out
to help him. He was fine, but he was way up in the tree
and refused to come down unless "Red Bean" came to
assess the situation. Well, no one knew who Red Bean
was..."

"Bert!" I said. The chuckle I was trying to hold in
escaped. "Please let me know if Alphonse is okay or not.
I'd feel horrible for laughing if he was seriously injured."

"Nah, he's fine. Your injuries are far worse than
his."

"Good!" I doubled over when I pictured how
hilarious Alphonse must have looked swimming through
mid-air.

"Bert arrived to help out, and he got majorly pissed
when everyone started chanting, "Red Bean" when he got
out of the car. He angrily motioned for Alphonse to come
down, but he refused. Bert wasn't in the mood to play
games, so he climbed the tree to make Alphonse come
down.

Alphonse scurried higher to get away from him and
lost his grip. Bert used his free hand to catch him by the

belt and Alphonse was left dangling in mid-air, screaming for help because he thought Bert was trying to kill him. Bert grew tired of the nonsense and yelled for him to shut up. Alphonse got really still, moaned loudly, then gripped his stomach. He was still a few feet above the ground when Bert dropped him, thus the bruised tailbone."

"I feel so sorry for poor Alphonse, but I *really* needed to hear that story!" I said, wiping the tears that had gathered.

"I'm glad you got to laugh, but *I* have to clean things up tomorrow. Bert's not happy and I've got some employees to discipline. They should've stopped Alphonse long before the wind carried him away. No one's admitted it yet, but if I had to guess, I'd say they were taking bets to see how much stuff he was going to put on, or something equally stupid. Plus, they should've been helping Bert instead of antagonizing him. That was wrong," he said.

"You can't tell me that you don't find it funny," I said, gently rubbing my sore cheeks.

"I find it freaking hilarious, but I can't let anyone else know that," he said with a smile.

"I can talk to Bert for you. He'll be fine. The rest of the offenders, they're *your* problem," I said with a chuckle.

Jackson was suddenly serious. "It's kind of awkward taking over the department like this. I still don't know the personnel that well."

"I'm sure you'll do just fine," I said encouragingly.

"Thanks for your vote of confidence. It means a lot to me."

"Of course. Well, I'm going to get cleaned up and get a little sleep before I go back to the hospital," I said, stretching. "If you get a chance, would you leave tomorrow evening open for me? There's something important that I'd like to talk to you about."

"Sounds serious. Is everything okay?" he asked.

"Everything's fine. I'm glad you're here," I said, going on tiptoe to give him a kiss on the cheek.

"Well, it was here or a holding cell. The choice wasn't a difficult one. Thanks again and goodnight, Emily," Jackson said.

I gave him a quick wave then went upstairs with the plastic bag the nurse had given me when I left the ICU. I tossed it onto the bed and Holden's tattered clothing flew out. A set of keys, a wallet, and his cell phone were still in the pockets of his pants. Curiosity got the best of me and I picked up the phone. It was there, the text I'd sent during the tornado, but had he read it? I prayed he had. Putting the phone on the nightstand, I reached for his wallet. Inside was a picture of us at our Fourth of July party.

I gently traced his outline on the photo as I thought about how screwed up things were. If Holden could get past what I'd done, could we ever be that happy again? In my heart, I knew it was something I had to try. I still loved him. My eyelids grew heavier and heavier until I eventually fell asleep clutching his wallet.

~.~.~.~.~

Knowing that I was going to visit Holden was plenty enough motivation for me to pull my sore, aching body out of bed. I was almost to DeSoto when I glanced at the clock on the dash. It would be another forty-five minutes before I'd be allowed in the ICU so I went in search of caffeine.

Fortunately, Linda's Donuts had not only survived the weather, but the little shop was open for business. Armed with a box of pastries for the nurses and a giant coffee for myself, I arrived just in time for the eight o'clock visiting hours. The nurses were appreciative of my offering, and they dug in as Holden's nurse updated me on his condition. If he continued to improve, they would remove the breathing tube. I was all smiles when I entered his room.

"Hi there, Holden," I said, sitting across from him and softly stroking his hair. "I've got good news. You might get that tube out of your throat today."

He struggled to open his eyes and his head turned toward my voice. Excitement coursed through me.

"Holden, can you hear me?" I asked. He squeezed my hand. "Oh, Holden! Hi," I said, gently touching his face.

"Well, look who's awake. It won't be long before that tube comes out for sure," the nurse said when she entered with a fresh IV bag. She swapped it out with the old one then began injecting various medications into Holden's IV port. He turned to see what she was doing.

"You heard that, didn't you?" I asked softly. He looked back my way and squeezed my hand. His lips began to move as he tried to say something.

42

"You can't talk right now, Holden. Very soon, okay?" I asked. He nodded, allowing his eyes to close.

"I'm sorry, but I'm afraid you're going to have to cut your morning visit short. The meds I gave him are going to make him sleep, anyway. Why don't you come back at twelve-thirty? He might be able to talk to you by then, and I'll be sure to give you some extra time to make up for your having to leave early," the nurse said cheerily.

"I'd like nothing more than to hear his voice. I'll be here."

"Good! We'll see you then, Miss Boudreaux. I'll give you a minute to say goodbye."

Holden's hand drifted upwards and touched my cheek. I kissed his palm then stood to leave. "I have to go, but I'll see you very soon." When I kissed his forehead, he reached for me and began mouthing words again.

"I'm sorry that I can't understand what you're saying. Tell me after lunch, okay?" I looked to see the nurse motioning that time was up. "I have to go, Holden. They're making me leave. Please close your eyes and rest. I'll see you really soon."

He slowly nodded his head and closed his eyes. I kissed his hand one more time before leaving the hospital.

Since I'd promised to update Jackson on Holden's condition, I drove past the demolished APSO DeSoto branch and continued to the small, gray portable building that was set up nearby. I climbed the grated metal steps to enter the temporary office and noticed that it was absolutely jam-packed with office furniture. I couldn't see anything that resembled a human.

"Hello? Anyone in here?" I cautiously asked.

"Hey, you!" Jackson said, suddenly popping up from behind a copier in the back of the room. "Step into my office."

"I'll come see you if I can figure out how to get there." As I carefully navigated the labyrinth, two deputies simultaneously appeared from different quadrants of the room.

"Didn't mean to startle you, ma'am. We're going to step out and give you some privacy, Chief. It's time for a break anyway," one of the uniformed officers said, ducking under equipment to get to the door.

"Yeah, we'll be right outside," the deputy closest to me agreed.

"No need to hang around. I've got things squared away here. Why don't you two run out and pick up some coffee?" Jackson suggested. "Here, take this. I want mine with two sugars," he said, fashioning a five dollar bill into an airplane and whizzing it across the room.

"You got it, Chief. Radio if you need anything else." The deputy slipped the bill into his pocket, but stalled as he approached me. The quarters were so tight that he had no choice but to press his body against mine if he wanted to leave the building.

"Pardon me, ma'am," he said, looking extremely embarrassed.

"Don't worry about it," I said once he got by me. "You know? If you would've done that a little slower, we might have enjoyed it more."

"Ma'am?" he nervously asked, flushing once again.

"She's messing with you, Jones," Jackson yelled from the back of the room.

"Oh," Jones said, letting out a nervous laugh. "Can I get you anything while we're out, ma'am?"

"Nah, I'm good. And please don't call me ma'am. I'm Emily," I said, pushing my hand out the short distance to shake his.

"You wouldn't happen to be Emily Boudreaux?" he asked.

"I am. Have we met?"

"Not exactly," he murmured.

"Everyone knows who you are, Emily," Jackson called. This time, I blushed.

Deputy Jones suddenly got very excited. "I heard all about the ax murder incident! Did you really throw the guy across the room so the deputy could get a clean shot at him?"

"What? Who told you that? Wait, let me guess; Alphonse, right?" I asked.

"So, I'm guessing that the baby oil in the kiddie pool incident didn't happen either?" he asked, a twinge of disappointment in his voice.

"No, that happened," I answered. His eyes went wide so I tried to justify my actions. "I only gave her a quick kiss because she deserved it. Wait, that doesn't make it sound any better, does it? I don't usually kiss strange women. Her daughter needed a breathing machine. Oh, never mind. Think what you want to think." I threw my hands up in exasperation.

I could hear Jackson's laughter from across the room.

"I have to get going now, but it was *really* nice to meet you," the deputy said, a cheesy grin still on his face as he closed the door.

I squeezed between a row of filing cabinets and some large machine and sat on the folding table that Jackson was using as a desk. "Thanks so much for defending me!" I playfully snapped while pushing my finger into his chest. "Had I known it was going to be this cluttered, I would've brought bread crumbs."

"You were holding your own. You must have good news—the old sense of humor's back," he said, rubbing the spot I'd poked.

"Holden's doing great! They might pull the breathing tube out today and he opened his eyes when he heard my voice."

"That's great. Does that mean he's out of the woods?" Jackson asked.

"I think things are looking better. Did you sleep well last night?" I asked, pulling off a chunk of Jackson's granola bar and popping it into my mouth. "I'm sorry. Do you mind?"

"No, not at all, help yourself. I slept like a rock. Thanks for letting me stay with you. It sure beats sleeping on a cot in a jail cell." He shuffled the papers on his desk and put them into a file folder.

"My pleasure. Have Bert and Alphonse made up yet? I tried calling Bert before I went to the hospital, but he didn't answer."

"I gave Alphonse the rest of the week off to give his tailbone time to heal. I think things will simmer down by then. What about you? Are you sore?" Jackson swiveled in his chair and put the folder into a nearby cabinet.

"Yeah, nothing I can't handle. In case you haven't noticed, I'm pretty tough. I should get out of here. You look busy, plus I need to hit a drive-thru before getting back to the hospital. Can I bring you something?"

"What? The bite from my granola bar not filling enough?" he teased.

"That, and the éclair I had this morning just didn't do it," I answered.

"Thanks for the offer, but no. I'm taking the coffee with me as soon as the guys get back. I've got lots of errands to run. I'll pick something up while I'm out."

"Claustrophobia setting in?" I joked, looking around the tiny, cluttered building.

"Funny. Remember, this building is only temporary," he said.

"I know. I'm just messing with you. At least you have an office! I have no clue what ESMR's gonna do about the Bienville station. Guess I'll see ya tonight?" I asked, carefully working my way to the door.

"What if we had dinner together? Didn't you want to talk?" Jackson asked.

"It can wait. I planned on staying in town because the last ICU visit is at eight-thirty. I wouldn't want you to wait that long to eat."

"Some other time, then?" he asked.

"Sounds good. I'll keep you updated on Holden's condition."

"Thanks, Em. Even though Holden and I aren't on the best terms right now, I still worry about him."

"Of course you do," I said with a knowing smile.

3

I found an open drive-thru and returned to the hospital just in time for the twelve-thirty visit. When the elevator doors opened I noticed a security guard stationed outside of the ICU. Even though his presence baffled me, I flashed a brilliant smile at the short, hefty man. When I reached for the door handle his expression remained ambivalent and he refused to budge.

"Hi, I'm here to see Sheriff Dautry. If you'll excuse me, I'd like to go in," I cheerily requested.

"Name."

"Emily Boudreaux."

He scowled. "Miss Boudreaux, I've been stationed here to inform you that you are now banned from this hospital. I insist that you leave immediately. Consider this a formal warning; if you're caught on the hospital grounds again, you will be arrested for trespassing. Do I make myself clear?" He uncrossed his arms, pulled back his shoulders, and stood straighter.

"I don't understand. I've done nothing wrong. Why do I have to leave? There must be some mistake," I argued.

"There's no mistake, ma'am. You aren't related to the patient therefore you have no rights to visitation. A formal complaint was filed on behalf of the patient and the CEO has ordered your immediate expulsion from the property," he stated.

"What are you talking about? This wasn't an issue before! Everyone around here knows of my relationship with the Sheriff! Who filed this so called complaint?" I asked loudly.

"Ma'am, you need to keep your voice down. The hospital administrator has banned you from the property and that's all you need to know. I must insist that you leave right now or you'll be arrested."

"Okay," I said, my finger in his face. "I can understand not being able to visit him because of this technicality, but why am I being banned from the facility. I've done nothing wrong. I want to talk to this CEO right now," I demanded, hands firmly on my hips.

My tirade was interrupted by an enormous, bald man in a designer suit and dark sunglasses. He cleared his throat before stepping aside to reveal a tiny, self-assured woman. Her custom-tailored, red pantsuit was accented with lots of gold jewelry and her long, salt and pepper hair was pulled back into a tight bun. Slowly tapping her foot, she crossed her arms and began to stare me down.

"Is this the woman?" she asked the hospital security guard.

"Yes ma'am, it is. I was just telling Miss Boudreaux that she's expected to leave immediately," he said anxiously.

I looked back and forth between the security guard and the mystery lady before deciding that more answers would come from her than the fidgety guard.

"Pardon me, but *the woman* would like to know what the hell's going on," I said snidely.

The haughty lady shot me a look of contempt. "She's just as crude as I thought she'd be. I'm glad I brought along my own personal bodyguard since it's obvious *you* can't handle her," she directed at the hospital security guard. His nervousness diminished and anger began to show on his face.

"I can handle her," he insisted.

"Unlikely. Just look at her appearance. If I had to guess, I'd say those injuries are no doubt the result of a bar brawl?" she asked, looking down her nose at me.

"I look this way because I was out rescuing tornado victims, and that was *after* surviving a building collapse. I have no idea who you are, but you have no right to judge me and you certainly have no right to keep me away from my fiancé. If you'll move aside, I'd like to see Holden now," I said impatiently as I tried to push past the security guard. Before I could reach for the door handle, he had me pinned against the wall. I desperately struggled to break free.

"You're hurting me!" I fussed. "You better let go right this minute!"

"You see? I can handle her just fine," the hospital security guard scoffed, giving my wrist an extra twist when he pushed the weight of his body against mine. I yelped with pain.

"That's quite enough," the older woman commanded.

"You heard her! Let me go! I want to see the administrator right now! I hope you get fired for what you've done to me!"

"I wasn't talking to him, I was talking to you. You're making a scene and you have no right to be here. Holden is *my* son, *my* blood. You're just his whore. You may speak to anyone you wish, but due to the incredibly sizable donation I just made to this hospital, I'm pretty sure you'll be wasting your breath," she said mockingly.

"Holden's mother?" I asked with disbelief while looking over my shoulder.

"Yes, Luciana Dautry," she answered.

"Look, I don't appreciate you calling me a whore or banning me from the hospital. I wasn't aware that you and Holden kept in touch anymore. If you'll contact Jackson Sonnier, Holden's friend, he'll tell you that I'm not just some floozy."

"That street urchin Holden used to cavort with? You're not doing yourself any favors, young lady. Get her out of here," she said, making a shooing motion with her hand.

A deputy was waiting for me when the hospital security guard shoved me through a delivery door at the rear of the hospital.

"She's a wild one. You're gonna have to keep an eye on her," the guard cautioned.

"A wild one, eh? Thanks for the warning."

"Whatever. She's your problem now," he said, retreating inside and slamming the door.

"I like feisty women," the deputy said, moving toward me with a smirk. He quickly scanned the area and once he was sure we were alone, he suggestively pushed his body into mine. I tried to move away, but he bent me over the hood of his car. After I was tightly handcuffed, he leisurely slid his hands up and down my body. Anger and revulsion pounded through my veins. He squeezed my breasts and I jerked around, desperate to throttle him. He rested more of his body weight on me to keep me still.

"You're going to be sorry that you groped me," I warned through clenched teeth.

His hot breath was in my ear. "I'm only frisking you for weapons."

"That's not true and we both know it," I said defiantly.

"Go ahead and tell them that I groped you. We'll see who they believe." He flicked his tongue against my earlobe then pulled me to stand upright. "Get in," he said, pushing me into the backseat of the car. It took all I had to remain quiet during the ride to Green Bayou. Though he was rougher than he needed to be when helping me from the car; I merely grimaced.

I waited until we were inside to complain. "You shouldn't be so rough! You're really hurting me."

He twisted the cuff and excruciating pain nearly sent me to the floor. "And you need to learn to keep your mouth shut. Wait, I guess I'm gonna be sorry for that, too?" he said mockingly.

Biting my lower lip, I worked to regain my composure. More than anything, I wanted to cry, but wasn't about to give him the satisfaction of witnessing it. Eventually, I was handed off to a female deputy who fingerprinted, photographed, and booked me, then put me in a holding cell.

I was lying on the lumpy cot, fighting back tears, when Bert walked in with a prisoner. I jumped up and grasped the bars.

"Bert! You've got to get me out of here!"

A wide grin spread across his face. Once his prisoner was released to the booking agent, he approached the holding cell.

"There are so many things I want to say to you right now, but I can't figure out which one I want to say first!" he said, amused.

"Cut it out, Bert. I want out of here now," I snapped.

"You need to be a good little girl if you want out of there. Oh, and the name's Captain Hebert, not Bert," he teased, tapping his name tag.

I conveyed my feelings about his joking with a nasty look. "Have your fun now, *Captain Hebert*. I'll get out eventually and I can make your life miserable," I warned.

"Is that a threat?" he asked, smiling smugly while leaning his shoulder against the cell. When he pulled a toothpick out of his top pocket and started sucking on it, I reached my hands through the bars and yanked his collar. His head thumped against the metal bars.

"What do you think Connie's gonna do to you when I tell her that you let me sit in here?" I whispered in his ear.

"Ouch!" He chuckled while rubbing his head. "Who knew you were so mean? You take all the fun out of it! Flip the switch," Bert yelled, signaling to the camera mounted in the corner of the room. There was a loud *buzz* before the door slid open. "Come on, let's get this sorted out. How did you wind up in here?"

"I was arrested when I went to visit Holden at the hospital, but first, let's have a talk about the jerk that brought me in."

"Was there was a problem?" he asked nonchalantly as we walked toward a row of vending machines.

"Yes! A big one! The dude was a total prick!" I loudly fussed.

Bert smiled apologetically at the several people who turned to look our way. He stopped walking to fish some money from his pocket. "I know how you get when you're angry. You want heads to roll, but then you get over it quickly. Are you sure you're not overreacting because you couldn't see Holden?" he asked softly.

After inserting a few bills into the machine, he punched some buttons to drop a bag of chips and two sodas. I crossed my arms and angrily glared at him.

"Okay. Fine. Let's talk in here." He quickly ushered me into an empty conference room and offered the bag of chips. When I declined, he shrugged his shoulders and began eating them. "Please tell me all about how you were wrongfully accused and gravely mistreated by one of

Atchafalaya Parish's finest," he said with an exaggerated eye roll.

"I want that pipsqueak who brought me in disciplined! He was rude, mean, rough, *and* he felt me up!" I said, rubbing one of my sore wrists.

Bert's expression turned very solemn and he put down the chips. He took a seat on the table, motioning that he wanted to see the marks. "You were serious? I really thought you were just angry about the situation. I can't imagine anyone on staff who would do such a thing. Obviously, someone's not who we think he is. Emily, you can bet your life I'll be taking care of this!" Bert said, angrily eyeing the puffy, reddened area. "First tell me, the entire story. Why did you get arrested for visiting Holden?"

"I was wondering the same thing," Jackson said, entering the room and tossing a file folder onto the table.

"Oh, great!" I said, repeatedly tapping my forehead against the table.

Jackson stopped me by gently pulling on my shoulders to make me sit straight. "Don't do that. Tell me what's going on."

"I was banned from the hospital and when I refused to leave, they had me arrested."

"What in the hell did you do to get banned from the hospital?" Bert asked, a look of admiration creeping upon his face.

"Don't get all excited. I didn't do anything; Holden's mother did."

Jackson's face fell. "Luciana's in town?"

"Luciana, ha! Lucifer would be a more appropriate name," I said with a scowl.

"Not good." Jackson walked across the room to look outside the window.

A confused looking Bert nudged my elbow. "What's up with Holden's mom?" he asked quietly.

"Other than her being the spawn of Satan? She made a huge donation to the hospital so they're letting her run the show. There was a security guard waiting at the ICU doors and after I asked to see Holden, he said that I was banned from the facility. I demanded an explanation and he pinned me against the wall. After Luciana called me 'Holden's whore', she demanded that he throw me out. Let's just say that he wasn't very nice about it," I said.

"Oh, really?" Bert asked, his jaw clenched. "What did this security guard look like? Do you know his name? I have a couple of people I need to take care of, Chief, I mean Sheriff," Bert said, angrily pacing up and down.

"I understand your anger Bert, but you need to calm down. Let's finish sorting this out first," Jackson said, sitting across from me. "Are you hurt, Emily?"

"Nothing too bad, although the deputy who brought me here was a little overzealous with his hands and the cuffs," I answered, showing him my wrists.

"I suppose that's the other situation you're itching to handle? I will not stand for the inappropriate touching of women, much less the use of excessive force. After you get done with this guy, send him to me," Jackson requested.

"You know it, sir. I'm raring to go," Bert answered.

"Get to it, but use discretion," Jackson advised.

"Yes, sir. I'll see you soon, Em. Call me if you need anything," Bert said, kissing the top of my head before leaving the room.

"I can't believe Luciana's in town," Jackson mumbled, staring out of the window once again.

"Well, she spoke very highly of you," I said sarcastically.

"I'm sure she did. Did she refer to me as the 'bayou trash' or the 'thieving redneck'?"

"The street urchin," I answered.

"That's a new one." He sat across from me and took my hand in his. "I'm sorry she found out about Holden's injuries. You can see why he doesn't have much of a relationship with his mother, can't you? Growing up, he had lots of money and I was poor as they came, but we both had terrible home lives. We took care of each other."

"I'm so sorry I ruined the relationship," I said sincerely.

"Don't be sorry. I didn't intend to fall for you, and I certainly don't regret the night we spent together. I've realized that Holden and I are different people now. Things wouldn't be the same between us regardless. I know this isn't the best time to be telling you this, but if you ever decide to give us a chance, I think we could have something really good," he said.

"But, Jackson, I love Holden. That's what I wanted to talk to you about the other night," I said softly.

"Please don't tell me that you've made up your mind," he said, sliding his chair closer to mine. "We never got the chance to date or to get to know each other. I feel as though Holden has an unfair advantage and he knew it when he gave you that ultimatum. And, now that he's hurt, well…"

"Look, I hear what you're saying, Jackson."

"I'm not asking you to commit to me, Emily. Just take some time to get to know me. That's all," he said, gently lifting my chin.

"I've had a long day and I'm not thinking clearly. You're welcome to stay with me until you find another place and I'll agree to get to know you better, but you shouldn't have false hope about it leading to something else. It would be great for you and Holden to repair your relationship one day," I said.

"Okay, but there's something else we need to discuss," he said ominously.

"I don't like your tone. What's wrong?"

"Remember the five missing prisoners?" he asked.

"Don't even say it!" I said, slamming my fist down on the table. "Why can't I ever have only one crisis at a time? Brad's missing. Who else?"

"Brad, his buddy we arrested near your boathouse, Donovan Guidry, and two of Donovan's guys."

"Oh, great! The ex-DA's on the lam with the guy who keeps trying to kill me. Lovely! Just wonderful! Excellent news! Can this day get any better!" I said, getting progressively louder. I jumped from my seat, mumbling gibberish as I paced back and forth.

"Come here," Jackson said, reaching for me.

"Don't, Jackson," I said, holding my palm up to stop him. "This is the only thing that's keeping me from crying hysterically right now."

He wrapped his arms around me and I started to sob.

"You have every right to cry. Let it out," he said, gently stroking my back. After five minutes, I had no tears left and Jackson's shirt was soaked. I started to hiccup.

"Am I free to go?" I asked softly.

"Yes. The administrator has agreed to drop the charges, as long as you agree to stay away from the hospital," Jackson said.

Feeling completely defeated, I wiped my eyes with a tissue. "I guess I don't have much choice. I'm ready to go home."

"I'll take you. Let's go down to booking and get your things, then we'll get out of here. Everything's going to be okay, you know?" Jackson said, giving my shoulder a pat that was meant to be reassuring. Even though my gut was telling me otherwise, I pretended to agree with him.

"Excuse me, Miss Boudreaux," someone called from behind me once we entered the hall. I turned to see the sadistic deputy hunched over and slowly walking toward me. Bert held him by the scruff of the neck.

"I don't mean to interrupt, but may I please have a word with you?" the deputy asked, his arm guarding his stomach.

I remained silent, but looked at him with interest. He was dripping sweat and his skin had a greenish hue.

"I must say that I was quite surprised to hear about your behavior, Deputy Lee. You do know that such behavior is absolutely unacceptable, don't you?" Jackson inquired angrily.

"I don't know what I was thinking, sir. Captain Hebert has well shown me the error of my ways and you have my word that nothing like that will *ever* happen again, sir. It's not an excuse, but the guard at the hospital told me…"

Bert interrupted Deputy Lee's speech by loudly clearing his throat. Bert shot him an evil look when he glanced up.

Still profusely sweating and bent at an awkward angle, Deputy Lee began again. "Miss Boudreaux, it's my sincerest hope that you'll accept my humble apology for what I've done to you. I should have listened to you when you asked me to get in touch with Captain Hebert or Sheriff Sonnier. I promise to be more sensitive to the plight of those I may be called upon to arrest in the future."

"Better," Bert said behind a cough.

"Is that good enough for you?" Jackson asked me.

"If he's sincere, then yes," I answered.

"Well, consider this a warning, Deputy Lee. One more complaint and you're done here. Understand?"

"Yes, sir," he said.

"Miss Boudreaux will be writing a detailed, formal complaint. Once that's done, you'll see me for further counseling and to sign the disciplinary paperwork," Jackson said.

"Yes, sir. May I be excused, sir?" Deputy Lee asked.

"Dismissed," Jackson said sternly.

The deputy bolted down the hall and the sound of the bathroom door slamming against the wall echoed through the halls.

"How many times did you punch him in the gut?" Jackson asked.

"Officially or unofficially?"

"Well, of course the number is zero, officially," Jackson said.

"Exactly," Bert said. "But unofficially, five or six times."

"You're going to visit the security guard next?" Jackson asked.

"I was just headed out."

"Carry on," Jackson replied, guiding me out of the building.

~.~.~.~.~

The first shift I worked after the tornado was quite strange. When Grant told me to meet him at the Bienville station, I laughed and reminded him that there wasn't a Bienville station anymore. He insisted that it was all taken care of and that I should be there for my usual five-thirty in the morning. It was still dark out when I parked my car next to the ambulance and walked over to where Grant was standing. An outdoor light lifted high on a metal pole softly illuminated the area.

"What in the hell is this?" I asked Grant, staring at the empty space where the ESMR-Bienville station used to be. "You said we had a station to work out of! *This* is not a station!"

"It's a top-of-the-line pull-behind camper trailer. I think a little gratitude is in order. You could be stationed out of a tent, you know," Grant scolded.

"A tent would be bigger," I grumbled as I pulled the door open to peek inside. "There's only one bedroom, Grant, and I can practically reach it from the here!"

"The dining room table becomes a bed, thus two rooms," Grant explained.

"I call the bedroom," Chuck said, peeking in from behind me.

"I didn't hear you walk up, Chuckiedoo?" I remarked. "Look, I'm extremely happy to see you, but I'm very sorry to say, you don't get the bedroom. I was here first. The bedroom is mine."

"Sweet, sweet, Emily, I'm very happy to see you, as well. But, you can't have the bedroom because I need the extra space to prop up my leg when we aren't running calls. I won't be able to do that from the dining room table. Unfortunately for you, my medical condition trumps your request. The bedroom is mine."

"Oh, but dearest Chuck, I've already thought about your medical condition and I'm fully prepared to hang a sling from the cabinet over the table. Actually, it'll work far better at keeping your leg elevated than a few chintzy pillows in a bed."

"Cut the crap you two. Keep it up and you'll be under the stars in sleeping bags," Grant warned. "Here are the keys to your new station. I'm going back to bed, so don't call unless it's a legit emergency. Understand?"

"Got it," I said, taking my key.

"Yes, sir," Chuck said.

"Okay, have a good shift, and behave!" Grant said, climbing into his SUV. I wrinkled my nose at him before I turned to look at the itty, bitty trailer.

"This is what I get for picking on Jackson because he's crammed into that tiny portable building. Karma, you sure are a nasty one," I remarked as I followed Chuck inside.

"How in the hell am I supposed to do anything in here?" Chuck asked, pointing into the bathroom. He stepped inside and I leaned forward to get a look at what he was complaining about.

"You've got to be kidding me! Is it possible to even turn around in there?" I asked.

"This is ridiculous! Look at how tight it is," Chuck said, sitting on the commode. His knees were flush against the opposite wall. "Uh-oh! Oh, no! I can't get up! My leg's cramping up on me. It hurts and I can't pull myself up. You have to help me, Emily."

I burst into peals of laughter. "You're kidding me, right?" I managed to ask.

"Does it look like I'm kidding? Owwww! Help me! It's hurting!" he exclaimed.

"What do you want me to do?" I asked, still laughing.

"Pull me up!"

"I can't get a grip on you from out here," I said.

"Come on, Emily, do something! It hurts really bad!" Chuck writhed in agony.

"Okay, stop squirming." I carefully climbed into the bathroom to stand between his legs. He was trying hard to control his breathing. "Really, Chuck?" I asked after his forehead came to a rest between my breasts when his hands encircled my waist.

"Like I'm doing it on purpose! Would you just hurry and pull me up!"

"I'll help you stand on the count of three," I said.

"Owwwee owww owwww owww! Just do it and pull hard!" Chuck insisted.

"I'm gonna pull hard and fast. Are you ready?" I asked, squatting between his legs to get some extra leverage.

"Hey guys, I forgot to give you…" Grant opened the camper door. I knew that we looked like deer caught in headlights. Though he paused, Grant's expression never changed, "…the key to the new supply closet at the hospital, which is near the x-ray department."

"This isn't what you think, Grant. I can explain," I said sheepishly.

"It never is, Emily. With you, it never is." He slowly shook his head. "I'm going home, and please, don't bother with an explanation."

"But, Grant!"

"Dah! Shhhhh!" He held his finger up to silence me.

"Grant!"

"Oh, for the love of God, please do it now, Emily!" Chuck screamed.

"I'm gone." Grant closed the door behind him.

It was a contortionist's act, but Chuck was finally freed. He said he'd rather do his business in the cane fields than brave the trailer's bathroom again. It really didn't matter because we were so busy that we didn't see the "station" until shift change the next morning.

Driving home, my body was exhausted, yet my mind raced. I needed to know how Holden was doing, but how could I get that information? I let my thoughts drift as I gently steered the car down the winding section of road that followed the bayou. There had to be some way around Luciana. I didn't know any of the nursing staff at DeSoto.

Suddenly, an idea came to me. I passed the driveway to my house and turned into Colin's. He might not have privileges at the hospital in DeSoto, but he had treated Holden after he was rescued, and Luciana didn't know him. It would be entirely plausible for the doctor who treated Holden in the emergency room to want to know how he was doing. I knocked on the door and when that didn't get a response, I rang the bell. Though he was dressed in shorts and a t-shirt, it was obvious that Colin was still half asleep when he opened the door.

"I'm sorry to wake you, Colin. I shouldn't have come so early, but…"

"Don't you dare apologize. Come in," he said, moving so I could enter the farm house he was refurbishing. "Want some coffee? I can fix a pot."

"I'd love some coffee if it's not too much trouble."

"Not in the least. Go on out back and I'll bring you a cup," he said.

I passed through the screened porch and made my way to the swing near Colin's dock. The sky still had traces of orange and pink and the murky water gently lapped at the bank. A raft of mallards swam by and I wished I had something to feed them. They quickly coasted to the other side of the bayou when they saw Colin coming toward the swing.

"I like it out here. I hope you don't mind," I said.

"Not at all. So what's up?" he asked, passing me a mug.

"Condensed version?"

"We can start with that if you want."

"Holden's mother, Luciana, came to town and had me banned from visiting Holden. I have no clue how he's doing and it's killing me."

"Why would she have you banned?"

"That's the thing—I have no clue."

Colin looked sympathetic, but remained silent.

"I was hoping you might be able to ask for an update on his condition. Luciana doesn't know that you know me, so if you call and tell them that you're the doctor who treated Holden after the tornado, they might tell you how he's doing."

"I don't think they'd give me that information over the phone, Emily," Colin interjected. My face fell.

"You're probably right. I shouldn't have bothered you with this. Thanks for the coffee," I said, standing.

He reached out for me. "Let me finish. They won't give me the information over the phone, but if I go in person with my ID, now that could be a whole different story."

"You'd do that for me?" I asked.

"Absolutely! Let me change and we'll head to the hospital."

"I can't go with you. Not only am I banned from visiting Holden, but I'm not allowed on hospital grounds. I'll be arrested for trespassing," I said sadly.

"Wow, that woman has a major chip on her shoulder, doesn't she? I know! We'll take the motorcycle.

As long as you keep your helmet on, no one will know it's you."

"That could work! You're the best, Colin!" I said, hugging him tightly.

"I'm glad I can help. Come on; let's get your information so you can get some sleep. You must've had a pretty rough shift?"

"Does it show?"

"It's obvious you've got a lot on your mind. It's expected. Why don't you write Holden a note and I'll see that he gets it? He may not realize what his mother's done," Colin suggested.

"That would be great!"

"Follow me inside. You can write while I change," he said.

4

I was kicking pebbles around the parking lot of DeSoto General when I spied the flashing yellow strobe light of a security vehicle. *Just play it cool, Emily. Look busy.* Using the key Colin had left in the bike's ignition; I unlocked the storage compartment and pretended to search for something important. The security officer rode right on by as I thumbed through the contents. I breathed a sigh of relief and started cramming things back in: the motor-cycle's registration, a spare house key, a picture of a beautiful, dark-headed woman. I lifted the visor of my helmet to get a better look. I recognized her as Miranda, Colin's dance instructor. *That explains why Colin backed off of pursuing me.* A smile crept across my face. I quickly locked the compartment and went back to kicking pebbles.

When Colin approached me his look was very solemn.

"What's wrong?" I demanded.

"We'll talk about it at the coffee shop down the street. Let's get out of here," he said, putting on his helmet.

"Oh, no! Is it that bad? He's not dead, is he? Please don't tell me he died," I said, hysteria rising.

"No, he's alive and stable. Get on and I promise I'll explain everything to you." He threw his leg over to mount the bike and as soon as my hands were around his waist, he took off for the little café about a block from the hospital. Instead of going inside he guided me to the patio. After we were seated he took my hand in his.

"Did you get to see Holden?" I asked anxiously. "Was he awake?"

"No, I didn't see him. I hate to tell you this, but Holden's not there anymore. He's been transferred to another facility. From what I understand, his mother used connections to get him into a top-notch rehab hospital somewhere up north. The nurse I spoke to couldn't remember the name of the hospital or even what state it's in. I didn't want to raise suspicion so I didn't push her for it. He was put on a medical flight yesterday morning. The nurse also told me that it's unlikely Holden will keep his leg. I'm really sorry, Emily," he said.

I slowly ran my hand down my face, stopping when my hand covered my mouth. We sat in silence for a while.

"But if he was stable enough to transfer, why didn't he let me know he was going? Do you have any idea how long he'll be in rehab?" I asked.

"If I had to guess, someone with his injuries, I'd say three to six months, maybe more. Depends on how quickly he heals, how well he does, and when the money dries up. As for why he didn't inform you, I can't say," he answered.

"Money won't be an issue. Well, I guess Holden's decided that he's finished with me. It's the only explanation. That must have been what he was trying to tell me," I said, heartbroken. "Would you mind bringing me home? I'm not feeling very well, and I'd like to get some rest."

"I'm sorry I didn't have better news for you."

"I know. I really appreciate your help," I said, choking back the tears.

"I know you do. Let's get you home," he said, pulling me in for a hug.

Several weeks later I still hadn't heard from Holden. I'd go to work then spend the rest of my time locked in my bedroom. No one, except for poor Chuck, bore witness to my downward spiral into desolation. Even though Jackson technically lived with me, he was rarely around, and I must say that I liked it that way.

When the phone rang I jerked upright and tried to get my bearings. I was in my bedroom and it was dark outside. I glanced at the clock and reached for the phone, clearing my throat before I answered.

"Hello," I said into the receiver.

"What's up, girlfriend? I haven't heard from you in forever! Are you busy?" Connie asked.

"No, I just woke up," I said, trying to stifle a yawn.

"Just woke up! Are you sick? Girl, it is eight o'clock! You've slept the entire day and half the night away! Whatcha gonna do now?" she asked.

"I don't know. I haven't gotten that far." I dangled my legs over the side of the bed.

"Well, Bert's working, Andre's with my parents, and it's the weekend. How would you like to get a few drinks at Chaisson's? It'll do you some good to get out of the house for something besides work. Don't think for one minute that I don't know you've been avoiding me," she fussed. I rolled my eyes and tried to think of an excuse to get out of it, but drew a blank. "Come on, Em! We can make fun of the karaoke singers," she threw in.

"Okay, do you want me to pick you up or are you coming here?" I said with a sigh.

"I'll come get you." She giggled.

"Fine, let yourself in if I don't answer. I'm getting in the shower."

"See you in a few!"

She sounded far too chipper for my liking. I thought about calling her back to cancel, but knew I'd never hear the end of it. It would be best to suck it up, so I pulled back my hair and climbed into the shower. Connie was sitting on my bed when I came out of the bathroom.

"Wow, you look great." I said, noticing the new blouse she was wearing.

"You really like it?" she asked.

"That shade of green is beautiful on you."

"Awww, thanks. Enough chit-chat, fill me in on the scoop. Any news about Holden?" she asked.

Leave it to Connie to get straight to the point. I breathed a long sigh and finished buttoning my shirt.

"No. I'm pretty sure that any hope of a relationship with Holden is officially dead and gone," I said sadly.

"My offer's still good. I can research rehab hospitals and we'll track him down."

"It goes beyond that, Connie. If find him, I'll have to get past Luciana. I almost have an arrest record because of her. Plus, it's not like Holden's attempted to contact me. Colin said Holden was conscious and coherent when he was transferred. You can't tell me that he doesn't have access to a phone. Holden tried to tell me something the last time I saw him, but he was still intubated. I guess he was trying to tell me to go away."

"I don't think Holden would say that," Connie said.

"It's been almost a month since the tornado and I've heard nothing. If he wanted to get in touch with me, he would've done it. I've had nothing but time to think this out and as much as I hate to say it, I think I ruined a good thing and it's time to move on." I tossed the tube of mascara that was in my hand onto the vanity. "Maybe I mistook the sign I was looking for."

"What do you mean?" Connie asked.

"Well, Jackson came out of nowhere to rescue me, and he's been a perfect gentleman since he's been staying here. I was never really sure if Holden could get past my sleeping with Jackson. Though it wasn't the one I was hoping for, maybe I did get my sign," I explained.

"But, you love Holden," she said.

"Yes, but if Holden felt the same way, he'd make sure I knew it. Maybe Jackson is the one I should be with, maybe he's not. Who knows? Geez, don't listen to me. My thoughts are all over the place. Do you think a few drinks will help me to see things more clearly?"

"I have no idea, but we are long overdue for some fun. Let's get out of here," she said, snapping her fingers and shaking her hips to an imaginary beat.

"After you," I said, following Connie. She danced her way down the stairs and right out of the front door.

~.~.~.~.~

Chaisson's Bar was packed when we arrived. Connie sidled up to the bar for drinks while I scanned the room for a table. A thin arm frantically waved up and down beckoning me—Alphonse. He was dressed in tight jeans, a brown turtleneck, and though we were in a dark barroom, he was wearing aviator-style sunglasses.

"I think you're being summoned," Connie said as she passed me a beer. "Dang, girl! He's gonna fly clean off that stool if he don't take it down a notch."

"You better be nice to Alphonse. Your husband's not sitting in a jail cell right now because of him," I reminded Connie.

"You're right. Let's go see what he wants." She sighed.

"How are you doing, Alphonse? I heard you were hurt during the tornado," I said.

"I was injured in the line of duty, but I live to serve, Emily. I couldn't let a tornado stop me from protecting the public," he said with utmost seriousness. Alphonse pulled his sunglasses down to sit on the tip of his long nose. "I live to serve," he said dramatically, slowly sliding the sunglasses back into place with his index finger.

"But you flew…" Connie started. I held my hand up to stop her.

"I'm so glad you're okay. You know what would be really great? If you went up there and sang a song." I threw an extra dose of sweetness into my request.

"I'm on it!" he said, jumping off of his stool so quickly that he took a tumble onto the floor. I winced for him. Just as quickly as he fell, he was back upright shaking it off. "I'm good! Nothing to see here, folks. Move along." He started to make his way to the stage and once he was out of earshot, Connie and I burst into hysterical laughter.

"You sure know how to handle him!" she commented.

"I've had lots of practice."

"Hi there, ladies. I'm glad I ran into you. Mind if I join you?" Jackson said from behind me. He was holding three beers.

"Since you come bearing gifts, I guess that's fine," I said, shoving Alphonse's stool out with my foot. Connie started elbowing me.

"Another sign that he's the one?" she whispered in my ear. I shook my head and cleared my throat.

"So, what brings you to Chaisson's?" I asked.

"Things are finally calming down at the department and I'm long overdue for a break. A beer seemed in order. What are we talking about?" Jackson asked.

"I was hoping to talk to Emily about her annual Halloween party," Connie said.

"I probably shouldn't throw one this year," I replied.

"If you ask me, I think you should. A party might help the guests put the tragedy of the tornado behind them. People are ready to kick back and have a good time. That's what we're doing here at Chaisson's, right? What better place to have some fun than at your costume party?" Connie reasoned.

"I don't know," I said after taking a long swig from my beer.

"You didn't ask for my opinion, but I think Connie's right," Jackson offered.

"Really?" I asked.

"People would have fun," he said, shrugging his shoulders.

I briefly considered it. "Okay, let's do it!"

Connie elbowed me in the ribs.

"Yow! What was that for?" I asked, cutting her some eyes. She raised her finger and pointed at the stage.

"…and I'd like to dedicate this song to the most beautiful woman in Atchafalaya Parish, Miss Emily Boudreaux. That's her in the back of the room over there. Could we get a spotlight on her?" Alphonse asked.

I turned beet red and tried to hide behind Jackson. The DJ placed a barstool on the middle of the stage and patted the seat. I was mortified when the crowd started chanting for me to sit up there. Connie took my hand and practically dragged me to the stage. Once I was seated, she raised her arms to encourage the crowd. I shot her a look and she returned a large grin before jumping down. Since I kept my hands over my eyes nearly the entire song, I couldn't see what Alphonse was doing. But, the catcalls coming from the crowd gave me a pretty good idea. I didn't have nearly enough beer in me to handle this! When Alphonse finally stopped singing, Jackson came to my rescue.

"Want to dance?" he asked.

"Oh goodness, yes!" I said, jumping from the stool.

"I heard the news about Holden. Are you okay?" he asked as we slowly swayed to the music.

"I don't know what to think. Did he call anyone from the department to let them know that he was leaving town?" I asked.

"No, not the department, word was sent to the Parish President via his mother. She felt it best not to disclose Holden's location because she didn't want anything to stand in the way of his recovery. She negotiated an agreement. His position as Sheriff will be held for one year, then if he's unable to return to his post, other options will be explored," Jackson explained.

"So you'll remain Sheriff until then?" I asked.

"Yep, got the call today. Although, I feel sort of awkward about it," he said.

"There's nothing to feel awkward about. You're a good man and you'll be a great Sheriff."

"Thank you. I'll try my best," he said.

The song ended and we returned to the table where Connie had another round of drinks waiting. She started to yawn before she finished her beer.

"I know it was my idea to come here, and I'm sorry to be a party pooper, but I'm tired! Are you ready to go home?" she asked.

"I'm feeling pretty wiped, too. Will you be leaving soon, Jackson?" I asked.

"A nice, warm bed doesn't sound half bad. I'll likely be right behind you," he answered.

"If it's okay, I'll just ride with you. It doesn't make much sense for Connie to bring me home if you and I are going to the same place," I said.

"I don't mind at all. Come on, we'll walk you to your car, Connie," he insisted. Once she was safe and secure in her SUV, we headed to his vehicle.

We arrived at Greenleaf and said a quick "goodnight" before entering our separate rooms. I took a fast shower and turned on the TV, but nothing held my attention. I kept thinking about Holden and wondering if I'd ever see him again. Pulling his wallet from my nightstand, I opened it and looked at our picture. I thought back to the Halloween party when Holden and I first talked. We clashed so badly back then, but as much as he got under my skin, there was something irresistible about him. I shook my head in an attempt to clear those thoughts and tossed the wallet back into the nightstand. It bounced off of his keys. I had his keys! Maybe there was a clue to his whereabouts at his house? If I could find him, then whether good or bad, I could get closure. Things might be starting to look up for me! I did my best to fall asleep as quickly as possible; I needed the rest. I was going snooping!

~.~.~.~.~.~

Jackson's SUV was gone when I came downstairs the next morning. Wasting no time, I gulped a glass of orange juice and set out for Holden's. Part of me wanted to stop and pick up Connie, but I decided against it. It was probably better not to have a witness.

After carefully navigating a maze of dirt roads and sharp turns, I finally arrived at Holden's—a beautiful, secluded log cabin that very few people knew existed. When I got out of the car, I noticed that the grass was freshly cut. I searched for a car. Someone was keeping up the grounds. Not seeing any vehicles, I went to the back door and slid the key into the lock. It opened so I went straight upstairs. If there were any clues to be found, surely they would be in Holden's office or his bedroom. I started with the office.

After digging through all of the drawers of his desk and thumbing through his files, I came up empty. I caught sight of the black mesh garbage can in the corner and swiftly rolled the chair over, but still nothing. I continued my search in the bedroom.

My fingers gently caressed the soft, red comforter on his bed. Suddenly, I longed to be close to Holden. I kicked off my shoes and climbed in, pulling the covers over my head. I deeply breathed in the scent from the pillow— it still smelled like him. It was so hard to keep my emotions in check. *What was I thinking by coming here?* If Holden wanted me to know where he was, he would've made it happen—plain and simple. Holden would never let anything, even an amputated leg, stand in the way of something he wanted. Obviously, I was right. He was over me. *I have to get out of here!*

While bending to put on my shoes, a noise from the hall caught my attention. I froze. Faint footsteps—

someone else was in the house and Holden's guns were in the office. He used to keep one in the nightstand, but it was clear on the other side of the room; no way could I get to it in time. I quietly dropped to the floor and slid under the bed. The footsteps grew louder as they got closer. I held my breath, desperately wishing for a weapon. My body began to tremble when a large pair of black tactical boots stopped at the side of the bed. I bit my lower lip so hard that I tasted blood. After a few seconds, the boots slowly backed away. While fighting the urge to breathe a huge sigh of relief, I heard the unmistakable *clicking* sound of a round being chambered. Whoever it was hadn't left the room and worse than that, I'd been discovered. I wanted to vomit.

"I know you're under the bed. Very slowly, I want to see some hands," a deep voice commanded. *What to do?* There was nowhere to go and nothing to fight back with. There wasn't much choice. One of my hands came out from under the bed and before the other one could be presented, I was dragged across the floor and flipped upright to stare down the length of a gun barrel.

A man dressed in head to toe black took a few steps backwards, yet kept the weapon trained on me. Instinctively, I curled into a ball and threw my hands over my face.

"What's your business here?" he demanded.

"Don't shoot! I'm a friend of the Sheriff's," I rambled as quickly as I could.

"Sure you are, honey," he said sardonically. Then his tone changed. "Hey, wait a second. Aren't you Emily Boudreaux?"

"Uh-hunh," I stammered, slowly moving my arms to see if I was still being held at gunpoint. The man holstered his weapon and extended his hand to help me stand. I looked at it warily.

"It's okay. I'm not going to hurt you," he insisted.

"How do you know my name?" I asked, still afraid to move.

"It's Crusher...Spencer Landry. Remember me from high school? Pete and I used to play football together," he said, waving his outstretched hand.

"Crusher? I haven't seen you since graduation. This is so awkward," I said, finally accepting his outstretched hand. "What are you doing here?"

"I was about to ask you the same thing. I've been given orders, and technically, I'm supposed to have you arrested," he said.

"What? I can't get arrested, I just came to see if..." I started, but Spencer lifted his hand to stop me.

"Relax; I know you're not normally a trouble maker. Let's go downstairs. I'm curious to hear the story of why you're suddenly into breaking and entering," he joked.

"You know, I didn't break anything, I only entered," I said, making my way down the stairs.

He laughed. "You haven't changed a bit, Emily."

I shrugged.

"Go ahead and tell me what you're doing here," he said, pulling out one of the kitchen stools for me.

Understanding that full disclosure wasn't the best option, I gave Crusher only the vaguest details.

"Holden gave me a key to his house a long time ago. I thought he might need someone to check up on the

81

place, but I haven't been able to reach him. So, I decided to come out and check on it anyway. That's my story, now you tell me yours. What are you doing here?" I asked.

"I own a security company in DeSoto and we were hired to protect this place. My instructions are to keep an employee here twenty-four hours a day until the five fugitives are apprehended. After that, I'm to check in on the property daily," Crusher explained.

"Were you able to talk to Holden? Was he the person who arranged everything?" I asked.

"No, it was all arranged through a representative of his," he answered.

"Do you know where Holden is?" I plied.

"I can't say," he answered. When he saw my face fall, he continued. "It's not because I'm forbidden to share that information or anything, it's because I really don't know. A messenger showed up at my office one day with a cashier's check to cover six months of round-the-clock protection. He said that if I needed anything else or had any questions, I should get in touch with some big shot attorney out of Baton Rouge. He handed me a business card and left. I'm sorry I don't remember the guy's name right off."

"Thanks, Crusher. I know you didn't have to share that information with me; it means a lot that you did. So, what happens from here?" I asked.

"Are you wondering if I'm going to have you arrested?"

"Yes," I said sheepishly.

"I'll get into so much trouble if I let you go," he started.

"I don't want you to get into trouble. Would you please ask for Bert Hebert or Jackson Sonnier when you call it in, please? I had a really bad experience with the last guy who arrested me," I interrupted.

"Excuse me! Would you let me finish talking, Emily Boudreaux?" He laughed. "I could get into trouble for letting you go, but seeing that you had a key and you didn't take anything, I'm not going to report it. Nothing against you, but you'll need to hand over that key."

"I understand. Thank you for not calling it in," I said softly as I pushed the key ring across the table. "Holden's gone. Time to move on," I mumbled to myself.

"I'm really sorry, Emily. You know it's just business—nothing personal. You don't need to worry about this place. My guys will take really good care of it for the Sheriff."

"I know. It was nice to see you, though. I'm really sorry it was under these circumstances," I said.

"It's all good. But, answer a question for me. What did you mean by 'the last time I was arrested'?" he asked, holding the door open. He followed me to my car, where I gave him another watered-down version of the truth.

"You're quite the rebel, aren't you? Let me give you a business card. You still live at Greenleaf Plantation, right? If you ever need anything related to security, I hope you'll give me a call."

"I sure will. At least two of the five fugitives have it out for me, so you never know," I said, tucking the card into my purse.

"Wow, hand the card back so I can give you my cell number," he said, scribbling down the digits. "Call me anytime; it doesn't have to be work related. Maybe we could get some dinner and talk about the old days?"

"That sounds really nice. Speaking of getting together, I'm having a Halloween party at my house and I'd love for you to come. Feel free to bring a date. Things get started around eight. Oh, and be sure to wear a costume," I said, putting his card back into my purse. "I hope to see you there."

"Sounds great. I'm just getting out of a relationship and I'm ready to have some fun. A costume party is right up my alley. Be safe and call if you need," he said, closing the car door for me. I nodded, giving him a quick wave as I drove off.

5

Connie wheeled a cart down the adult costume aisle of the Halloween party store. "How many people are you expecting at the party?"

I shook my head when she picked up a naughty nurse outfit. "Around twenty-five, and no. Try again," I replied.

"What? You don't think Bert will like it?" she asked, striking a pose as she held the costume against her body.

"In your bedroom maybe but not in public. That thing shows all of your zippity and half of your doo-dah," I said, putting it back on the shelf to hold up a black and white striped outfit. "Here, you could be his prisoner of love."

"Very funny!" Connie said, rolling her eyes before looking through other costumes. "Are you and Jackson dressing up together?"

"Why would we? We're not a couple."

"He lives with you, and there's nothing that says you have to be a couple to dress together for Halloween," Connie said, modeling a long, black wig.

"I don't like the black hair on you. Try the blonde wig," I suggested.

"Oh, I like it!" She turned so she could see her reflection in the mirror. "That settles it. I'm going as a mermaid and Bert can be a sailor."

"Cute!" I said as she started rummaging for the things she needed to complete their costumes.

"Twenty-five people, huh? Anyone I don't know?"

"I don't think so." I picked up a princess costume. Connie wrinkled her nose and shook her head, so I put it back on the rack. "There's a guy who may show up that you probably haven't met—Crusher Landry. Do you know him?"

"No, never heard of him. Crusher? What kind of a name is that?"

"It's his nickname because he was a linebacker in high school. He played football with Pete. His real name is Spencer."

"Wait, Spencer Landry? As in the Spencer Landry who owns Tac-Eagle Enterprises?"

"I don't know. Hold on, he gave me a card." I started to dig around in my purse. "Here it is. Yep, that's him. How do you know about his company?"

"When Grossie LaPointe, that loud-mouthed owner of those strip clubs in New Orleans, started getting death threats he hired Spencer. He'd be dead, too, if it wasn't for Spencer and his men. A guy came out of a crowd and started firing down Bourbon Street. Spencer took him down and saved a bunch of innocent bystanders in the process. It was plastered all over the news for weeks. Where were you?"

"Who knows? It depresses me that my life has more action than the news, so I try to avoid watching," I answered.

"Wow, Spencer Landry. He's like a local celebrity. I hope he comes!" Connie gushed. "Are you going to date him?"

"What! No! Remember, it wasn't that long ago that I was ready to commit to Holden."

"It's been almost two months," she said.

"And your point is?"

"You're no spring chicken, Emily. You need to move it along," she suggested.

"I'm thirty!" I said, shooting her a nasty look.

"Is that supposed to be a rebuttal? Because that's the point I was going to use to win my argument."

"What am I going to do with you, Connie?" I asked, holding up a low-cut vampire gown.

Connie nodded her head. "I can't wait to see it on you! I'll wait here while you try it on," she said, plopping on the bench outside of the dressing room.

"Do I have a choice?" I asked.

"What do you think?" she returned, settling in and crossing her legs.

"Guess not," I said, entering the room. The costume looked okay, but I knew it needed Connie's approval.

"So?" I asked, stepping out to do a twirl in front of her.

"I love it," she said.

"You don't think it's too revealing?" I asked as I adjusted myself.

"Not even. It's very sexy! I think it looks wonderful."

"Really?" I asked, turning to see how it looked from behind.

"Get it!" she said. "I saw a guy costume out there that would match it perfectly. What size do you think Jackson wears?"

"You were just trying to set me up with Spencer Landry. Now you're picking costumes for Jackson. Six weeks ago you wanted me with Holden. Would you pick a person, Connie?" I demanded.

"Until you're at that altar saying, 'I do', everyone's fair game, girlfriend," she said.

I sighed.

Once I came out of the dressing room, she tossed the male version of my costume into the basket.

"What am I going to do with you?" I asked.

"You're going to keep on loving me, like you have been." She laughed.

"Let's get out of here. You're beginning to stress me out," I said, giving her a playful push toward the checkout counter.

"Spencer Landry or Jackson Sonnier? Oh, yeah," I heard Connie singing under her breath. I rolled my eyes.

~.~.~.~.~

I was admiring my makeup job in the mirror when a gentle rap sounded at the door. I capped the tube of blood red lipstick and went to answer it.

"I'm sorry to bother you, but I don't know where to go from…" Jackson began. "Wow, you just took my breath away."

"Oh, stop!" I said, ushering him into my bedroom. "Your costume looks great. Do you need help with your makeup?" I asked, but Jackson didn't answer. "Hello, Earth to Jackson."

"Makeup? Sure," he said, shaking his head. "Wow, you look, wow!"

"Have a seat." I laughed, pushing him into a chair. After some strategic smearing of gray and white costume makeup, Jackson looked just as vampy as I did.

"Are you finished?" he asked.

"Yep, what do you think?" I asked, moving so he could inspect my work.

He came to stand behind me so he could admire our reflection in the mirror. "I think we look pretty awesome," he answered.

I leaned my head to rest on his shoulder and closed my eyes to savor the moment that Jackson's strong arms encircled my waist. It felt good to be held. He turned me to face him and gently lowered his lips to brush against mine.

"Emily! Where are you?" I heard Connie yelling from downstairs. Using my thumb, I quickly wiped my lipstick from Jackson's mouth.

"I'm sorry, I shouldn't have…" Jackson said, taking hold of my wrist.

"It's okay. Don't apologize."

"Emily!" Connie called.

I gave Jackson an unsure smile before yelling down. "We're upstairs, Connie!"

"I should've guessed you'd be up here getting ready. You two look great!" she said when we met her in the hallway.

"And so do you! You're lucky that it's not supposed to be too cold tonight, hot momma!" I joked, referring to the sequined bikini top Connie wore with her mermaid costume.

"What? This old thing?" she asked, putting her hands on her hips and wiggling. You had to love her!

"We should go downstairs. Would you mind helping me put out the food, Connie?" I asked.

"Not at all! Chief, uh, Sheriff, uh…" Connie stammered.

"Jackson's just fine," he said with a smile.

"Jackson, Bert's outside setting up the bar."

"And that's where I'll be if you need me," he said as he left the room.

"I interrupted something, didn't I?" Connie inquired, her arms crossed and her eyes squinted.

"No, let's go downstairs."

"You're lying!" she said, right on my heels.

"Cut that out! It was nothing."

"What was nothing?" she asked.

I let out an exasperated sigh. "The very insignificant and brief kiss that Jackson and I shared right before you came upstairs."

"I knew I interrupted something!" she squealed.

"You did not! Besides, it wouldn't have gone any further." I pulled open the refrigerator door and handed a food tray to Connie.

"I guess we'll never know," Connie said sadly.

"You're crazy," I said jokingly. The doorbell rang. "If you don't mind finishing up in here, I'll answer that."

"Not a problem. I've got this," Connie said, shooing me out of the kitchen.

Chuck and his girlfriend, Bridget, were at the door. Bridget and I met in quite an interesting way. A group of men had set up a kiddie pool, filled it with baby oil, and were taking turns wrestling with bikini-clad women. One of those women was Bridget. After providing care for a man with a back injury, I discovered that the only reason Bridget participated was to support her special needs daughter. We kissed for the crowd, she got lots of money for it, and then I set her up with Chuck. They were perfect for each other.

"Hi, Chuck! You look wonderful, Bridget!" I exclaimed when I saw their football player and cheerleader costumes. "How's your daughter?"

"Samantha's just fine. She's with her grandmother tonight. I gave your phone number in case she needs to reach me. I hope you don't mind," she said.

"Not at all." I ushered them in.

"Did Chuck tell you the good news?" she asked excitedly.

"I don't think so. What news?"

"I start paramedic school on Monday! I passed all of the tests and Chuck was able to pull some strings to get me into this session. You two have inspired me to do something better with my life. I really want to help people," she said, giving Chuck's arm a tight squeeze.

"Really? That's wonderful news, Bridget! I know you'll do fine. Let me know if you need help with anything."

"Thanks, Emily! I really appreciate it." She and Chuck went to join the others in the backyard.

A steady stream of guests arrived. They appeared to be having a good time, but I just wasn't in the mood to party. I stayed around the food table most of the night. *I should probably reign in the stress eating before my clothes get too tight to wear.* I tossed the potato chip in my hand aside and picked up a carrot stick.

"Would you like me to get you something from the bar?" Jackson asked.

"A glass of red wine would be great." I munched on a celery stick until he returned. "I thought Connie was nuts when she suggested these, but I'm glad she did. They're pretty cool," I said holding up the plastic, antique-looking goblet we'd picked up at the Halloween supply store. After nearly draining my cup, I perused the food table for something else to eat.

"Is that Spencer Landry over there?" Jackson asked, tapping me on the back to get my attention.

"It probably is since I invited him. Where?" I asked, looking in the same direction he was.

"The guy dressed as Caesar," he answered.

"Yep, that's Spencer. I didn't realize you knew him."

"I've seen him around, but we haven't met," Jackson said.

"Well, I went to high school with him. Come on, I'll introduce you." I took Jackson's hand and led him across the yard, but stopped mid-stride. "Never mind, I'll introduce you later."

I quickly turned and bolted into the house; Jackson stayed right behind me. I ran up the stairs and into the bathroom before dropping to my knees in front of the toilet. Jackson softly stroked my back as a series of dry heaves started. After they subsided, I rolled to sit on the cold, tile floor and carefully leaned my head against the wall.

"Emily, what's wrong? Are you sick?" Jackson asked, taking my face in his hands to feel for fever.

"You didn't see her?" I asked.

"See who?" he said, sitting next to me.

"Roberta. She must've come with Spencer. She was dressed in what I'm guessing is meant to be a toga," I answered.

The tension between Roberta and I went way back. Strutting around in her extra-thick makeup and extra-small clothes, she worked to seduce any male who crossed her path. She had unapologetically and incessantly flirted with every man I'd been involved with. She worked as a cashier at the local gas station, Jerry's Gas and More, and at The Blue Claw restaurant as a waitress. Needless to say, we did *not* get along!

"Hold on a second," Jackson said, walking into the bedroom to peer out of the window.

"I see what you're talking about. She's not wearing much of a costume, is she?" he said, coming to sit next to me again.

"I can't believe I'm getting this upset." Another round of dry heaves was coming. Luckily, I was able to quash them with some deep breathing.

"If the sight of her makes you that upset, she shouldn't be here. I'll ask them to leave," Jackson said.

"No, wait. That would be rude. Just give me a second." I stood at the sink and rinsed with mouthwash.

"Are you kidding me? You're up here, sick to your stomach because you literally can't stand the sight of this woman and you don't want me to get rid of her because you're worried about being rude? What are you going to do? Hide up here for the rest of the night while she has a grand old time at *your* party?" Jackson demanded.

"I might. I'm getting a headache," I said, climbing into bed and draping my arm over my eyes.

"Hello, I'm not sure what you did with Emily Boudreaux, but I'd like to speak to her please," Jackson kidded.

"What's that supposed to mean?" I asked, moving my arm so I could peep at him.

"It means that I miss your spunk. What happened to the woman who planted one on a bikini-clad stripper so that a little girl could get a breathing machine?" he asked.

A smile started to form in the corner of my mouth. "Speaking of, did I tell you that Bridget's starting paramedic class next week?"

"No, but that's great. I'm sure your influence had something to do with that," Jackson said.

"Chuck had everything to do with that," I corrected.

"You can't tell me that you didn't have a part in it, too," he said. "Now, whose house is this?"

"It's my house," I answered quietly.

"I can't hear you! Whose house is this?" Jackson asked loudly.

"It's my house!" I returned.

"Again! Louder!"

"It's my house!" I yelled.

"And whose damn party is this?" he shouted.

"It's my damn party!" I hollered back.

"Then get your ass out there and enjoy your damn party!" he said, pulling me off of the bed.

"Hell yeah! This is my house! My party! My time to shine! Screw the skank!" I yelled.

"Not even if you paid me." Jackson laughed. "Now, that's the Emily I know." He drew me in for a kiss. It didn't feel right, so I pulled away.

"Wait a second," I said, plucking the glued-on fangs from my incisors. "Now, let's give that another go." I offered my lips to him. This time it felt fabulous, so fabulous that I started to push my body tightly against his. I pressed him against the wall and ran my hands under his shirt, eagerly feeling his strong, muscular chest.

"What's gotten into you?" he breathed.

"I don't know, but all of a sudden I feel like throwing you on that bed and having my way with you," I whispered into his ear. He shuddered.

"Wait, how much have you had to drink?" he asked. I pulled away and looked at him with surprise.

"A few glasses of wine. Why do you ask?"

"It's not that I wouldn't want to take advantage of you if you were drunk, it's just that it would be so unethical," he answered. I ran my fingers through the hair at the nape of his neck as I looked deeply into his eyes.

"You really care about me, don't you?" I asked.

"Yes, I do," he answered.

I kissed him again making sure it was slow and gentle.

"Oopsie, I was looking for the little girl's room. Wow, look at you, Emily. Two Sheriffs within months of each other. Is that some sort of record?" Roberta giggled.

"First of all, you shouldn't be up here and secondly, you're one to talk! You knew that Holden and I were together and you took advantage of his concern for your well-being by making moves on him!" I yelled.

"He seemed to like it," she said smugly.

"You wish! He only pretended to like you to get what he needed—evidence to lock up your abusive, ex-DA boyfriend!"

"That's not true! Holden wanted me!" she insisted.

"Holden thought you were a joke!"

"Take that back, you bitch!" Roberta said, suddenly finding her grownup voice.

"I see that you're capable of speaking something besides baby! Kudos!" I fired off.

"You better take that back! I don't have cooties!" she said, thrusting her lower lip out in a pout and shoving her hands on her hips.

"I didn't say cooties! Never mind, it's too easy," I mumbled under my breath. "The guest bathroom is *downstairs*."

"You owe me an apology," she said, tapping her foot.

"I owe you an apology? The only thing I owe you is a beating!" I shouted.

Roberta's eyes grew wide as I charged her. She started to run away, but when she saw that Jackson had me around the waist, she smiled a smug grin.

"Let me go, Jackson!" I said, struggling to get free.

"Calm down, Emily. She's obviously drunk and it's not worth it," Jackson said, trying to quiet me down.

"You heard him! Another one of your guys has just sided with me," she taunted before she turned to go downstairs.

"I'm good," I said to Jackson after taking a deep breath. He released his hold on me, so I worked to fix my costume. "Ugh, that woman knows how to push my buttons!"

"It's over now," Jackson said, taking my face in his hands. "Come on. I'll tell Spencer to get her out of here."

Once downstairs, we discovered that Roberta had not rejoined the party, but had decided to pose in front of the doors with her breasts nearly exposed and a finger between her teeth.

"Why waste time playing around with her? This is what I bring to the table, Sheriff. You interested?" she teased.

Jackson wasn't quick enough to stop me this time. In an instant, I shoved Roberta through the doors and pinned her underneath me.

"Don't you even think of looking in my direction ever again, you stupid whore!" I shouted, steadily pummeling her. Somewhere in the chaos, Roberta managed to drag her nails across my cheek. "Oh, no you didn't!" I said drawing back my fist and giving her a punch she'd remember for a long time coming.

Roberta writhed to get on top of me, but I was pulled to my feet before she could do any damage. Bert held on to me tightly, while Spencer helped Roberta up. Blood trickled out of one of her nostrils, her eye was swelling, and clumps of her bleached-blonde hair lay all around us.

"I don't look as bad as she does, do I?" I quietly asked Bert while I tried to slow my breathing.

"Hell no! You whooped ass." Bert laughed.

"I'm sorry, Spencer. I should've clarified that you were welcome to bring anyone *but* her," I said, wiping the corner of my mouth.

"Because she knows that her men always come to me, eventually," Roberta said, pulling her toga to cover herself. When I charged again, it took Jackson *and* Bert to pull me off of her.

"I'll get her out of here," Spencer said apologetically. "I had no idea she was like this. I'm really sorry, Emily. I apologize for ruining your party."

"It's not your fault, Spencer. You couldn't have known," I said, rubbing the kink out of the back of my neck.

"What are you apologizing to her for?" Roberta squeaked.

"Let's go," Spencer said firmly. "Good night and sorry again."

"Okay, folks! The show's over! Time to wrap up the party! It's getting late!" Connie yelled to the guests. "I'll see everyone out if you want to go upstairs and get cleaned up. Don't worry about anything down here. Bert and I have this. Is it still okay for us to stay the night in the guest house?"

"Of course! Thank you, Connie. You know I love you, right?" I asked.

"I know. How'd it feel to knock the crap out of her?" she asked excitedly.

"Pretty damn good," I answered with a smile.

"The men might've been gaga over the fake boobies bobbing up and down, but we women were cheering you on. I think each one of us has thought of popping the tar out of that woman at least once. You're our hero," she joked.

"Oh, stop. Thanks again," I said, giving her a quick kiss on the cheek. I went upstairs, showered, and had just crawled into bed when Jackson knocked on the door.

"Come in," I said.

"How's it going?" he asked.

"I'm a little embarrassed about what I did."

"Embarrassed about what happened with Roberta or what happened with me before she interrupted us?" he asked.

"Her," I answered.

He smiled, stretching out beside me so he could prop up on his elbow. He slowly traced the scratch marks Roberta left on my arm. "When she struck her pose downstairs, did she do anything for you?" I asked.

99

"Why would she? She's not my type. You're more intelligent, have a better personality, and you're way more beautiful than she could ever be."

"Good answer." I smiled and rolled to face him.

"It's the truth," he said softly, touching the tip of my nose.

I casually draped my leg over his and he pulled me closer to his body. I tucked my head under his chin and he held me in his arms until I fell asleep.

6

The buzzing of the doorbell woke me the next morning. Slightly cracking an eye and sneaking a peek at the clock, I groaned—it was only nine in the morning. Jackson, still holding me in an embrace, began to stir.

"You can go back to sleep if you want to. I'll get the door," I said, pulling on a robe.

"No, I think I'll come down and start some breakfast." He thrust his arms high overhead in a stretch before following me down the stairs.

An older woman, holding the largest bouquet of flowers I'd ever seen, stood on the front porch. She continually shifted her weight from one foot to the other to keep upright. Sure that she'd topple over any second, I threw the door open and helped her inside.

"Whoa! That's quite an impressive arrangement, but I think you have the wrong house," I said, reaching out to help hold the vase.

"This is Greenleaf Plantation, isn't it?" she asked, flustered.

"Yes."

"Are you Emily Boudreaux?"

"I am."

"Then I'm at the right house. If you'll tell me where you want this," she said.

"The dining room will be fine; it's just right through here," I said, going through the doorway first. "I can't imagine how many flowers are in that bouquet!"

"Three dozen sterling roses, a dozen stargazer lilies, a dozen purple irises, wax flowers, as well as other assorted fillers and greenery. I was told to use purple, lots of purple." She removed her glasses to wipe her brow.

"It's very beautiful. If you'll wait here I'll get my purse."

"No need. The tip's already been included. I hope you enjoy the flowers. I'll show myself out. Good day to you," she said quite monotone. I ignored her lack of enthusiasm and appreciated the flowers. After hearing the front door latch, I reached for the card.

I can't apologize enough for last night.
I hope we can still be friends. Please call me.

Crusher

"Looks like someone's got a new fan," Jackson said from behind me.

"Crusher sent apology flowers," I answered.

"That's one hell of an apology."

"Jealous?"

"That's not how I do things," Jackson answered.

"Good to know." I followed him to the kitchen. "Care to elaborate on that point?"

"I'm not the jealous type. It's obvious that you're beautiful; men will be attracted to you. It's a fact of life. How can I be jealous of that?" he asked, pouring pancake batter onto the griddle.

I propped my chin on my hands. "So you're telling me that even if we were in a committed relationship and another man showered me with attention and gifts, you wouldn't be the least bit jealous?" I questioned.

"I don't think so, because I'd trust that if you wanted to pursue something with another man, you'd be open and honest about it." He held out a strawberry slice for me to sample.

I shook my head. "Unlike the night I caught Holden with Roberta and went running to you," I said, putting my head down.

"Apples and oranges, Emily. I'm not Holden. I believe that honesty is a two-way street. Come on. Open up. These strawberries are extra sweet."

I raised my head and accepted the fruit. He was right—it was delicious. "Holden said the only reason he didn't tell me about Roberta was so the case would remain solid. He was scared I'd start acting differently and people would get suspicious," I said.

Jackson turned off the stove and walked over to me. He took my hands in his. "I'm not going to bash Holden. He did what he thought was right. I can only speak for myself. That being said, I would tell you everything, and I wouldn't be jealous because I'd make it my life's mission to treat you so well that you wouldn't give anyone else a second thought," he said.

Suddenly, I wasn't feeling so well. "If you'll excuse me for a minute, I'd like to get dressed before breakfast," I said, climbing from the stool. Jackson continued to hold my hand.

"I'm sorry, I shouldn't have said anything," Jackson apologized.

"I appreciate what you said. I'm still recovering from a rough night and I think I might be coming down with something. That's all," I said with a reassuring smile. He gave my hand a gentle squeeze before releasing it.

After getting upstairs, I splashed some cold water on my face. So many things about me had changed since moving back to Green Bayou—like the scratches across my cheek and arm. I couldn't believe I'd gotten into a fight with Roberta! It was so unlike me. Had I made the right move by coming home? If ever there was a good time to leave, this was it. Oh, who was I kidding? Green Bayou would always be home. I sighed heavily before going into the closet and pulling on a pair of black shorts and a stretchy top. Bert and Connie had joined Jackson in the kitchen by the time I went downstairs.

"You don't look any worse for the wear, Big Brawler," Bert joked. I gave him a pair of evil eyes. "Oh, come on! You know you've been wanting to do that. I had no idea you were such a scrapper!"

"Bert, leave her alone! Are you okay, sweetie?" Connie asked, pouring me a mug of coffee.

"I'm fine. I'm just tired and I'm not feeling well today," I answered.

Connie reached out to feel me for fever. "You're not warm. Is it your stomach?" she asked.

"Yes, I'm probably getting an ulcer from all the stress," I said, gently smacking my forehead against the table.

"Don't do that," Jackson said, pulling me upright. I gave him the most pathetic look I could muster. "And don't do that either. Eat your breakfast." He gave my shoulders a tight squeeze. The pecan pancakes he made were delicious, but I couldn't get more than a few bites down.

After breakfast, Bert and Jackson decided to go fishing. I didn't feel like going out in the boat, so Connie and I stayed behind. She "ooed" and "awed" over my flower arrangement.

"Are you going to date Spencer?" she asked.

"Who said anything about dating? He sent these to apologize for bringing Roberta to the party," I said.

"Hello, Miss Naïve, no he didn't," Connie said sarcastically.

"Crusher and I know each other from high school. That's all," I said defensively.

"A bouquet of daisies says 'Sorry I brought a slut to your party. Will you forgive me?' This says, 'I messed up big time and I don't want to ruin my chances with you.' He's going to ask you out," Connie said assuredly.

"You're so wrong," I returned.

"I'm wrong? Me? Let's take a quick trip down memory lane. How many times have I been right about things like this?"

"Lots," I said, covering my face with my hands. I slowly massaged my temples.

"So are you going to go out with him when he asks you?"

"Stop talking about dating. You're making my stomach churn," I told Connie. She looked at me with concern.

"How long have you been feeling like this?" she asked.

"Since I found out that Holden left town," I answered.

"Is it just your stomach?" she asked.

"It's the stress. No need for you to jump into your Nurse Ramrod shoes," I complained.

"Answer the question, Emily," she said, tapping her foot.

"Okay, I've had headaches, nausea, and my appetite fluctuates. Stress," I asserted.

Connie stared me down with an unsure look on her face. She tapped her lower lip with her finger before her face suddenly brightened.

"When was your last period?" she asked, pointing her index finger at me.

"What? Why? Noooo. No way," I said, shaking my hands to shoo her away.

"Emily?" she said sternly.

"I'm on the pill," I said.

"Emily?"

"Okay, so I missed a period. Stress can make you do that."

"And so can being pregnant," Connie said with a smile.

"Did you not hear me when I told you that I'm on the pill?" I fussed.

"You work in the medical field! You know as well as I do that the only method that's one hundred percent guaranteed is not having sex."

"I'm gonna throw up," I said, running for the downstairs bathroom.

"You go do that. I'm going to town for a test. Don't you dare leave!" she ordered, running for her purse. I heaved my reply.

Connie must've spent most of the trip to town with the accelerator mashed against the floorboard. It seemed like a few seconds had passed when she tore back into the house.

"Here it is!" She panted holding the white, plastic bag high above her head.

"Stop being so cheery about it. This is nothing to celebrate," I said. "Not that it really matters because *I'm not pregnant*. It's stress."

"Oh, really?" she asked, reaching her hand out to squeeze one of my breasts.

"Ouch!" I yelled, slapping her hand away.

"Stress doesn't make your boobies hurt. You're pregnant," she said with a huge smile. "Now, go pee on the stick so I can gloat."

"Let's go upstairs in case the guys come back early."
I begrudgingly took the bag from her. She stayed right on
my heels.

Carefully following the directions on the package, a
positive result showed in the window before I'd even
capped the end of the stick. Uncontrollable trembling took
over my body, so Connie grasped my hand to see the result
for herself.

"Oh, Emily! You're going to be a mommie!" she
said excitedly. "This is so wonderful!"

I sank to the floor, tears filled my eyes. Feeling as
though I couldn't catch my breath, I pushed my forehead
into my knees. Connie gently rubbed my back.

"Oh, no." I gasped.

"It's going to take a little time to get used to the
idea, but it's going to be fine. Just you wait and see," she
said. "I'm so excited for you and …" The smile slowly
disappeared from her face.

"Now do you see my problem? There are two
possible fathers, and one of them I can't even find," I
sobbed. "Why, oh why, did this have to happen now?"

"Are you thinking of maybe ending…" Connie
cautiously started to ask.

"No! That's not an option." I pulled toilet tissue
from the holder and blew my nose. After a few minutes of
silence, I finally spoke again. "Okay, I'm not going to feel
sorry for myself. I have to get a game plan. Like it or not,
this is going to happen."

"My obstetrician, Dr. Nelson, is awesome. You'll
love her. I'll go with you to all of your appointments. You

know I'll be right there with you the entire time," Connie offered.

"I'm so glad I have you in my life. I love you," I said, giving her a tight squeeze.

"I love you, too. You're going to be a great mom and now Andre's gonna have a playmate!" she said. "When are you going to tell Jackson?"

"After everything's confirmed by the OB doctor. I know that these tests are supposed to be accurate, but I don't want to say anything until I'm absolutely sure," I answered.

"I completely understand. What about Holden?"

"I'm not sure about that one, yet. Give me a few days to come to terms with this and something will come to me," I said.

"I know it will. Come on. Let's leave a note for the guys saying we went into town to get a pedicure. Maybe it'll help you relax," she said.

"Connie, pretty toes are the last thing on my mind."

"That's my point. This is huge and you need time to process it. You can fret here or you can fret in a massage chair with someone pampering you. Take your pick."

"Well, when you put it that way."

She put her arm around my shoulder and gave it a squeeze. "Everything's going to be just fine. You'll see."

~.~.~.~.~

Thanks to Connie's connections, I was able to see Dr. Nelson two days after the positive home test. She told me that my lab results confirmed it—I was pregnant. Secretly, I wondered how often the lab gave false positives.

"How do you feel about an ultrasound? It'll help me to get a closer estimate of your due date," the doctor explained.

"An ultrasound? Sure, I'm fine with it, I guess." I said, looking past the doctor to Connie. Connie nodded her head to say she thought the ultrasound was a good idea.

"Great." She pulled the machine closer to her. "Would you mind getting the lights, Connie?"

She turned them off and the screen on the machine lit up the room. Dr. Nelson began moving the wand until she found what she was looking for. "There, do you see it?" she asked, freezing the image and pointing to the screen. "That's your baby."

Reality smacked me and it smacked me hard. I could no longer deny it; there was no false positive. I was going to be a mom. A tear slid down my cheek, but I quickly wiped it away.

"From the measurements I'm getting and taking into consideration the information you gave me about your last cycle, I'd say you're between seven and eight weeks pregnant. I'm going to give you June seventh as a due date." She placed the wand back in the holder. "I'm all done here; you can get dressed and meet me up front. We'll schedule your next appointment and get you a 'Future Mom' goodie bag. Do you have any questions for me before I go?"

"I do, Doctor, and this is a little embarrassing…" I started.

"I can assure you that whatever it is, I've been asked it before." She sat on the stool and gave me her undivided attention.

"Two men could potentially be the father," I said softly.

"We can certainly do paternity testing to determine which gentleman is the biological father, and there are a couple of options available. We can get a sample in-utero or we could wait until after the baby's born. In-utero is generally safe, but like anything, it does carry potential risks. If you decide to wait until after the baby's born, the risk factor is eliminated. I'll be happy to set you up with a dependable lab. The decision is entirely yours. If you choose in-utero, it can be done in a just few weeks, once you're past your first trimester."

"Thank you, Dr. Nelson. I really appreciate it," I said.

"Anytime, I'll see you at your next appointment. Oh, here's a picture of your baby," she said, handing it over with a smile before she exited the room.

"Well, what do you think?" Connie asked, moving my hand so she could see the picture.

"She's nice. Thank you for recommending her," I said, pulling on my clothes.

"What about the testing?"

111

"I'll have to run it by Jackson. If he agrees to wait, then I'll need to find a way to get word to Holden to see if he agrees, as well."

"How are you going to do that?" Connie asked, passing me my purse.

"Crusher Landry," I said.

"What? How's Spencer supposed to help you find Holden?"

"Word was left that if Spencer needed anything he was to get in touch with this attorney out of Baton Rouge," I answered.

"Ahhh, I see," Connie said.

"Since we're already in DeSoto, would you mind if we stopped by Copies 'n Coffee so I can make duplicates of the ultrasound picture and jot a quick note to Holden. Hopefully, Spencer will be at his office."

"I don't mind at all. Who knows, maybe Holden will come home? You know how he is with Andre; just imagine how he'll be with your baby. Even if it isn't his, I'm sure he'll still want to be involved," she said.

"I'm not as confident as you are. Too much time has gone by without hearing anything from him. I can feel the disconnect."

"He was hurt pretty badly. Maybe he just needed time to heal. Let's see what happens once he gets the letter," Connie suggested.

"Yeah, we'll see," I agreed.

~.~.~.~.~

Spencer's secretary buzzed him to let him know that Connie and I were waiting and he joined us in the waiting room in no time flat.

"Emily! It's good to see you. Did you get the flowers?" he asked.

"I did. They were gorgeous, and totally unnecessary."

"I'm glad you liked them and they were completely necessary. That's what happens when you take a chance on someone you don't really know. I stopped to get gas at Jerry's on my way back to DeSoto, Roberta and I started talking, anyway, I'm sorry."

"You had no way of knowing my history with her. Apology accepted."

"Good. That makes me feel better. Now, what can I do for you? You here to take me up on that security system?"

"Not exactly. I have a favor to ask of you."

"Just name it," Spencer said, leading us into his office.

"I have a letter I need to get to Holden. I thought you could send it to the attorney in Baton Rouge and maybe the lawyer could get it to him. I wouldn't ask if it weren't extremely important," I pleaded.

"I don't know…" He rubbed the back of his neck.

"Crusher, it's very, very important. I wouldn't dream of asking otherwise. Would you please do this for me?"

"Okay, I'll see what I can do," he said, taking the envelope.

"Thank you so much!"

"Don't thank me; it's nothing." He tossed the envelope onto his desk then took a seat on the corner. "I'm glad you stopped by, Emily. I was wondering, do you have plans for dinner?"

Connie nudged me with her elbow, her way of saying "I told you so." I gave her a look that said, "Stop it".

"I'd love to, but something unexpected has come up and I have to deal with it before I can commit to anything else. You understand, don't you?" I asked.

He stood silent for a few seconds. "If you'd rather not go…"

"It's not that, I promise. We'll get together soon, okay?"

"Sure, whenever you're ready," he said, rising to escort us out.

"Great, I'll keep in touch," I promised.

"Feel free to stop by anytime you're in town," he offered before we left.

Once we were in the car, Connie couldn't keep quiet. "I so should've bet money on that one! I told you he wanted to date you!"

"Seriously, with everything that's happening, this is what you want to harp on?" I asked.

"Just tell me I was right and I'll drop it," she sang.

"You were right," I said dryly. She started to wriggle and dance in her seat.

"Tell me again, who was right?" she asked, pointing to me.

"That's the opposite of dropping it, Connie," I said smartly.

"Fine, it's over, but just so you know, I was right!"
She laughed.

7

Later that evening, I found Jackson watching the sunset from the back porch swing.

"Hey. I don't mean to interrupt the quiet, but can we talk?" I asked.

"Sure, sounds serious. Is everything okay?" he asked, sitting up so I could join him.

"Everything is fine. It's just that I'm not sure where to begin," I said, nervously wringing my fingers. Jackson took my hand in his.

"Whatever it is, you'll feel better once it's out. Just tell me," he suggested.

"Okay. You know how I've been feeling yucky lately and thought it was because of stress? Well, I went to the doctor today and it's not stress. She estimates that I'm between seven and eight weeks pregnant."

"You're going to have a baby? I'm excited for you! What can I do? I'll help with whatever you need," he said.

"Jackson," I said, scooting closer to him. "I'm not telling you this because I want your help, I'm telling you because there's a chance that you may be the father."

His face went ashen. "The father? I assumed that Holden... But we only... I didn't do the math, I thought that..." Jackson stumbled for the right words to say.

"I was where you are not that long ago. Just take some time to let it sink in. You don't have to say anything, yet."

His cheeks pinked back up. "I don't need time. How do we find out if it's my baby?" he asked excitedly.

"The doctor said that we can do an in-utero test as early as a few weeks from now, but even though it's minimal, there's a risk of miscarriage. Or, we can wait until after the baby is born to have it tested and there'll be no risk involved. It's up to us to decide," I answered.

"Ultimately, it's your decision. I'll support you no matter what you want to do, but if it were up to me, I'd say why take a risk if it's not necessary? I'm okay with waiting," he said.

"That's how I feel, too." Relief flooded through me.

"What about Holden?" Jackson asked.

The tension came back. "I gave Spencer Landry a letter to give to Holden's attorney in Baton Rouge. I have no other way of getting in touch with him." I sighed. "If he answers back and wants the test, then I'll schedule it. Other than that, we'll wait until the baby comes."

"Well, that's settled." He softly patted my hand.

"Would you like to see a picture?"

"Would I!" he said eagerly. I pointed out the tiny spot that was the baby.

"Jackson, I'm really sorry about this. I promise you, I *was* on the pill. This was a total accident," I explained.

"There's nothing for you to be sorry about. I'm not sure what kind of response you'll get from Holden, but I want you to know that I'd like to be a part of this baby's life. I want to be there for the both of you. I'm okay with being Uncle Jackson and I'm all right with being Daddy; whichever way it plays out. When's the baby due?" he asked.

"June seventh."

Jackson was lost in thought for a minute or so before he snapped out of it. "Do you need me to do anything for you? Want me to rub your feet? Are you thirsty? What about cravings? Do you have any yet? Do you need me to run to the store?" he rambled.

I put my hands on either side of his face and drew him close. "Thank you for taking this so well. You're a good man, Jackson Sonnier. Don't ever let anyone tell you otherwise," I said, giving him a brief kiss on the lips.

"That means a lot to me. I try," he said.

I suddenly pulled away from him, and Jackson looked confused when I gasped.

"What's wrong?" he asked.

My eyes glazed over. "Celeste and Don Boudreaux. I have to tell my parents. Oh, no! I have to tell my parents," I said, starting to panic.

"Emily, you're an adult. I'm sure they'll be very supportive once the shock wears off," he said soothingly.

I started to paw at him. "No, you don't understand. You don't know my parents. A grandchild changes everything. They're going to come back to Green Bayou for good! Oh, my gosh! How long do you think we have before I start showing? I can probably blame my pooch on bloating when they visit for Thanksgiving, but what am I going to do for Christmas? I'll think of something. If I do this right, I might be able to hold out on telling them until their Mardi Gras visit. Mardi Gras is in April this year, so that buys us maybe five months! Okay, I've got five months."

"Emily, you can't withhold that kind of information from them for five months!" Jackson fussed.

"You're right." I inhaled slowly and deeply to calm myself down. "I'll wait until Thanksgiving so I can tell them in person."

"That's not very far off. I guess I need to get busy and find a house," Jackson said.

"Why? Because of my parents? Please!"

"Won't they be upset having a stranger living in their home?"

"They stay in the guest house when they visit. You'll need to meet them to understand, but no, I assure you, you don't have to worry about upsetting them," I insisted.

"Good, because I'd really like to be with you during the pregnancy. I don't want to miss a thing."

"That means a lot to me, Jackson." I propped my head on his shoulder.

"Anytime," he said, giving me a gentle squeeze.

~.~.~.~.~

The week before Thanksgiving I showed up on Connie's doorstep a sniveling wreck. She quickly pulled me inside.

"What's wrong? Are you hurt? Is something wrong with the baby?" she asked.

I shook my head.

Bert came around the corner to see what was going on when he heard the commotion.

"Who do I need to have a conversation with?" he asked gruffly when he noticed my distressed state.

"It's okay, Bert. Tone down the protective brother routine a bit and give us a minute for some girl talk. Okay?"Connie asked.

"Are you sure you're okay?" he asked.

"I'm sure. I just need to talk to Connie," I said in between gasps.

"Alright then. Wanna go play outside, little man?" he asked, bending down to scoop up Andre.

"Jess, we go pway, Daddy," Andre said, jumping up and down.

"Okay, okay," Bert said, smiling as they went out of the door.

"Come sit down," Connie said, passing me a bottle of water and placing a box of tissues in front of me. I tried to take a sip, but ended up choking on the water instead. "You're scaring me, Emily. What's wrong, sweetie?" she asked, pushing my hair out of my face.

I handed her the certified letter I received in the mail that day. She opened it and started to read aloud, "'On behalf of my client, I am formally notifying you that any and all communication is not only unwanted, but will be considered harassment.' That bastard!"

"I guess that answers the question about the DNA testing." I sobbed.

"But, I tell you what, he can't pretend that it's not his baby if it is! I was hoping it wasn't Jackson's baby, but now I want it to be his! At least he's supportive! Ewww, I'm so mad! You have rights that you can pursue, no matter what this jackass of an attorney says!" Connie spewed.

"But if this is how he wants it, I'm not sure he should be involved. Jackson's been so good to me, Connie. Even if it's Holden's baby, the DNA doesn't matter so much to me anymore. I want my baby to be loved and wanted, not just supported."

"Do you love Jackson?" she asked.

"Not exactly, but I could see myself loving him one day. When we kissed on Halloween night, I did feel something."

"You lied when you said I didn't interrupt anything! You said it was no big deal!" she fussed.

"You do realize that I don't have to run *everything* by you, right?" I blew my nose.

"You're upset, so I'm going to pretend as though you didn't just say that," Connie said, crossing her legs and pursing her lips. She smiled after realizing her theatrics had helped me to stop crying. "I know you still love Holden, but it's been months since you've seen him and now this letter—it looks like he's made his decision," she said softly.

"You're right. I'm not just thinking about myself anymore," I said, drawing in a deep breath while wiping my eyes.

"I'm sorry to interrupt, but I can't contain this little monster anymore," Bert said from the doorway. A very excited Andre bounced up and down in his arms.

"NeeNee! I slide down! I slide down!" he yelled, extending his arms out for me to take him.

"You're not interrupting," I said, hugging Andre tightly. "Were you playing on your slide?"

"I want balls-balls!" Andre shouted.

"Not tonight. Nannie will take you to get balls-balls soon though," I said.

"That child and his spaghetti and meatballs," Connie started. "I can't pass Papa Leonardo's restaurant without him pitching a fit!"

I couldn't help but laugh. "I can't help it if the child knows good food. Speaking of good food, Bert, you're going to be off for Thanksgiving, aren't you?" I asked.

"Sure am! I can't wait for dinner with Celeste and Don. Please wait until I get there to tell them that you're pregnant?" Bert begged. Connie gave him a good, hard slug in the arm. "What was that for?" he asked.

"You know what that was for!" Connie said.

I shook my head then gave Andre a quick kiss before handing him off to Connie.

"I'm going home," I said. "Thanks for listening."

"Not a problem. You know I'm here if you need me?" Connie asked.

"I know."

"Okay, I don't have to be there in person when you tell them, but can I be on speakerphone?" Bert called from the other room.

"Don't you worry, he'll get his," Connie said, closing the door. I was so grateful to have them in my life. Besides being there for me, they sure kept things interesting!

Jackson and I were sharing a pizza in front of the TV when he reached over and turned it off. I looked at him expectantly.

"Your parents are supposed to be here tomorrow and I'd like to do something special for them. Any ideas?" Jackson asked.

"That's an incredibly sweet gesture, but you have no clue what you're getting into," I warned, reaching for the remote.

"I want to make a good impression." He pulled the remote out of my reach. I placed my hand on his thigh.

"You don't need to worry about that. I'm sure they'll love you."

"I'm so used to being on my own. I can't tell you the last time I participated in a family event; much less met the parents of someone special. I feel like I'm back in high school," Jackson remarked.

"Oh, it's not that bad. What about your mom? Don't you celebrate the holidays with her?" I asked.

"No, she favored Kent and I chose not to be there when he was visiting. Since his death, she's asked me to stop by quite a few times, but I haven't."

"Why not?" I put my plate on the coffee table and gave Jackson my undivided attention.

"I'm not ready to see her. She'd prefer that I lie to her about Kent, and I'm not willing to do that. She wants me to tell her that he was a brave deputy who was killed in the line of duty. She doesn't want to hear the truth," Jackson answered.

"I'm sorry." I offered him a sympathetic smile. "I shouldn't be going on about my family when you've had such a hard time with yours."

"You have nothing to apologize for. I'm fine. Not seeing her is my decision and I'm okay with it. Why am I nervous? If your parents are anything like you, then I'm sure they'll be wonderful people," he said. "Can I get you anything from the kitchen? More pizza? Another drink?"

"No," I said with a laugh. "You're going to spoil me!"

"It's a risk I'm willing to take. Are you sure there's nothing I need to know about your parents before they get here? No helpful hints or tips?" he asked again.

"You don't need any tips. Just be yourself," I said, inching closer to him so I could rest my head in his lap. He slowly stroked my hair.

"Are you tired?" he asked.

"Yes, I find myself wanting to crawl into bed way earlier than I used to." I yawned.

"The books I've been reading said that you'd most likely experience fatigue. It's normal," he said.

"You've been reading pregnancy books?" I asked, rolling to look at him.

"Does that surprise you?"

"A little. I don't know what to say."

"You don't have to say anything; I want to do it. Go on upstairs and get some sleep. I'll take care of the dishes and lock things up tonight," he said.

I rose from the sofa, stretching one hand overhead and rubbing my eye with the other. "I'm going to take you up on that. Good night, see you in the morning," I said, moving in to give him a kiss on the cheek.

"Good night, Emily. I hope you sleep well."

I did.

~.~.~.~.~

"Emily, there appears to be a strange man flitting about the house. Should we be concerned?"

I was convinced it was just a dream, but when I opened my eyes, I found both of my parents staring down at me. "Mom? Dad? What's going on? You weren't supposed to be here until tomorrow."

"The traffic on the interstate wasn't as bad as usual and we made excellent time. I don't mean to harp on the subject, but the man dragging boxes out of the garage, should I call someone?" Dad asked.

"Big guy, strawberry-blonde hair?" I asked through a yawn.

"Yes," he answered.

"No, Dad. He's the acting-Sheriff, Jackson Sonnier, although I'm not exactly sure why he's taking boxes out of the garage." I pulled back the covers to get out of bed, dipped my feet into a pair of slippers, then walked to the window to see what was going on out there.

"The acting-Sheriff? Have you got some sort of an arrangement with APSO that we're unaware of?" Mom asked.

"Mother!" I shot out.

"Emily!" she shot back.

"Dad, tell Mom that her comment was totally uncalled for!"

"Celeste, that comment really was uncalled for," he said.

"Since she's moved back to Green Bayou, how many APSO men has she been involved with? Think about it, Don?"

"She's right, Doodlebug. The numbers are rather high," he said.

"High? There was Pete, Holden, and now Jackson. Three in more than three years is not a high number, plus Jackson and I aren't even dating, per se," I argued, throwing hand quotes into the air to stress the word "dating".

"So why is he going through our things?" Dad asked.

"And I wasn't just referring to the men you've dated, I'm talking about all of the Sheriff's department personnel that you interact with on a regular basis. Not that they aren't lovely people, it's merely an observation that has often piqued my curiosity," Mom stated before I had the chance to answer my father.

"Dad, I'm not sure why he's going through our things, but I'll find out shortly. Mom, it's coincidence. I spend a lot of time with them because of my job. We tend to run into each other pretty often on calls and I've become friends with many of them," I answered through the bathroom door. My parents continued to look upon me with interest after I exited wearing sweatpants and a sweatshirt.

"Why are you staring at me that way?" I asked.

"Darling, that outfit does nothing for your figure," Mom said, shaking her head.

Dad turned to look out the window. "I'd really like to know what he's doing with our things."

"It's way too early for this!" I fussed, throwing my hair into a quick ponytail. "I'll be right back. It would be great if you could make some coffee." I gave my mom a kiss on the cheek. "Welcome home," I said, moving to kiss my dad. "Good to see you."

I left them mumbling to each other and went to the garage to find Jackson.

"Hey there! Whatcha got going on?" I asked, nodding my head at the boxes.

"I remember you telling me that your Mom likes the house fixed up for Christmas. I found the decorations and thought I'd put them up for ya'll," he explained. I suppressed a sigh of content.

"That is the nicest, sweetest, most thoughtful thing you could do! Mom and Dad will love it!" I said excitedly.

"It's not worthy of all that. I just thought it'd be a nice thing to do," he said.

"It's incredibly nice!" I slung my arms around his neck and hugged him tightly. He laughed while reaching behind to unfasten my arms.

"I think there's only one box left in there. Would you mind checking these to see if I've forgotten anything?" Jackson asked.

"It's going to have to wait. You've been spotted by the folks and they're in a tizzy to meet you," I said.

"Your parents are here?" he asked with surprise. "I thought they weren't due in until tomorrow."

"They weren't. My parents never stick to a schedule. Let's go inside so I can introduce you," I said.

"Now?" he asked nervously.

"Would you relax?" I took him by the hand and led him to the house.

The aroma of buttery pancakes, salty bacon, and freshly brewed coffee greeted us when I opened the door.

"Mom, you didn't need to fix breakfast," I said, shallow breathing to curb the nausea.

"I like being in a kitchen that's larger than a closet. Hi, I'm Emily's mother, Celeste. You must be Jackson," she said, handing her spatula off to me so she could thrust her arm through his. "Emily tells me that you're the Sheriff now and that you've been taking care of her during these trying times. Her father and I are so very grateful." She escorted him to the kitchen table. "Tell me about yourself."

"Later, Mom. The poor man just got inside," I

said, hurriedly pushing the spatula back into her hand so I could tug on Jackson's elbow. "Come meet my dad."

"But Emily, I…" my mom started. I took Jackson's hand and he turned to offer a quick, awkward wave to my mom as he trailed behind me. Dad was sitting on the sofa, flipping through channels on the TV.

"Dad, this is Jackson Sonnier," I said. My dad's eyes left the television set to give Jackson a quick onceover.

"You're the guy taking Holden's place at APSO?" Dad asked, looking back at the screen.

"Yes, sir," Jackson answered.

"Emily tells me that you're staying here because your place was destroyed by the tornado," he said, steadily clicking the remote.

"Yes, sir," Jackson said, turning to give me an unsure look.

"You like football?" Dad asked.

"Yes sir, I used to play in high school."

"What position?"

"Linebacker," Jackson answered.

"Good man. Have a seat." Dad said, nodding to the sofa. "Why were you emptying my garage?"

"Dad!" I fussed. "Jackson, I'm so sorry."

"What? It's a fair question," Dad said, kicking his feet up on the coffee table.

"I was getting out the Christmas decorations. I intended to have them in place before you arrived, sir."

"Really?" Dad asked, finally looking away from the TV screen. Jackson nodded. Dad's jaw set to the side and he appeared to be in deep thought. He snapped out of it after a few seconds passed. "I like him. What do you feel like, Jackson? A soda, some coffee? Get him whatever he wants before he finishes with the lights, Doodlebug."

"Not now," Mom said, coming into the room to turn off the TV. "Breakfast is ready."

"Come on, Jackson. Celeste usually puts out a pretty good spread. Let's get something to eat," he said, giving him a hearty smack on the back. "You know, after breakfast, I'll help you hang those decorations and then maybe we could toss around the old pigskin once we're done? I used to play some ball, myself."

"High school?" Jackson asked, following my dad into the kitchen.

"College, but my career was cut short after I was injured," he said dramatically. "We played pretty cut-throat back in those days."

"Too bad your injury had nothing to do with football," Mom said, passing around glasses of orange juice.

"Please don't tell the story, please don't tell the story," I softly mumbled to myself.

"It's one humdinger of a story, Jackson. You've got to hear this one!" my dad said, slapping the table.

I suppressed a groan.

"Don, I don't think that Emily's comfortable with you sharing the story. Perhaps we should talk about something else. Tell him, Emily," Mom said.

"Dad, could we please talk about something else?" I pleaded.

"Come on! It's a great story!" he said excitedly.

"Poor Jackson hasn't been able to get a word in. Let him talk, Don," Mom encouraged.

"I wouldn't mind hearing the story." Jackson leaned back to get more comfortable in his chair.

"You see! I told you he'd want to hear it!" Dad said triumphantly.

I closed my eyes tightly to keep from rolling them. Five minutes into his tale, I put my fork down and massaged my temples.

"...and then Sandman and Rattlesnake said that they saw it when they were camped out one night hunting rabbits near the old, abandoned Bourgeois place," Dad continued. Jackson seemed enthralled by the story.

Ten more minutes passed and I couldn't take it any longer. "Sandman and Rattlesnake dressed up like the mythical swamp monster, the Rougarou, and scared Dad so much that he filled Sandman's ass full of buckshot! Dad ran away, tripped on a cypress knee, and broke his ankle, for Pete's sake!" I yelled.

My parents look mortified, but only slightly less so than I did. I immediately started to cry.

"Is there a problem, Emily?" Mom asked, concerned. "Obviously, something is stressing you. Do you know what it is, Don?"

"She hasn't told me anything. I guess you're just as clueless as I am," he answered.

"What do you think it could be?" Mom asked, gently rubbing my back.

"I don't know, maybe you should ask her?" Dad said.

"She may prefer to talk to you about it," Mom replied.

"I think that if she preferred to speak to me about it, then she would've already asked to have a word with me. Isn't that right, Doodlebug?"

Jackson looked as though he was having a hard time keeping up with my parents' banter. I raised my head and reached for a napkin to dot the tears from my eyes.

"There's something that I need to tell both of you," I interrupted.

"Maybe I should leave. Those Christmas lights aren't going to hang themselves," Jackson said, rising from his seat.

"Sit!" I demanded. Looking quite uncomfortable, he slowly sank back down.

"Mom, Dad, I'm not sure where to start, so I'm just going to say it," I said, shutting my eyes tightly. "I'm going to have a baby and I'm due in June."

I didn't hear the screaming or ranting that I'd expected. Picturing them clutching their chests and gasping for breath from the dual heart attacks I'd obviously given them, I waited to hear the *thud* of the bodies hitting the floor. I didn't hear anything, so I slowly opened one of my eyes. They stared at me; Mom with a hand over her agape mouth and Dad with a contented grin on his face.

"I'm gonna be a grandpa. That's the best news I've gotten in a long time! I don't want to be called Grandpa, though. Which sounds better Poppie or PeePaw?"

"Don, hold it for just a minute. Emily, what did Holden say when you told him?" she asked, waving her hand to quiet my father. I lowered my head.

"He wants nothing to do with the baby," I answered.

"I don't know if I believe that," Mom insisted.

"I tried telling him and I was threatened with a restraining order. Holden and I are finished, Mom. He's made it very clear, via his attorney, that he wants nothing more to do with me," I explained.

"That doesn't sound like Holden," Mom said with surprise.

"Well, after meeting his mother, I can say with confidence that the apple must not have fallen far from the tree," I said sadly. "Plus, there's more."

Mom looked at me with anticipation while Dad sat back in his chair and hooked his thumbs through his belt loops. Jackson reached under the table for my hand, giving it a gentle squeeze.

"Go on," Mom insisted.

"I'm embarrassed to say this because it's out of character for me, but I did something that I'm not very proud of…" I began.

"Go on, Doodlebug," my dad encouraged.

"She's agreed to let me help her with the baby because of the Holden situation," Jackson said. I looked at him with surprise. "She didn't want me to at first, but I guess I grew on her. That's why I'm still living here."

"Well, I think it's quite admirable of you to want to do that," my dad said sincerely. "But, you shouldn't have to step in for Holden."

"No sir, I shouldn't, and I'm not doing it for Holden. I'm doing it because I care for your daughter," Jackson said.

"So you two are a couple?" Mom asked, confused.

"Not exactly," Jackson said, looking to me.

"Maybe one day," I answered with an appreciative smile.

"There's only one thing I'm concerned about. How are you with all of this, Doodlebug? Are you okay?" Dad asked.

"I wasn't so sure at first, but the baby appears to be healthy, and despite horrible morning sickness, I'm healthy, too. I'm excited," I answered.

"Then I couldn't be more thrilled!" he said. "PeePaw Don or Popee Don? What do you think, son?" Dad asked, giving Jackson a nudge with his elbow. "We can talk about it while we hang Christmas lights. Ready to head out there?"

"Sure, I'll be right out," Jackson said. "If it's okay, I'd like to talk to Em for just a second."

"Celeste, why don't you come outside with me? You can tell me if you want to make any changes this year," Dad suggested.

"As a matter of fact, I'm thinking about adding more lights around the boathouse," Mom started as they walked out of the door. As soon as it latched I turned to Jackson, but his finger was against my lips to shush me before I could get a word out.

"Your parents don't need to know about the paternity question unless it becomes an issue," he said. I leaned in to rest my head against his chest.

"You're amazing."

"I just try to do the right thing, that's all," he said, shrugging his shoulders after I pulled away. "I should probably get outside and help your dad."

"Thank you for being so patient with my parents," I said.

"Your Dad's great. There's no need for thanks. I wish mine could've been like that," he said, moving toward the door.

"Jackson," I called. When he turned I went up on my toes to kiss him. Startled, he pulled away at first. After the shock wore off, he gently lowered his lips for a slow, lingering one that left me weak in the knees.

"I could get used to that," Jackson whispered, his thumb lightly stroking my lower lip. He smiled before going out of the door.

"So could I," I said after he'd walked away.

8

We were happy to have Bert, Connie, Andre, Chuck, Bridget, and Bridget's five-year-old daughter, Samantha, join us at Greenleaf for a Thanksgiving feast. The food was tasty, the desserts scrumptious, and the conversations, though varied, were mostly fun and light-hearted. After dinner the big excitement began.

The men were watching the football game on the back patio while the women sat around the kitchen table drinking coffee. Andre started pulling on my skirt, begging me to take him outside.

"Mommie, can I go outside, too?" Samantha asked, peeking from behind Bridget's chair.

"Not right now, sweetheart. Let Momma talk to Mrs. Boudreaux for a few more minutes and then I'll take you outside," Bridget answered.

"I don't mind taking her with us, if it's okay with you," I said. "We can see if the fish are jumping. We might even see an alligator!"

"Yay! Can I Mommie? Can I?" Samantha begged.

"If Miss Emily's sure she doesn't mind, then yes," Bridget said.

"Yay! Let's go, Miss Emily," Samantha said, taking my hand and pulling me toward the door. A jealous Andre ran ahead of us and used his little body to block the path.

"No!" Andre fussed, his arms crossed over his chest.

"Andre Peter, that's not nice," I said, lightly scolding him. "Samantha's coming with us."

Andre pitched a crying fit so Connie came to see what he was whining about.

"If you don't want to share your Nannie, then you can stay in the kitchen with Momma," Connie said to Andre. She took the screaming child with her; I continued out of the door with Samantha.

"Are you guys still eating?" I asked when I spied the men munching on mixed nuts and potato chips.

"We're snacking. There's a difference," Bert said. "What did you do to my kid? I heard him screaming for you."

"He's jealous because we added a plus one to the fish viewing party," I said, holding up Samantha's hand as I looked down at her. Her big doe eyes were on Bert.

"I'm sorry that I made Andre cry," she said softly.

"You have nothing to be sorry for. You didn't make him cry; his Nannie did," Bert said with a smile.

"Bert!" I shouted.

"I'm kidding! He's just tired, Samantha. Nothing that a good old nap won't fix. Would you like to try to catch some of those fish out there?" Bert asked.

"Can I really? I never caught a fish before!" Samantha said.

"Sure! Do you mind if I loan her a rod from the boat shed, Don?" Bert asked.

"Absolutely not! I've got some bait in there, too. Fix her up with whatever she needs," Dad said.

"What do you say to Mr. Don, Samantha?" Chuck prompted.

"Thank you," she said, twirling her golden-blonde pony tail around her index finger as she looked to the ground. She was adorable without even trying!

"Let's follow Mr. Bert," I said.

She thrust her hand into mine, swinging her arm up and down as we walked to the boat shed. Bert spent time showing her how to bait the hook and cast into the water before they took a seat at the end of the dock. It wasn't long before Samantha got her first nibble. Even though she didn't catch the fish, she giggled with excitement.

"You and Connie should think about trying for a little girl," I remarked after observing them for a while.

Bert turned his attention to me. "Who knows? Maybe in a couple of years."

"I got one, Mr. Bert! I think I got one!" Samantha yelled as she tried to reel in the line. Bert reached for the pole.

"Yep, you've got something on there!" he said. "You're doing great, just keep reeling it in."

"It's getting hard for me to turn it, Mr. Bert!" Samantha said, struggling with the pole. Bert kneeled behind her to help.

"I think it's gonna be a big one, Samantha!" Bert exclaimed.

All hell broke loose when the fish surfaced.

A very jealous Andre bolted through the back doors, running towards Bert as fast as his little legs would carry him. "My daddy!" he yelled.

Samantha's catch turned out to be a pre-historic ogre of a fish called an alligator gar, which not only scared the hell out of her, but me, as well.

"It has teeth! The fish has teeth!" she yelled. An ear-piercing shriek tore through the air when she looked back to see the extremely long, slippery fish snapping its jaws and flopping around on the dock. Samantha was gone like a rocket, screaming and running toward the house.

Even though there was a massive back yard for the kids to run through, they somehow managed to plow right into each other. The shrieking stopped and the sound of sobbing children took its place.

"Oh, no! Are they bleeding?" Bert asked, throwing the rod aside to assess the damage. Chuck ran across the yard to check on the children, as well.

Because Bert no longer held the rod, the fish vigorously flopped in my direction. It seemed eager to sink its sharp, jagged teeth into the first thing it could find—me! I did some serious screaming of my own. Panic took over and I desperately wanted to get to get away, but the fishing line tangled around my foot. I took off, dragging it all behind me. Every time I tried to kick the monstrous thing away from me, it snapped at my shoes.

Jackson and Dad tried to come to my rescue, but Dad had just put a handful of mixed nuts into his mouth when he started towards me. He suddenly stopped and his hands went around his throat to signal that he was choking. I stopped screeching and twirling in circles long enough to see that my dad was turning blue.

"He's choking! Help him!" I yelled, pointing to the patio.

"What do I do, Chuck?" Jackson hollered, skidding to a stop and turning to run back to help Dad.

"Bert, watch her. I got it, Jackson. You take care of Emily," Chuck said, dashing back to help Dad.

I wanted to help, but the fishing line was now completely entwined around my feet; I tripped and fell before I could manage two steps. My ankle twisted on the way down and to add insult to injury, the fish got a nip at my hand. I drew my injured appendage to my chest. The fish looked as though it wanted more! My shrieking started all over again.

Once he was sure that Chuck had the situation with my dad under control, Jackson made a mad dash for me. He whipped out his pocket knife, cut me free, then tossed the fish across the yard. He knelt beside me to finish untangling the line from my feet.

I desperately looked over to where Dad was still choking. Chuck reached around Dad's midsection and performed the Heimlich maneuver. It took three good thrusts, but whatever was blocking his airway finally dislodged and came hurtling out of his mouth.

"He's good, everyone! Relax, Em! Don, go inside and drink a little water! You'll feel better," Chuck yelled, leaving Dad to race back to where Bert was trying to soothe the two wailing children.

Jackson pulled me to stand, but my ankle throbbed. I couldn't even attempt to walk on it, so he put my arm around his neck and helped me hobble to the house.

We weren't even to the back porch when we heard a loud *kathunk*, followed by, "Oh, my God! I'm so sorry, Don! Someone was screaming and I... Let me get you some ice," Connie said after nailing Dad in the head with the door.

"I'm bringing triage tags to the next get together," Chuck sighed, holding Samantha in his arms.

"I'm so sorry, Chuck. How is she?" I asked, softly patting her back.

"She's gonna have a goose egg, but she's good. She's starting to wheeze, though. Time for us to go so we can give her a breathing treatment."

"I understand..." I began, but Dad cut me off.

"Hey, Em! I think I'm bleeding," Dad yelled from across the yard. Dark red fluid poured from a gash on his forehead and began to dribble down his face. "Yep, I'm bleeding," he said, leaning forward so the blood would drip directly onto the ground.

"Oh, my gosh. Get me over there!" I said to Jackson, who didn't hesitate in picking me up and running me over.

"Do you want me to stay and help?" Chuck asked.

"No, go on home! It's okay. Get Samantha her treatment," I said.

Connie came out of the door with a plastic bag filled with ice; Mom was right behind her.

"Oh, no! Let me get you a bandage, Don! I didn't know you were bleeding!" Connie said, jumping past my mom to get something to cover the wound.

"That sure is a lot of blood. Is he going to be okay, Emily?" Mom asked, looking extremely pale.

"He's going to be fine, Mom. Head wounds bleed a lot," I answered.

"That's good to know." Her eyes rolled up in her head and her knees buckled. Jackson practically tossed me into a chair so he could catch her before she hit the ground.

"Goodness gracious!" Connie said when she walked out with a dishcloth. "Hold this over your cut, Don. Press it hard and it'll help to stop the bleeding. Celeste, can you hear me? She's starting to come around. Will you put her on the swing over there, Jackson? Oh, and make sure she has some pillows under her knees."

"Sure," Jackson said, hoisting her into his arms.

"Is your mother okay, Emily?" Dad asked, peeping from between the folds of the dishcloth.

"Connie says she's fine, Dad. No need to worry," I answered.

"Wow, you're quite a strapping man, aren't you? What's your name, gorgeous?" Mom asked with a giggle as she leisurely ran her hand across Jackson's chest.

"Mother!" I shouted. Her eyes flew open to see a beet-red Jackson carrying her.

"What happened?" she asked, snapping to attention.

"You passed out when you saw the blood I lost. You remember? It happened just before you started feeling all over Emily's boyfriend," Dad said shortly.

"I did no such thing," she snapped.

"We all saw it, so don't deny it. I can carry you, too, you know? Want me to prove it to you?" he asked, tossing aside the blood-soaked dishcloth.

"No!" Connie and I said at the same time, stopping him in his tracks. Bert, carrying Andre, came up behind us.

"How is he?" I asked.

"I think we're going to need some stitches," Bert said, holding the bottom portion of his shirt over Andre's mouth.

"Oh, no!" I said.

Bert removed the shirt, so I could see where Andre's teeth had gone through his lower lip. He whimpered in his father's arms.

"What happened to you? You're bleeding, too!" Connie said, looking at my hand.

"The garfish bit me after I twisted my ankle," I said.

"That's it! Everyone load up! We're going to the hospital and no arguments from any of you. Now move!" Connie announced, her finger pointed at the door. It did no good to protest. We filed out the door and into our vehicles. Mom, Dad, and I got into Jackson's SUV, while Bert and Connie followed with Andre in their car. I knew that Colin was scheduled for the ER, so we decided to meet up at the newly renovated hospital in Bienville.

Oh, what a sight we were, the seven of us entering the hospital! Mom loudly fussed over Dad's wound, and Andre couldn't decide which of his parents he wanted to hold him. Bert would take him, but then he'd thrust his arms out and start crying for Connie. As soon as Connie held him, he'd whine for Bert again.

Jackson carried me even though I argued that I was quite capable of hobbling. Taking notice, Dad insisted on carrying Mom to prove to her that he could still do it. He was just trying to lift her when all of the raucousness lured Colin from the nurses' station.

"What happened? Was there a car accident or something?" Colin asked.

"I don't know if you'd believe the story if I told it," I said.

Colin arched an eyebrow high in the air.

"Okay, Samantha caught a fish, Andre was jealous, they plowed into each other, the fishing line got tangled around my ankle, Dad choked, I sprained my ankle, and Connie smacked Dad in the head with the door causing Mom to faint when she saw the blood."

Colin looked at each one of us, but didn't miss a beat. "Okay. Jackson, I'll have you take Emily to the x-ray department. Bert and Connie, you can take Andre into this room," he said, opening the door for them. "Any loss of consciousness, Don?"

"Nope, just loss of some blood. Celeste is the one who lost consciousness," Dad said, lowering the rag so Colin could see his wound.

"Not a problem. I'll get you fixed up good as new. Did you hit your head or hurt yourself when you fainted, Celeste?" Colin asked.

"She didn't get a chance to because she was rescued by 'Strapping Boy' over there," Dad said, nodding his head towards Jackson.

"Would you let it go, Don? Maybe I thought it was you holding me," she said defensively.

"Oh, I could see where you'd make that mistake," he grumbled.

"Emily, would you tell your father to drop it, please?" Mom requested.

"Dad, Mom didn't mean anything by it."

"I'm sorry. I feel like I did something wrong, but I swear I was just trying to help," Jackson insisted.

Dad gave Jackson a solid pat on the shoulder. "Awww, you gotta relax, boy. I'm just giving the Mrs. a hard time," he said, amused. "Where do you want me, Doc?"

"In this room right here. Let me duck in and see the little one first and I'll be in to patch you up next, okay? I'm calling x-ray right now if you want to go ahead and take Emily down there, Jackson. There should be a wheelchair in that closet behind you."

"See you guys in a few," Jackson said, quickly pushing me down the hall. It was obvious that he couldn't wait to get out of there.

Fifteen minutes later, the radiology tech finished taking pictures, and I was moved to the stretcher next to Dad's.

"If we aren't a pathetic bunch," I commented.

"It could always be worse," Dad said. Mom gave him a look, so he quieted down. Soon after, Colin came into the room.

"Bert and Connie are bringing Andre home. He only needed two stitches and he did great. Connie said that she'll call you later, Emily," Colin relayed.

"Thanks, I'm so glad he's okay."

"Which one of you wants to go first?" Colin asked, washing his hands.

"Fix Dad up first," I requested.

"No, you should take care of Emily first. Don can wait," Mom insisted.

"It makes more sense for Dad to go first. My x-rays aren't even back yet. There's not much Colin can do for me right now, anyway," I returned.

"He might not have the x-rays, but he could check the spot where that nasty fish bit you," Mom said.

"You mean finned?" Colin asked.

"No, she means bit. Did I leave that part out?" I asked.

"Yes," Colin said, shaking his head as he glanced at my hand. "Don, I don't think you're going to need stitches. I know it bled a lot, but head wounds often do. I'm going to butterfly it and you should be good as new. The nurse will go over head injury protocol with you when I finish. Emily, stay put. You're next."

Mom was so busy doting over Dad that they soon forgot about me. I seized the opportunity to roll onto my side and get a little rest. Jackson softly stroked my hair and I nearly fell asleep. Colin was putting the last strip into place when the tech came into the room with my x-rays. Colin placed a bandage over Dad's cut then sent him down the hall to consult with the discharge nurse.

"I guessed that you'd rather not have them in here. I know how they can be," he said with a smile. He slapped one of the pictures onto the lighted viewer.

"You are very correct, sir. So, what's the damage?" I asked after he'd inspected the x-ray for a bit.

"It's just a sprain. We'll wrap it and get you a set of crutches. I want to clean out the fish bite and I'll probably give you a course of antibiotics, too," he said.

"Antibiotics…oh," I said, looking at the ground.

"It's just a precaution. You aren't allergic, right?" he asked, flipping through the chart.

"No, no allergies, but Colin, I'm pregnant. You'll need to make sure that any meds you give me will be safe for the baby," I said.

"What?" he asked, rolling his stool across the room to stop at the stretcher. "You're messing with me, right? You Boudreaux's have such a crazy sense of humor."

"Nope, not this time. I'm due June seventh," I said.

His mouth briefly hung open. "I guess it's obvious that I'm shocked. I'm not sure what to say. Congratulations?" he asked.

"I've come to terms with it," I answered. "So, yes. Congratulations are just fine."

I could tell by the look he was giving me that Colin wanted more details about the pregnancy. I didn't feel like explaining the whole Holden situation to him. Luckily, Jackson's presence served as a deterrent.

"I'm really happy for you, Emily. Since we're making confessions, I might as well tell you that I have some news of my own. I'm getting married," he announced.

"Married, really! I didn't know you were dating! Who is she? Do I know her?" I asked excitedly.

"Do you remember Miranda, the dance instructor?"

"Yes," I answered.

"We began spending time together after my dance lessons and we realized that we had a lot in common. I fell hard, Em," Colin explained.

"That's so great! Why didn't you say something before now?" I asked.

"Because you were having such a hard time with things. It didn't seem right to go on about how happy I was," he answered.

"I wish you had. The distraction would've been nice. Tell me about it," I insisted as he worked at cleaning my wound.

"This is the first marriage for both of us. Miranda's from DeSoto, but she'll move in with me once we're married. She comes from a large family with strong religious values. You'd think that would turn me off, but I love it. They've accepted me into their family with open arms and I've never been happier. We're going to be married on February twenty-eighth, so try to keep that date open."

"I'm so happy for you, Colin! Maybe we could all have dinner sometime?" I suggested.

"I'm sure Miranda would like that. Call me when you're feeling better and we'll set it up." He scribbled on a prescription pad, tore off a page, and handed it to me. "Here you go. Keep the area clean and call me with any issues."

"Thanks, Colin," I said with a smile.

He gave my knee a soft pat. "You take good care of her now," Colin requested.

"You have my word," Jackson said, helping me from the stretcher. "Are you okay?"

"I'm fine. I'm beyond ready to go home and put this day behind us."

"Home it is," he said.

Sometime during the drive to Greenleaf, I caught a second wind (aka—pregnancy hormone surge). As Jackson helped me up the stairs and into my room, I rested my head against his tight, broad chest. Mom was right; he was quite the strapping man. Suddenly, I was overcome with lust. Damn hormones!

"I guess you want to get cleaned up? Should I get your mom for you?" he asked, gently placing me on the bed.

"I really hate to bother her; she's had a pretty rough day and she's keeping an eye on Dad. I thought that maybe you could help me," I said, my finger gingerly stroking the first button of my blouse. The look on his face showed that he was interested, so I slowly unbuttoned it.

"How can I help?" he asked, his voice getting deeper.

A devious grin came upon my face as I casually tossed my shirt aside. "You could help me finish getting undressed."

Taking his cue, Jackson slowly raised my skirt so he could leave a trail of soft kisses along each thigh. My breath caught.

"Should I stop?" Jackson asked.

I shook my head and closed my eyes. It seemed like a lifetime had passed since I'd felt a man's lips on mine and my body quivered in anticipation. His fingers lightly stroked my cheek then slid down my throat. His hand gently cupped the back of my neck.

"I'd forgotten how good you feel," he breathed in my ear.

I pulled away from him. "I want to feel you, too. Okay?" I asked, hurriedly untucking his shirt.

"Absolutely." He stood on the side of the bed, unbuckling his belt and tossing it onto the floor. His shirt soon followed. I bit my lower lip when he reached for the button of his pants.

He joined me on the bed, bombarding me with slow sensual kisses that soon gave way to something far more demanding. I pushed my hand between our bodies to feel his growing hardness and he sucked in a deep breath. I moaned loudly.

He jerked back. "Wait! Maybe we shouldn't do this. I'm worried I'll hurt you."

I took his face in my hands. "Don't worry about that. I'm feeling no pain right now." My lips once again found his and he gently lowered me to lie flat.

"You are so unbelievably sexy," he breathed.

Jackson used his finger to lightly trace circles around my stomach. It left its path and came to a rest on the clasp that secured the front of my bra. His hungry eyes were fixed on mine.

"Do it," I encouraged. Once he unclipped it, his lips lightly kissed the spot where the clasp used to be. Slowly teasing and tormenting me, he reacquainted himself with my body. It was torture, yet I hungered for more.

"I want you inside me," I whispered.

He smiled. "Not yet. Patience."

He began using his finger to plot a course then he used his tongue to trace it back. By the time he finished, I was quivering.

"Oh, please Jackson. It's been so long. I can't take anymore," I pleaded.

"Promise you'll tell me if it's uncomfortable for you, okay? I don't ever want to hurt you." His hand was on my cheek.

"I promise," I said with a slight shiver.

Poised above me, he entered slowly. I turned my head to the side and opened my mouth as intense pleasure consumed me.

"Oh, you feel so good," I breathed. Jackson moaned.

Yes, maybe he was the person I should have been with all along. My breathing quickened, and as we settled into a steady rhythm, love showed in Jackson's eyes. I returned his look of adoration.

"I've wanted this for a long time," Jackson confided.

"Wanted what?" I asked, my hand softly touching his face.

"For you to look at me that way. I've fallen hard for you, Emily. There's no point in denying it any longer."

At that moment, my feelings toward Jackson intensified. I drew him closer, offering up my lips to him. He readily accepted, quickening his pace. He brought me to the brink.

"Oh, Jackson! Jackson! I want this so bad!" And then it came. I felt as though I was floating. His release was right after mine. He collapsed next to me then pulled me into his arms.

Once my breathing slowed, I rolled onto my side to softly skim my fingernails across his chest.

"That feels nice," he said, kissing the top of my head. "How are you feeling?"

"My ankle's a little sore. Aside from that, so much better than I've felt in a long while."

"I'm glad to hear that. I've been worried about you," he said.

"Why are you worried?"

"Do you really need to ask?" he said, amusement in his tone.

"No, I guess not. Don't worry about me; I'm okay," I assured.

"Good. I still want to be here for you and the baby."

"I know you do," I said.

"Would you like to get married?"

"What?" I asked, sitting up.

"I wasn't sure, but because of the baby, I thought you might want to get married."

"That's incredibly sweet and generous of you, but no. I'm not in a rush to get married," I said, resting against him again.

"You'll let me know if you change your mind?" he asked.

"I'll let you know," I agreed. "Thank you."

"I haven't been this happy in a long time. You've shown me what it's like to lead a normal life."

"Normal? You were here this afternoon, weren't you?" I laughed.

"You know what I mean," he said.

"Yes, I do. Now see if you can figure out what I mean," I said, positioning my body on top of his.

"You're ready for a repeat performance?" he asked.

"Very good, Sheriff Sonnier."

9

The next few months were wonderful! Christmas was tranquil—no injuries and no drama. Then in early February, we attended Colin and Miranda's spectacular wedding. It took place at a massive cathedral in DeSoto. I'd never seen Colin look so happy and Miranda was absolutely radiant when her father gave her away. At the reception, when Jackson wasn't bringing me plates of food, he was whirled me around the dance floor. We couldn't have asked for a better time. Mardi Gras came in March, and I was elated to have an excuse to eat as much King Cake as I wanted. I happily blamed my new sweet addiction on the baby.

The size of my belly seemed to have a direct effect on the amount of time Mom and Dad spent at Greenleaf. The bigger I got, the more they stuck around, so I hit the local travel agency for brochures and suggestions of places they might like to visit. I did my best talking up the various locations, knowing that if I got them to bite, it would afford me a couple of weeks of freedom. My fear was once the baby actually came, the quiet little family of three that I'd so happily imagined would suddenly turn into a disruptive, rowdy family of five. I shuddered to think of how the conversations with my parents would go.

Don, please tell Emily that it's better if she uses a circular motion when putting lotion on the baby. Emily, you should use a circular motion. Don, tell Emily that the baby should be wearing long sleeves. Emily, the baby needs a sweater. Don, tell Emily that she needs to eat more calcium-rich foods. Emily, eat some cheese. Don, tell Emily that the baby's been on the right breast too long. Emily, switch boobs.

It was a horror that I didn't want to consider, so I threw myself into my work. Bridget, Chuck's girlfriend, finished the classes required to become an Emergency Medical Technician-Basic, and after riding with us for a while to learn the ropes, she took my spot as Chuck's partner. She continued with her paramedic classes on her days off and some weekends. I'd get a new partner when I returned to work, but that was fine. Chuck and Bridget were great for each other; they deserved to be together. Since I was too far along to work in the field, Grant happily made concessions by assigning alternative duties, namely— *his* paperwork. My days were spent at headquarters in DeSoto auditing medical reports.

My feelings for Jackson flourished and we settled quite comfortably into a routine. He was home nearly every evening, Wednesdays were reserved for dinner and a movie, and our weekends were spent exploring nearby towns. He again offered marriage, but I declined. I probably should've jumped on his proposal, and I wasn't exactly opposed to it; I just didn't want our marriage to feel forced or rushed simply because I was having a baby. He was incredibly attentive and caring, escorting me to every doctor's appointment, every ultrasound, every midnight ice cream and nacho run. After several years of turmoil, life was finally serene.

About ten o'clock one morning, I left headquarters to meet up with Jackson for one of my doctor's appointments. I walked into the new APSO office and I found Alphonse sitting in the glass-enclosed dispatcher's cubicle. He smiled broadly when he saw me, waving wildly as he buzzed me through to the back.

"Do you know what the baby is yet?" he asked, coming from behind the counter with outstretched arms. His hands stopped inches from my distended belly. "Can I?" he asked excitedly.

"I told you that we're not going to find out until the baby's born. We want to be surprised and yes, go ahead," I said.

Alphonse gently rested his hands on my stomach. He jumped backwards when he felt the baby kick. "Whoa! I don't think the baby likes me much, Emily," he said, scratching his head.

"Babies do that, Alphonse," I explained. "Isn't that why you've been touching my stomach whenever you see me—to feel the baby kick?"

"That's why people do that? I thought it was 'cause they were measuring how fat the lady done got," he answered.

I tugged on his ear and pulled him upright. "Don't you *ever* say that to a pregnant woman again, Alphonse! The next one might knock you clean out," I warned.

"I'll keep that in mind," he pouted, rubbing his ear. "The Sheriff's in his office."

"Thank you," I said, sighing loudly as I made my way down the hall.

The door was open so I was able to see Jackson sitting behind his desk thumbing through a stack of papers. I stopped to watch him. He looked quite handsome in his uniform. He must've felt my presence, because he suddenly looked up from his work. His face lit up as he came to meet me.

"Come inside. Did you want to sit for a minute before we go?" he asked, pulling out a chair for me.

"Sure," I said, enjoying the shoulder massage he gave once I was seated.

"How are you feeling today?" he asked.

"Pretty good. The baby's kicking up a storm."

His hands drifted from my shoulders to my stomach and it felt like the baby did a somersault. "That is the most amazing thing ever. Does it hurt?" he asked.

"No, but it feels strange," I answered. "After the appointment, I'm going to pick up a few things for supper. Any requests?"

"What are you craving? It must be pretty weird if you're asking me for suggestions."

"You don't want to know," I said with a smile.

"Try me."

"Cracklins and bananas," I answered.

"Fried pork skin and bananas? Even though it sounds revolting, you should get it." He grimaced.

"You'll be really grossed out to know that I want to dip them in tartar sauce," I said, resting my hand on my stomach. "How does Mexican sound?"

"Far better than tartar sauce dipped bananas," he replied, giving me a light kiss on the lips. "Are you ready to go?"

"Sure am," I said, accepting his outstretched hand so I could stand.

~.~.~.~.~

Dr. Nelson said that everything was right on schedule for thirty-six weeks, so after the appointment, Jackson returned to the Sheriff's Department and I went to Green Bayou to shop for groceries. I turned down the dairy aisle and noticed that Connie and Andre were there, too. As soon as he saw me, Andre eagerly bounced up and down in the front seat of the cart, his little arms outstretched, begging to be held.

"Andre Peter, sit yourself down. Nannie can't hold you right now," Connie gently fussed before turning her attention back to me. "What are you fixing for supper tonight? I'm taking any and all suggestions because I'm fresh out of ideas."

"Mexican, but I'm still trying to decide between fajitas and enchiladas."

"Enchiladas sound so good," Connie slowly drew out. "I know what we're eating, but I'm not cooking! We're going to Casa Verde! Sorry to abandon you, but there's a margarita calling my name." She parked her empty basket in a nearby doorway and removed Andre from his seat, perching him on her hip. "Kiss your Nannie goodbye so we can get home to Daddy." Andre threw out his arms and puckered his lips. He looked so adorable that I laughed.

"Bye, you two! Love you!" I said, still laughing as I steered my cart through the aisle.

Enchiladas sounded good to me, too. I tossed several packages of cheese into the basket then walked toward the Mexican food aisle for jalapenos. I was craving something spicy, but the heartburn that was sure to follow weighed on my mind. Remembering the new bottle of antacids on my nightstand, I reached for the largest jar on the shelf.

"Since when do you eat jalapenos?" a voice asked from behind me. I froze, my hand still grasping the jar. My eyes closed as I worked to keep my composure. *It can't be.*

"Holden?" I asked, my voice shakier than I wanted it.

"Are there so many men in your life that you don't recognize my voice anymore?" he asked, teasingly.

Overwhelmed with emotion, I pulled my hand away from the jar and tried to control my breathing. I wanted to hug, scream, and slug him all at the same time. When I glanced over my shoulder to see if it was indeed him, his condition shocked me. He was thinner than before and the well-groomed beard he wore was something I hadn't seen since we first met. A cane was firmly planted in his right hand, but he was walking. When I turned to face him, the semi-smile that he was wearing completely disappeared. His shock gave way to anger.

"I heard you'd moved on with Jackson, but this is a real slap in the face." He nodded toward my very pregnant belly.

"Are you kidding me? If anyone has the right to be upset, it's me! You didn't even have the guts to tell me to my face that you wanted nothing more to do with me. You had to get your high-priced, Baton Rouge lawyer to do your dirty work for you. Don't you for one second expect me to apologize for moving on, Holden Dautry," I argued.

"What in the hell are you talking about? I don't have a lawyer in Baton Rouge and I *never* said that I wanted nothing to do with you. You're the one who sent that message, and I got it loud and clear, Angel Lips."

"Yes, I did send you a letter, but it said nothing about moving on. And, I was told to never do it again or I'd be arrested for a second time!" I fussed.

"When were you ever arrested?" he asked incredulously.

"When I went to visit you at the hospital in DeSoto," I snapped. "It was horrible. I was ridiculed, groped, and manhandled." I subconsciously rubbed my wrist.

"By one of *my* deputies!"

"Yes, by one of *your* deputies. Jackson and Bert took care of it."

He shook his head. "Okay, obviously there are some major details missing here. We need to talk, and I don't think the middle of the grocery store is the right place. I'm living back at my house now. I want you to meet me there," he requested.

"I don't know if I should, Holden," I said, moving away. He stopped me.

"What? Do you need to check with *Jackson* before we sort this out?" He quickly ran his hand through his hair and sighed loudly. "I'm sorry. I'm blaming you and I shouldn't. I promise to be civil; I shouldn't have lost my temper. It's just that I was surprised to see you, you know, like that," he said, pointing at my stomach.

My anger dissipated. "I know, I'm huge. Okay, we'll go to your house to talk it over. It's good to see that you're walking. The last I heard, they weren't sure if you'd be able to keep your leg." I said, following him to the parking lot.

"They underestimated my determination." He held the door of his sports car open for me.

I shook my head. "It'll take me days to get in and out of there. I'll just take my car, okay?"

"If that's how you want it. I'll see you at my house in a few minutes," he said, shutting the door and driving off.

Once in my car, I fought the urge to bawl my eyes out. Just when I thought I'd resolved my feelings towards Holden, he was back in my life! Things were going so well with Jackson. I pulled out my cell phone to call him.

"Sheriff Sonnier," he answered on the third ring.

"Jackson, it's me. There's something I need to tell you," I began.

"Sounds serious. What is it? Are you okay?" he asked.

"I'm fine, but Holden's back in town and he wants to meet with me at his house," I said. Jackson remained quiet. "Should I go?"

"Do you want to go?"

"I don't necessarily want to go, but I feel as though I should. I need to tell him about the baby," I replied.

"Wait, I thought you did tell him. What about the letter you sent through the attorney?" Jackson asked.

"I don't know if he ever got the letter. He said that he doesn't have a lawyer in Baton Rouge and when he saw me, he assumed that the baby was yours."

"Emily, what does this mean for us? If he didn't know…"

"Nothing changes between us. I'm coming home to you," I answered.

"We can't pretend that this isn't going to change things. We'll talk about it more when you get home. Will you promise me that you'll leave if you begin to feel stressed?" Jackson asked.

"Don't worry. Are you sure you're okay with this? Maybe we should wait and go together?"

"I know it's something that needs to be done, and it's probably best that I not be there," he answered.

"You could be a huge jerk right now if you wanted to. Thank you for understanding, Jackson."

"Call me if you need me," he said.

I ended the call and turned down the trail that led to Holden's house. My heart sank when I saw him struggling to get out of his car. I wanted to help, but knew it was best to let him do it on his own, so I pretended to dig around for something in my purse. He didn't need to see the tears that were welling in my eyes. After I was sure I had my emotions firmly in check, I entered the house, grabbed a bottle of water, and took a seat next to Holden.

"I'm not sure where you want me to start," I said, nervously picking at the label on the bottle.

"Why don't you start by telling me how long I was out of the picture before Jackson knocked you up? Was I still in the ICU or did you wait until I was transferred?" he asked.

My jaw dropped and all of the anger I'd tried so desperately to get under control started to rage. It took everything I had not to yell at him.

"You promised that you'd be civil. If you're going to criticize me, there's no reason for me to be here. I need to go," I said as calmly as I could, rocking to gain enough momentum to get off of the sofa.

Holden reached out to stop me. "Don't leave. That was wrong of me to say. I'm sorry. I'm frustrated and I'm taking it out on you. Please don't go," he insisted.

Though I sat back, I refused to look at him. "I'll only stay if you promise not to do that again."

"I won't. Even though I got your message, a part of me hoped that we might be together again. I wanted to come here and win you back, Emily. It's not your fault that I'm too late. I should be happy for you."

"Clearly, we both got letters that neither one of us sent. What message are you talking about?"

"The message that was sent to the rehab hospital; the one saying you wanted nothing more to do with me because you and Jackson were in a relationship," he explained.

"Holden, I didn't even know where you were. The only message I sent went through an attorney in Baton Rouge, and it didn't say anything about leaving you. He threatened to press harassment charges against me if I tried to contact you again."

"Okay, I'm confused. Why don't you start at the beginning and don't leave anything out," he requested. I moved closer, turning to face him.

"Do you remember any of the times I visited while you were in the ICU at DeSoto General?" I asked.

"I vaguely remember seeing you, but I thought it was a hallucination," he answered.

"It wasn't a hallucination. The first couple of days, I was at every visitation. I tried getting the staff to let me stay with you, but the nurses said it was impossible," I explained.

"Why did you stop coming to visit?"

"Because your mother had me arrested."

"What! Why would my mother have you arrested?"

"I visited with you before breakfast one day, but had to wait until noon to see you again. When I showed up, a hospital guard was waiting for me at the doors. Your mom came down the hall with a huge security guard, saying that I wasn't family; I was your whore and she wouldn't allow me to visit you anymore. Obviously, it mortified and upset me," I said.

"She called you what?" he asked with disbelief.

"Your whore," I answered matter-of-factly and he shook his head. "Of course, I stood up for myself and the next thing I knew, I was pinned against a wall and forbidden to step foot on the hospital grounds. Since she'd made a very sizable donation to the hospital, your mother insisted that it was pointless to fight it. I filled you in on Deputy Grabs-a-lot. I was handcuffed and put in a holding cell until Jackson and Bert came to help me."

"Who was this guy? I want a name and I want it now!"

"I told you, Bert took care of it for me."

"Fine. Then skip ahead and tell me about this attorney," he said, his jaw tightly clenched.

"After I was banned, I came to your house to look for clues about where you'd been transferred, but Spencer Landry caught me."

"What in the hell was Spencer Landry doing in my house?" he asked, his face turning redder and redder with each new revelation.

"He was hired to keep it secure. His orders and payment came from the attorney in Baton Rouge. Any questions or issues were to be run through the lawyer. I asked Crusher, that's what we called him in high school, to forward a letter to the guy in the hopes that it would get to you. Instead, I got a very nasty, threatening response," I explained.

Holden lowered his head to massage his temples with his fingertips. "The message that you sent, did it say that you couldn't see a future with me because my injuries were so severe? That you decided to be with Jackson because he offered you more than I could give you physically, emotionally, and otherwise," he asked.

I looked at him with skepticism. "I can't believe you thought I'd ever say such a thing!"

"Just like you believed that I didn't want to see you anymore?" he shot back.

"I'm not feeling so well. I need some air," I said, walking to the deck and drawing in a deep breath. Holden's cane thumped against the floor as he came out to join me. He put his hand on my shoulder.

"Are you okay? Should I get you to a doctor or bring you home or something?" he asked.

"No, I'm fine," I said, running a protective hand over my stomach. I grabbed the rail when the baby gave me a solid kick in the ribs. "The baby's been kicking a lot lately and some of them are pretty hard."

"May I?" he asked, holding his hand close to my abdomen. When I nodded, he put his cane aside to gently place both hands on my stomach. A smile spread across his face when he felt the baby moving around.

"It might be yours," I said softly.

"What might be mine?" His face searched mine for an answer.

"The baby. It's the message I was trying to get to you. I needed to know what kind of paternity test you preferred. But, since I'm due June seventh, we'll have to wait until the baby is born to find out. After you said that you wanted nothing to do with me, Jackson stepped in. Early in the pregnancy, we decided to wait until after the birth to test, since it's the least risky. He's been great to me and the baby."

"I'm sure he has," Holden said, pulling his hands away.

"You can't be mad at me or Jackson about this!" I insisted.

"I'm mad as hell, but no, it's not directed at you or Jackson," he said. "I assure you, my mother will be dealt with. Just let me know how we're handling the situation? Am I the no good son of a bitch who left you high and dry during your pregnancy or are you just telling everyone it's Jackson's?"

"Holden Dautry!" I snapped. "I forgot how much you infuriate me sometimes! Everyone assumes that the baby is yours. The only people who know otherwise are me, you, Connie, Bert, Jackson, and my doctor. That's all."

"What about your parents?" he asked.

"They assume that you're the father. I was going to tell them, but Jackson said that we shouldn't until we had the results of the paternity test."

"And why would he say that?" Holden asked mockingly.

"Because he didn't want me to have to disclose to my parents that I slept with him. He did it to protect me," I said, looking down at my feet.

"I don't understand? Aren't you and Jackson together?"

"Yes, but not until I was four months along. Before then, he lived at Greenleaf, but only because his apartment was destroyed by the tornado. He stayed in a guest room," I explained.

"Is he still running the department?"

"Yes," I answered.

"What do you want from me?" Holden asked.

"What do you mean?"

"Do you want me to disappear so you, Jackson, and the baby can live happily ever after?" he asked.

"No! I'm going to tell you just what I told Jackson. I want you to be as involved with the pregnancy as you want to be. If you want to be at the doctor's appointments, in the delivery room, or anything else, that's fine," I said, taking his hand in mine. "I never tried to hide this from you. I wanted you to be a part of this."

"I realize that, but there's a lot to think about," he said.

"Yes, there is. We both need some time. I really should go; Jackson's waiting," I replied.

"Emily…" Holden said, stopping me. His words never came.

"Welcome home, Holden," I said before I walked away.

10

Even though it was obvious that Jackson was anxiously awaiting my arrival, I appreciated that he didn't immediately start grilling me. I kicked off my shoes and eased onto the sofa; Jackson scooped my legs into his lap and gently rubbed my feet.

"I figured with everything going on that I'd pick up the Mexican food you were craving from Casa Verde. It's in the kitchen. I hope that's okay?" he said.

"It's more than okay. I'm starved."

"Good, I'll bring you a plate," he said, leaving the room.

My head was throbbing so I closed my eyes.

"Are you okay?" he asked when he returned.

"I'm fine. It's been a long day," I said, struggling to sit upright. Jackson's face showed his amusement and he reached out to help me up.

We small-talked through dinner, and once the dishes were cleared I knew I had to tell him what happened at Holden's. He'd waited long enough.

Jackson intently listened to my retelling of the story before he asked questions. "How are you feeling about all of this?" he asked.

"Confused. Part of me wishes that he would've stayed away. For the first time in a long time, I feel normal. I like our routine," I said, snuggling up to Jackson. "As soon as I walked into Holden's, I could feel the contentment being sucked away," I confided.

"His coming back to town certainly changes things, but we'll manage. Nothing has to be decided tonight. You've had a very stressful day and you're looking tired. Are you ready to go upstairs and relax?" he asked.

"That sounds great. I could go for a nice, warm bubble bath."

"On it," Jackson said, rising from the sofa.

"You're so good to me." I thrust my hand out so he could help me stand.

"I'm happy to be a part of this. You're not the only one who enjoys the normalcy. I've searched for it my entire life. I don't want it to end." He pulled me in for a hug.

"I don't want to lose it either," I said softly, even though intuition told me that it was already long gone.

~.~.~.~.~

Jackson left for work early. I cuddled with his pillow and quickly fell back to sleep. I was startled when I woke and found Holden sitting across from me.

170

"Holden! You can't do this anymore. You can't just walk in here whenever you feel like…"

"You picked me," he blurted. His beard was gone, his skin glowed, and his sapphire-blue eyes sparkled.

"What are you talking about?" I asked, rubbing my eyes so I could better focus on him.

Though he grimaced when he stood, he managed to walk to the bed without the help of his cane. He lay next to me, propped on his side.

"I don't think it's appropriate for you to be in the bed with me, Holden."

"Emily, you picked *me*. I talked to the doctors and nurses at DeSoto General, Grant, and Colin. I know everything that happened. Not only did you save my life, but you stayed with me. You picked me over Jackson. You wanted to be with *me*," he said.

"I picked you, at that time. But, your mother came and I didn't hear from you, Holden. Things have changed," I said, trying to scoot myself to the edge of the bed so I could roll out.

"I want to talk about this," he said, reaching out to stop me.

"There's nothing to talk about. I'm with Jackson. He's good to me and he's excited about the baby."

"Do you love him?" Holden asked.

"Yes, I do," I answered.

"You don't say it very convincingly," he remarked.

"Who do I need to convince? I love Jackson," I snapped.

He leaned forward, taking my face into his palms as he leaned in to kiss me. The jolt that went through my body nearly cut my breath.

"Tell me you didn't feel anything," he challenged.

"Holden…"

"You've gotten comfortable with Jackson. I'm the one you love."

"I can't do this, Holden. I'm not going to throw away the great thing that I have for a rollercoaster ride with you. I have a baby to think about," I said.

"A baby that might be mine," he remarked.

"Yes, but even if it's yours, Jackson will still be a great influence in the baby's life. He doesn't need to get in the trenches like you did. He's happy being home with me every night and trusting his men to do the stakeouts and the drug raids."

"You think that I'm incapable of that? It's easy for him to slide into that role because I laid the groundwork that got the department to that point! Do you remember the mess I had to clean up? Jackson slid into a position that I poured my blood, sweat, and tears to get right," Holden said.

I shook my head because I didn't want to hear anymore.

"Tell me you didn't feel anything when I kissed you."

"Holden, I…"

He stopped my answer by kissing me again and this time I felt it in my toes.

"I think you should leave," I said, my voice not sounding nearly as confident as I wanted it to be. He moved to stand near the door.

"Fine, I'll go, but you better get used to seeing me more often. I don't give up on something I want, and you know it," he said, finally leaving the room.

Throwing the covers over my head, I prayed for sleep. There was so much to think about and I wasn't ready to sort it all out. Half an hour later, I was finally just dozing off.

"Emily, are you feeling okay? It's eight o'clock in the morning and you're still in bed."

"Mom, eight o'clock is not late. What are you doing here? I thought you were coming in tonight," I said.

"Your father's terrible at judging arrival times. We came into Louisiana last night, but we didn't want to wake you, so we spent the night at a lovely RV park. Now, let me see you!" she exclaimed. I rolled out of bed, holding my nightgown taut so she could see how much my stomach had grown. "Oh, my sweet girl! You look absolutely adorable!"

"Thanks, Mom," I said, giving her a hug. "Mom, can I talk to you for a minute?"

"Sounds serious," she said, sitting on the edge of the bed. The smile was gone from her face.

"Everything's great with me and the baby," I said hurriedly and she let out a sigh of relief. "It's Holden. He's come back to town."

"Oh, my," she said.

"Mom, things have been going so well with Jackson and after the incident with Holden's mother, I was actually grateful that I wouldn't have to deal with her anymore."

"What incident with Holden's mother?" she asked.

"After the tornado hit, she had me arrested when I went to visit Holden in the hospital."

"She what! Why is this the first time I'm hearing of this, Emily Clothilde Boudreaux?"

"She used her connections to have me banned from DeSoto General," I said.

"I've heard stories about Luciana Dautry, but I had no idea that she was actually that big of a witch," Mom replied.

"That's not all she did. She had her attorney send a letter to me on Holden's behalf. He knew nothing about it, and while that was happening she sent Holden a message saying I wanted nothing to do with him."

"She did not!" Mom exclaimed.

"She did," I said sadly.

"Come give Mom a hug." She held her arms out to me. It felt good to be comforted by her. "My dear, sweet Emily, trust me when I say that everything will work out. Time heals all wounds. I think you need a distraction from your problems and I know exactly the thing to help."

"What's that?" I asked, sniffling.

"A baby shower! We'll have a lovely party and then Dad and I will help you fix up the nursery! Doesn't that sound fun?" she asked.

"I have been looking forward to getting the nursery set up. You're right. I need time to sort everything out before I make any decisions," I said, giving Mom a half-smile.

"Then it's settled. We're having a baby shower on Saturday. I think I have Connie's number programmed into my phone." She pulled it out to scroll through the address book. "You leave it to us. It'll be great. Now, go downstairs and say 'hi' to your father. We'll talk about all the other stuff tonight. Hello, Connie? Hi! This is Celeste Boudreaux," my mom started before making shooing signals with her hands. I shook my head, shutting the door behind me.

I wandered down the stairs and found my dad watching TV in the living room.

"Doodlebug!" he said, standing so he could hug me. "And, Doodlebug part two!"

"Oh, Dad!" I said, hugging him back.

"Where's your mother?"

"Upstairs planning a baby shower with Connie," I said, taking the remote from him.

Nothing on the guide caught my attention, so I settled back to watch a special on local sports legends with him. He took my hand in his and gave it a little squeeze. I loved how Dad could sum it all up without saying a word.

11

The guests in the den were all talking amongst themselves and I had a serious hankering for a second piece of cake, so I excused myself to pop into the dining room. Connie soon joined me.

"You and Mom went way overboard with this baby shower!" I said, admiring all of the food and decorations. "And this cake! Yum!"

Connie cut a wedge for herself. "It is delicious, isn't it? Are you having a good time?"

"I'm having a great time. Thank you so much!"

The doorbell rang and we eyed each other curiously.

"I wonder who that can be."

"Whoever it is, they're taking being fashionably late to a new level. The shower started nearly an hour ago," Connie said, following me into the foyer.

"I'll get the door," Mom sang. She buzzed by me so quickly that the lavender scarf she was wearing stuck straight out behind her.

"Who's she expecting?" I asked Connie.

"I don't think you hire strippers for a baby shower, so your guess is as good as mine," she said.

I felt the blood drain from my face when the door opened to reveal Luciana Dautry. A fake smile was plastered on her perfectly made-up face when she extended a pastel-green package to my mom.

"Celeste, I'm so glad that you called. Your home is quite lovely." She took it all in as she walked through the foyer.

"Thank you, Luciana. We do enjoy it when we aren't traveling. I'm so glad you could come. It's very important that we show our support to our children," Mom said, ushering her down the hall.

I looked at Mom with disbelief and she gave me one of her biggest smiles.

"Emily, I'm sure you remember Mrs. Dautry," Mom said, giving me a look that warned me to be polite.

"Yes, ma'am," I said with far less aggression than I was feeling.

"Celeste, Emily, you'll have to forgive my tardiness. I seem to have double booked myself today. I do hope you understand," Luciana said.

"Oh, but of course. Would you care for some refreshments?" Mom said, holding her hand out to guide Luciana in the right direction. As soon as they were out of earshot, Connie and I simultaneously started rambling.

"Did you know she was coming?"

"I didn't know she was coming."

"Why in the hell did my mother invite her? And, what's up with her being so nice to that woman?" I asked.

"Damn, I wish I could drink, because I could sure use a stiff one right now."

"I *can* drink. Follow me to the bar so I can slip some rum into my punch," Connie said. Before I could get there, Mom found me.

"Emily, Luciana is on the back patio and she wishes to speak to you."

"She's the last person I want to talk to. I tell you how she treated me and you invite her to my baby shower? What were you thinking?" I demanded in a hushed tone.

"I was thinking that she only has one child and that child is about to be a father. It's only right that she have the opportunity to get to know her grandchild. If she chooses not to do so, then that is on her conscience, but if we don't allow her to, then it's on our consciences," she explained.

"Do you always have to be so darn PC?" I grumbled. She reached out to fix my hair.

"You know I'm right," she said with a slight smile.

"Yes, ma'am." I sighed.

Mom hugged me tightly then I walked outside to find Luciana. She was admiring the view of the bayou from the seat she had taken. Sitting opposite her, I kept my back rigid and my gaze forward. She was the first to speak.

"I just left Holden's and he is quite upset with me for what I did. Poor thing often views my assistance as interference. Supposedly, the baby you're carrying is my grandchild. Though I strongly recommended a paternity test to him, I've been informed by Holden that it's his place to make that demand, not mine. If it is true that he's the individual who accidentally impregnated you, I feel somewhat better knowing that you're Don and Celeste's daughter. You come from a respectable family, far from the poor white trash that Holden usually fraternizes with. Now, because I've said that, I don't want you to think that my mind has been changed about the situation. Holden needs to know for sure that it is indeed his child you are carrying before he invests too much time and energy into the situation. He also needs to return to his family. I'm sure you realize that he might not be walking today if I hadn't taken matters into my own hands, so you'd be remiss to expect an apology from me. I stand firmly behind my decisions," Luciana said.

"The decisions by which you stand, I suppose, are the forged letters that you sent to us? I listened to you, now you can return the favor. You may very well be the grandmother of this child, but I'll dictate how much influence you have in his or her life. You made a lousy first impression and an even worse second one. It's quite apparent why Holden was conservative when it came to sharing stories about his family. You judged me without knowing anything about me. You're nothing but a superficial woman and unless there's a major change in your attitude, I want nothing to do with you. You can show yourself out; we gave the butler the day off," I snipped.

"Perhaps I was premature with my comments about your family. I got an entirely different impression when I spoke with your mother, or maybe you simply lack couth. Your generation has no respect," Luciana said, rising to leave.

I came out of my seat in a way that I hadn't since my pre-pregnancy days.

"You're calling *me* uncouth? You have the nerve to come into my home and…" I started yelling, but my mother came outside to stop me.

"Emily, is there a problem?" she asked, smiling as she joined us on the patio.

"You should have a talk with your daughter about etiquette and decorum," Luciana insisted. "I'll be leaving now. I'd appreciate my wrap."

"I'm sorry that you wish to leave. Emily, a brief word while I gather Luciana's things? I'll meet you at the front door if you care to say your 'goodbyes' to the other guests," Mom said. I looked at her with disbelief.

"Thank you, Celeste. You see, it's not so difficult to be gracious. You could learn a lot from your mother," she directed at me.

It took everything I had to remain calm when I followed my mother into the pantry off of the kitchen. "How could you side with her?" I demanded.

"I didn't side with anyone. I heard you raising your voice and I didn't know why. I brought you in here so you could tell me what got you so upset," Mom explained.

I filled her in on the conversation, but the expression on her face never changed. I tossed my hands in the air and sighed with discontent.

"Emily, why don't you find Connie? It's obvious that you and Luciana do not get along, so I'll show her out."

"Whatever," I said, hurrying off to find Connie. I caught her by the sleeve of her dress and before she could protest, I pulled her to come along with me to the empty dining room. I gently closed the doors so we wouldn't be disturbed.

"What's going on?" she quietly asked. I was whispering the story to her when we heard voices from outside the door. Holding my hand up to stop our conversation, I put my ear to the door to eavesdrop.

"It's her," I mouthed to Connie. She kicked off her shoes and tiptoed to join me.

"...you understand what I'm saying, don't you, Celeste? The youth of today have no respect," Luciana said.

"I understand that you had quite the conversation with Emily. I extended an olive branch to you, because I hoped that you'd reconcile with my daughter. I thought that we, as grandmothers, could enjoy watching that precious baby learn and grow, but evidently, you have no intention or desire to do so. From the bottom of my heart, I believe that Emily and Holden would still be together if you hadn't manipulated them. Yes, I know all about what you did and I think it's deplorable that a mother would do such a thing to her own flesh and blood.

Unlike a certain person standing before me, my child's happiness is all that I care about. That being said, if you *ever* do anything to hurt or insult my daughter again, I'll make your life so fucking miserable, you'll rue the day you met me. How's that for decorum? Here's your wrap. Do have a safe journey home," Mom said extra-cheerily.

Connie and I raised our hands to our wide-open mouths. Connie stifled a laugh, but I was too shocked to even blink. After we heard the front door close, we dashed to the kitchen where Mom soon joined us.

"Everything okay?" I asked Mom.

"Just fine. I hope she didn't upset you too much," she answered in her normal, cheery tone.

"Nah, I'm not going to let her ruin my shower." I gave Mom a big hug.

"I'm glad to hear it, my sweet girl. Now, get out of here and go mingle with your guests," she said, pushing me toward the parlor.

"Okay! I'm going. Why so demanding, Celeste?" I jokingly fussed.

"Celeste! Someone's gotten a large dose of moxie. You best take it down a notch, Miss Smarty-pants," Mom cautioned.

"I love you, Mommie."

"That's what I thought," she said, laughing.

I did my duty, graciously thanking each and every guest for attending as I showed them out. Mom, Connie, and I were resting in the den when Jackson, Bert, and Dad returned with pizza. The mood was light and carefree as we sat around the dinner table recapping the day. The laughter stopped when the doorbell rang.

"Everyone stay where you are. I'll answer it," Dad said, tossing his napkin onto the table. Our noisy conversation continued, but when he returned, the room got eerily silent. Holden was standing behind him.

"I'm sorry to interrupt your dinner, but I came to speak to Emily. May I have a word in private?" Holden asked.

Jackson rose from his seat.

"This has nothing to do with you, Jackson," he said, holding his hand up in warning.

"You're crazy if you think I'm going to stand aside and let you upset Emily," Jackson asserted, taking a protective stance in front of me.

"Fine, you can stand there and listen to what I have to say. In fact, all of you can hear this. Emily, my mother manipulated me, not because I was clueless about what she was doing, but because I felt sorry for myself. There were doubts that I'd ever walk again and it bothered me to think of you giving up everything to take care of me. I convinced myself that it was best to leave things as they were. My plan was to come back to town, tie up a few loose ends, and leave.

All of that went out the window the moment I laid eyes on you at the store. I was fooling myself. I never stopped loving you and I never will. We belong together, Emily," he said.

The room was absolutely silent, so much so that I was sure everyone could hear the rapid pounding of my heart. Jackson's fists were tightly clenched, but he remained quiet.

"Bert and I should get going," Connie finally said, rising from the table. My parents stood too, but Holden stopped them.

"No, I want you all to hear this. Bert and Connie, you're our good friends. Hell, you're the closest thing Emily has to siblings. Celeste and Don, you've always treated me like family. I want no secrets. I've been cleared by the doctors and I'm taking back what's mine. Effective immediately, you're Chief Deputy again," he directed to

Jackson. "I expect you to be out of my office by Monday morning. Also effective Monday morning, Bert, you're promoted to Major. Things got lax while I was away and it's time to get the department back into check. There's absolutely no reason why five missing prisoners should still be fugitives. I want a task force created and your top priority will be getting them back into custody. Do you understand, Bert?" Holden asked, the authoritative tone back in his voice.

"Yes, sir," he answered.

"And as for you," he said, directing his attention at me. "Tell me that you don't love me."

"Holden, I don't think we should discuss this right now. This isn't the right time or the right place," I said looking at Jackson.

"Don't look at him. Look at me and tell me that you don't love me," he demanded. "Never mind, I know how to tell what you're feeling." He rushed forward, his lips met with mine.

Jackson pulled him away from me, pinning him against the kitchen counter.

"Tell me you felt nothing and I'll give you my blessing to be together," Holden insisted, no longer fighting Jackson's grasp.

I couldn't catch my breath when looking between Holden and Jackson. They both stared at me expectantly. The longer I waited to answer, the looser Jackson's grip on Holden became. Finally, he released him to walk over to me.

"Emily, do you love him?" Jackson asked quietly.

"I don't know," I said, looking away once I noticed the hurt in Jackson's eyes.

"I think you do," he said, leaving the room.

"Jackson! Don't go." I followed him into the foyer. "I never lied about loving you."

"But not like you love him. I'm the good old standby and I always knew it. That's probably why I'm not as angry as I should be right now. You know what they say about things being too good to be true? You should see how your face lights up when you see him. You absolutely glow. That never happened with me."

"That's not true, Jackson. I'm happy with you. Stay here; I'll ask Holden to leave."

"No, you're comfortable with me. There's a difference. I want you to be happy. Talk things out with Holden. If by some chance you two decide that it's not going to work between you, then I'd be honored to spend my life with you, but you need to be sure. I'm not going to live a life where I constantly have to wonder if you're secretly wishing you were with him. That's not fair to any of us. Do you understand?"

"I understand what you're saying, but you don't have to go, Jackson."

"Yes, I do. You're not the only one who has to sort things out. It's not over between us, though. We still have the baby to think about," he said.

"Of course." I nodded.

"I'm going upstairs to pack a bag and I'm going to check into a hotel until we can figure out how we're going to handle this," he said.

"Are you sure?"

"Yes, I need time to process this," he said. "Let's just say our goodbyes now. I'd rather not face everyone else."

I nodded, giving him a hug and a light kiss on the cheek before he disappeared upstairs. I wasn't ready to face the people in the kitchen either, so I ducked into the dark, empty parlor until I heard the front door close. After hearing Jackson drive away, I slowly walked into the kitchen. The conversation hushed and all eyes rested on me.

"I've had a really long day," I said meekly. "I think I'd like to go upstairs and get some rest."

"Certainly, sweetheart," Mom said.

"We were just leaving, weren't we Bert?" Connie asked.

"Sure were. Later, girlie," he said, kissing my forehead before softly patting my stomach. "Later, little one."

"I'll call you tomorrow," Connie said, hugging me. "And, I want to know every detail," she whispered into my ear.

They showed themselves out and my parents retreated to the guest house. After locking the door behind them, I turned to see that Holden was no longer in the kitchen. Sighing heavily while tromping up the stairs, I couldn't wait to get into bed. As soon as I crossed the threshold, Holden startled me by gathering me in his strong embrace. I tried pushing him away, but it did no good. His lips rested near my ear.

"I love you and I'm sorry that my pride kept us from resolving this long ago. Even when we were apart, I never stopped thinking about you. Emily, we're meant to be together. Please, tell me you feel the same way," he pleaded.

"It does no good to deny it. I feel something too, but..."

His lips found mine. When he tried to unzip my dress, I quickly wiggled away from him.

"Holden, please stop. I don't think you should be here. It's far too soon."

"Do you realize how long it's been since I've felt you next to me? I know you're probably confused because you have feelings for Jackson, but please let me hold you tonight. I've missed you so much, Emily. I want to be near you, to touch you, to know you're really here with me," he said softly. His hands immediately went to my stomach. "There's so much lost time I need to make up for. Please let me stay? I swear all we'll do is talk. I'll sleep in the chair if that makes you feel better." His eyes twinkled and he smiled when he felt the baby move.

He got to me. "How can I say no when you look at me that way? You promise that we'll only talk? You won't try anything else, and that includes kissing, too!"

"You have my word." He pulled his shirt over his head and tossed it onto the chair. I was about to scold him, but instead, I gasped when I saw the fresh scars.

"Oh, Holden," I said, instinctively reaching out to touch one of them. "How much do you remember about this?"

"If you're worried that I remember the pain, don't," he answered. When he removed his pants, I could see that his leg was scarred far worse than his torso. "This will continue to heal. I had several surgeries and most of it's titanium now, but considering that I wasn't supposed to keep the limb, I'm not going to complain."

"The doctor's weren't very optimistic at first," I said, walking to the bathroom.

"From what I've heard, I owe my life to you," he said, sliding under the covers.

"I only did what I was trained to do," I called while slipping on my nightgown. I joined him in the bed and he propped up on his elbow to look at me.

"You're being modest. I know everything." His finger lightly stroked my cheek. I closed my eyes and bit my lower lip. I'd forgotten how much his touch affected me. The baby kicked and I was pulled from my trance.

"Holden, you know that we can't just jump back into a relationship like nothing ever happened, don't you? We have some very serious topics to discuss," I said.

"Like?" he asked, raising an eyebrow.

"Like your mother, Jackson, the baby if it's Jackson's, the baby if it's yours, nearly everything that happened after you gave me that ultimatum before the tornado hit, as well as Roberta and how we'll handle situations like that in the future. There are lots of things we need to iron out," I said.

"Disowned; he'll get over it; we'll arrange some sort of visitation schedule; I'll be the happiest man ever; I was an ass so we'll disregard all of that; and I'll work on keeping you better informed without threatening the integrity of any future cases. There, all our problems solved in less than ten seconds," he said, trying to kiss me.

"It doesn't work like that you know it. What are you doing? You gave your word."

"I thought that maybe you'd cave once I got close to you. It's been a long time," he said, optimistically.

I pushed him away. "Stop it. I'm serious. We're supposed to be discussing these things. Did you know that your mother was here today?"

"Why was she here?" he asked, sitting up. "What did she say? Was she rude to you?"

"It's not important right now. Look, it's been a long day and I'm worn out. Let's just forget the talking part and sleep. We'll pick up where we left off in the morning after we're rested," I encouraged as I reached over to turn out the light.

Once I was settled comfortably on my side, he nudged my hair out of the way to whisper into my ear. "Let me make love to you."

A wave of excitement coursed through my body. I did my best to contain it.

"No, go to sleep now, Holden or I'm going to put you in a guest room," I said, moving away from him. Lying in the dark, I worked to make my breathing slow and rhythmic. Holden must have assumed I was sleeping. He moved in close and his arms wrapped around me. My skin tingled from his touch. Though Jackson still had a piece of my heart, I was thankful to have Holden back in my bed.

12

The next morning, my parents and I decided to finish the nursery. Though Holden was eager to help us, he was scheduled for a brief meeting at APSO headquarters. He insisted on finishing the crib assembly once he got back, so Dad helped out by putting the changing table together. Mom and I were lost in conversation, discussing how we could best decorate the freshly-painted walls, when a knock on the doorframe startled us.

"I hope you don't mind, but I let myself in," Jackson said.

"Not at all," I answered with a sheepish smile.

"Don, would you help me start lunch?" Mom asked.

"Huh, oh, sure," he said, putting down the instructions he held in one hand and the screwdriver he had in the other. "What's on the menu?"

"I don't know yet, Don. Let's go downstairs and see what we come up with," she suggested.

"I could go for a roast beef poboy. Do we have the stuff for a roast beef poboy?" he asked.

"I'm not sure, Don. We need to check the refrigerator—downstairs," Mom said with a slight trace of agitation in her voice.

"Not roast beef, fried oyster poboy. Yeah, fried oyster sounds good, doesn't it?" he asked, pulling off his glasses to clean them.

"Okay, but we'll have to go out to get an oyster poboy," she said, waving her hand in a gesture that said, "Come on".

"I don't feel like leaving the house. Do you have any leftovers of that casserole you made the other night? Or maybe we should just order in?" he said.

"Don!" Mom snapped before clearing her throat and smiling.

"What? Doodlebug, are you having any cravings? What would you like for lunch?" he asked. Mom slapped her palms against her thighs before throwing her hands up in exasperation.

"Dad, I'd like some hot wings from the new place that opened up off the old highway. There's a menu on the fridge. They have ten different wing flavors, but I can't decide which ones I want. Maybe you could pick for me?" I asked.

"Hot wings! I'm on it," he said, rubbing his hands together as he left the room.

Mom looked at me with an expression that was a mixture of embarrassment, frustration, and relief. She mouthed the words, "thank you" before closing the door.

"Hi," Jackson quietly said once we were alone.

"Hi," I returned, taking a seat in the rocker situated in the corner of the room.

191

"I came by because I know Holden's at the office right now. I did a lot of thinking last night," he said, slowly pacing the room.

"Did you?" I asked, following him with my eyes.

"I did, but first tell me how things are with you."

"Okay, considering," I answered, nervously wringing my hands.

He sat on the ottoman across from me and reached out to take my hands in his. "How did things go with Holden last night? Are you okay? Was anything resolved?" he asked.

"He's been fine. No, nothing's been resolved. I was too tired to discuss everything with him last night."

"But he's treating you well?"

"I'm not sure what you want to hear," I confessed.

"I want the absolute truth," he requested.

"For the most part, I guess he's acting like the old Holden," I said.

"I know you're feeling conflicted, Emily. I want you to know that it's okay for you to be happy that Holden's back. I'm not sure how to say this without sounding callous, but a part of me is glad he's here," Jackson said.

"What are you saying?"

"I'm saying that we lost a bit of ourselves when we settled into our routine. Not, that it wasn't great! This isn't coming out right. I want what we had, but I want it for my future. That's not right either," he said, running his hands through his hair.

"You felt obligated to be with me?" I remarked.

"No, not obligated. I wanted to be with you more than anything. You're all I could ever hope for, but you weren't yourself when we were together. I had to see you with him to realize that we were just going through the motions."

"I'm sorry if you feel that way, Jackson. I never lied about loving you," I said sincerely.

"I know you love me and I love you, but there are different kinds of love. What you and Holden have is different than what we have—had. You and Holden have passion. How much trouble have you gotten into since we've been together?"

"None," I said, shaking my head.

"Exactly. That's not you, Emily." He smiled. "You need to be wreaking havoc somewhere. All of Green Bayou is in an uproar. They haven't had anything to bet on or talk about since we've been together," he joked.

"That's not fair. Stop trying to make me laugh," I said. When I looked away, he reached out to touch my cheek.

"Oh, how I wish I'd found you first," he whispered, before clearing his throat. "I'm going to make the decision easy for you, Emily. I'm leaving you."

"You're leaving me?" I was taken aback.

"Yes, now there's nothing left for you to figure out. You need to be with Holden."

"Yes there is! What about the baby?" I said, placing my hand on my stomach.

"I don't want you to stress out about that. I was there for most of the pregnancy. Holden's got a lot of appointments to catch up with and now that you're going once a week, he has an opportunity to do that. It's only fair. I do expect you to keep me informed, though," he said.

I couldn't hold the tears back any longer. "You never cease to amaze me. You're probably the most selfless man I've ever met. Are you sure about this, because I'm not so convinced? I'm going to miss you being here."

"Please don't cry, Em. I'm going to miss you, too. I'm not being selfless; I just have the sense to know when it's time to let something go. Trust me on this. You're better off with him. I enjoyed our time together, but I need to move on and so do you," he said with a half-smile. "I brought over some boxes so I can finish packing up my things."

"Have you found a place?" I asked.

"No, not yet. I'm going to use some of my vacation time to take a trip. I've got a lot of thinking to do and I'd rather be alone as I try to sort things out. I've got a few loose ends I need to tie up now that Holden's back in command then I'm headed to the mountains," he said.

"I understand. When will you be back?" I asked.

"I'm not sure."

"You are coming back, aren't you?"

"Yes." He rose to kiss me on the forehead. "I'll be in the bedroom packing."

"Can I help you?" I offered.

"Nah, there's not too much here. I'll get it. You go on downstairs and have lunch with your parents," he insisted.

"Promise me you'll keep in touch and you'll let me know if you need anything?" I said, holding out my hand so he could help me to stand. Once I was up, I wrapped my arms around his neck. "You deserve to be happy, Jackson. Thank you so much for loving me," I said.

He nodded as he moved away. "One more thing. Emily, always remember that anything I've done, I've done because I love you."

"I will," I promised, dashing a tear away when he left the room.

~.~.~.~.~.~

A couple of weeks passed and I still hadn't heard anything from Jackson. Though I missed him, I began to come to terms with his leaving. He was right; I hadn't been myself in a very long time.

Holden had a renewed vigor and zest for life that was contagious. He made me feel so alive! We weren't together as a couple romantically, but Holden and I did try to spend every spare minute together. He was right there with me when my next visit with Dr. Nelson came around. I loved watching his face light up when he heard the baby's heartbeat. The doctor gave me a clean bill of health and said that everything was right on schedule. After we finished up with the appointment, Holden followed me into the parking lot.

"Why don't you come back to the house with me?" I asked.

"I wish I could, but I have a lunch meeting and I can't get out of it," he said.

"Later then? Mom and Dad are in the Cayman's so it's just you and me tonight."

"It amazes me how they do that. Your dad sees a picture of a resort in a magazine and two days later, they're there," he said.

"Someday, that might be us," I said.

"Hopefully sooner, rather than later," he said with a smile.

"Don't eat too much at lunch. I'll cook for us tonight," I said, leaning against my car.

"Why don't you let me cook?" he asked.

"What did you have in mind?"

"You tell me."

"Boudin on the grill and sweet potato fries," I answered.

Holden laughed at me. "In a Cajun sausage kind of mood? Pork and rice or crawfish?"

"Pork and rice, and make sure it's extra-spicy," I answered.

"I can make that happen. I'll stop by the meat market, if you don't mind picking up everything else we need from the store. I'm not sure what time this meeting is supposed to wrap up," he said, giving me a gentle squeeze.

"Not a problem. Oh, man! I could go for some red velvet cake with a side of cheesecake ice cream. Doesn't that sound awesome?"

"Get to the store and I'll see you tonight." He laughed.

"Hey! I'm entitled," I protested, running my hands over my abdomen.

"I'm not going to argue that point," he said, raising his hands in surrender. "Be safe and I'll see you in a few hours."

"I will. See you soon." I got in the car and headed to the store.

~.~.~.~.~

I should've stopped for groceries down the street from the doctor's office, but my hankering for ice cream refused to waiver. It would surely melt by the time I got home from DeSoto, so I stopped off at the market in Green Bayou to buy what we needed for supper.

Since I planned to gorge on sweets for dessert, I figured a little extra exercise would do me some good. After picking the parking spot furthest from the store, I took my wallet from my purse before finally stepping from the car. I wasn't about to lug the extra twenty pounds of junk it held. Note to self—clean out purse! A soft, refreshing breeze greeted me when I put my purse in the trunk. It was such a beautiful day!

Suddenly, the hair on my arms stood at attention and the smile left my face. Something was off, but I couldn't place what.

Before I could react, a hood was thrown over my head and I was pushed inside the trunk of my car. *Scream! You need to scream!* I couldn't. The lid slammed shut and the driver sped off, sending me rolling to the back of the car. With my fists, I banged as hard as I could against the metal. The driver turned a corner then came to an abrupt stop.

I desperately clawed at the covering to rip it from my face, but the trunk clicked opened before I could manage it. The kidnapper secured my hands, and despite my struggling, I couldn't get free. There was a loud smashing sound; my hope sank. It was my cell phone being shattered into pieces. No one would be able to track me.

"Why would you do this to a pregnant woman? Please, listen to me. It's not too late. Just run off and no one will have to know about this. I didn't see anything. You can have my purse, the car, anything. Just please let me go," I pleaded.

The trunk closed, but this time the driver didn't speed off. Whoever it was began to drive very cautiously. I needed to stay calm and pay attention to the turns being made, but I couldn't. My mind raced. *How long will it be before someone notices that I'm missing? Mom and Dad are away, so they won't be able to help. I already talked to Connie today, so she won't think anything of not hearing from me. Holden will realize that I haven't been home, but that won't be until after his meeting.* My kidnapper would have a good five hour head start. I felt sick.

We traveled for nearly half an hour before I recognized the sound and feel of a shell road. Another fifteen minutes went by and the car finally came to a stop. I listened for any clue that might tell me where we were, but all I could make out were the occasional sounds of two men arguing. I felt around for anything I could use to get free. *Maybe I could use the tire iron?* Unfortunately, there was no time to get a game plan—the trunk opened and I was dragged out kicking and screaming.

"Stop that fighting right now. You have a baby to think about," a familiar voice cautioned.

"Who are you and what do you want?" I asked, turning my head in the direction of the voice.

"You'll find out in good time. I don't want you to fall, so I'm going to pick you up and carry you to where you need to be. I'm telling you this as a courtesy, so I hope that you'd extend me the same by not resisting. Do we have an understanding?" he asked.

"If you intend to hurt me, I'd at least like to know who's doing it and why," I argued.

"It's not me, I just do what I'm told," he said, lifting me into the air. *Why couldn't I place his voice?* Concentrating didn't help, it just frustrated me more.

He carried me through two doorways before placing me on a worn, uncomfortable mattress. I gasped when I felt the cold, hard steel of a knife blade press against my wrists. My hand restraints were cut away, but my mouth went dry when I realized that very blade might soon plunge deep into my chest or slide across my throat. The panic I was feeling honed my hearing: the sound of the knife blade clicking back into place was to my right—the shuffling of boots on a dirty floor, some movement and then the creaking of bedsprings to my left, and finally, a faint sigh before a set of footsteps moved away and out of the door. As soon as the lock slid into place, I ripped the hood from my head.

Rapidly blinking my eyes and trying to focus, I was shocked to find that I wasn't alone.

"They got you, too?" a feeble voice asked.

A battered Roberta was sitting on the twin bed opposite me. Though I despised the woman, it shocked me to see her in such a state. One eye was swollen nearly shut; the other had a bluish-purple tinge around it. Dried blood was crusted around her nostrils and her cheeks bore small nicks and large abrasions. As she stared forward, her fingers repeatedly touched a swollen, puffy spot on her lower lip. She looked exhausted and defeated; her eyes were vacant when she looked my way.

I barraged her with questions. "What's going on Roberta? Do you know where we are? Who did that to you? How long have you been here? Have you tried to get away?"

"They don't know that I know this, but we're at old man T-Jack's place. I recognize it because I used to meet Sheriff Rivet out here," she said. My stomach churned.

Pete had filled me in on the wild escapades that used to take place at T-Jack's, a small run-down house in the middle of nowhere. Sheriff Rivet used to get so sloshed that his deputies would take turns picking him up after his long hours of debauchery. Though everyone knew it happened, no one discussed it. Old man T-Jack's death occurred not long after Sheriff Rivet's, so the place was supposed to be abandoned.

"Do you know who did this?" I asked, heaving myself from the bed so I could check out Roberta's injuries.

"Only one of them; Spencer Landry," she said.

The voice—it was Spencer's! I felt the blood drain from my face as a flood of questions barraged my mind. Roberta was still talking.

"I thought he was different." She sniffled. "After that night at your party, Spencer told me that he saw beyond my bimbo routine and that he thought I had something to offer the world besides my body. I don't know if you heard, but he'd hired me to work at his office, and I was doing a good job, too," she said.

I shook my head, moving closer to better inspect her cuts. Though her clothes were dirty and torn, she wore a nice skirt and jacket set. It was disheveled, but her hair had once been in a neat up do or a bun. She truly looked the part of a business woman.

"No, I didn't hear," I said, gently touching one of the gashes on her cheek. "Did Spencer do this to you?"

"I don't think so. They wear disguises when they come in and the one who was doing the hitting was a lot thinner than Spencer," she answered.

"Did they do anything else to you?" I asked carefully.

"One of them tried to once, but Spencer stopped him. He said, 'I never agreed to let you have your way with her. Remember, she's supposed to be let go, unharmed, after you get the information you want,'" Roberta said, mimicking Spencer.

"What information?" I prodded.

"I don't know. I got smacked around a couple of times and that's when they started fighting. Next thing I know, I'm put in here," she explained.

"How long have you been here?" I asked.

"Since this morning. I got to work early so I could catch up on some filing. Next thing I know, everything went black and I woke up in the trunk of a car. I found these, and believe me, they still hurt," she said, raising her skirt to show two red marks left by a taser gun. "Did they get you like that? I hope not. Wouldn't the shock hurt the baby?"

"No, I wasn't tasered. I was put in the trunk of my car, but wasn't knocked around or roughed up or anything," I answered. Damn, if Roberta kept up the caring act, I might have to start liking her. "Thanks for asking," I threw in.

"Sure. I hear that Sheriff Dautry's back in town. That was the best news I'd heard in a long time," she said. My thoughts of reconciliation vanished just as quickly as they had appeared.

"Yes, he's back," I said curtly.

"I don't know what they intend to do with me. If Spencer has any control, I might have a chance of surviving, but if the others have their way, I'm not so sure," she said, weeping.

"Don't talk like that, Roberta," I said, trying to sound reassuring.

"I want to apologize for what I did to you. I don't want to die with all of this guilt on my conscience. You have to know that the only reason I tried to steal your men from you is because I was insanely jealous," she said.

"Jealous of whom? Me?" I asked with disbelief. "Why?"

"I never got treated good, I mean well, so when I saw how Pete doted over you, I wanted to feel what that was like. One time, I called from Jerry's Gas and More to tell the dispatcher that I needed an armed escort to make a deposit. When Pete got there, I put every move I could think of on him, but he never gave me the time of day," she said. I didn't want to think about Pete. Roberta needed to shut up!

"You're forgiven," I said rudely, struggling to rise so I could walk away from her. She reached out to stop me.

"Wait, I haven't told you about Holden yet," she said.

"I know all I want to know about you and Holden."

"I didn't mean to upset you. I just wanted you to know that I'm sorry," she said.

I nodded, moving over to the window. There were bars over it, but being able to see out helped me feel less trapped. After a while, I walked to the door and put my ear to it hoping to hear any trace of conversation. The loud buzzing of the generator and the humming of the tiny air conditioner that was nailed into the wall made it impossible.

"Do you know how many people are here? You mentioned Spencer, the person who hit you, and the person who groped you. Are there more?" I asked.

"Yes, two others watched," she answered.

"And they were all in disguise?"

"Spencer wore all black and he had this black ski mask kind of thing on. The rest of them wore some strange looking Mardi Gras masks and street clothes," she answered.

"Can you remember anything else about any of them? Tattoos? Scars? Anything that stands out to you?"

"The super skinny guy that was feeling me up, he had really weird eyes."

"What was weird about them?" I asked.

ining.

"Did he have long, stringy black hair?" I asked, sighing.

"Yes!" she answered. "It was greasy and nasty."

"I know who's holding us hostage. Now, we need to figure out what they want," I said.

"Who is it?"

"Donovan Guidry and his posse. They escaped from prison after the tornado."

"Uh-oh," Roberta said.

"What uh-oh? I don't like uh-oh."

"Donovan probably wants his stuff back," she mumbled.

"What stuff, Roberta?" I asked, walking back to where she lay on the bed.

"Just some stuff," she said, sitting up and looking around the room.

"What stuff!"

"I don't know for sure it's what he's after." She nervously chewed at one of her fingernails.

"Answer me, Roberta. What stuff?" I said, carefully enunciating each word.

"The drug stash and the six hundred thousand dollars that I hid," she answered.

"What!" I exclaimed. "You hid drugs and money for him?"

"Not for him, from him," she explained. "I was going to turn it over to Sheriff Dautry, but he refused to meet with me after Donovan was arrested. Then the tornado hit and I didn't trust the new Sheriff, so I just held on to it."

I stared at her with disbelief.

"Where is it, Roberta?" I asked, rubbing my throbbing temples.

"It's in a really safe spot. Somewhere no one would ever think to look," she said.

"Good, but where?" I demanded.

"Why do you need to know?" she asked.

"Really? It's going to be like that, Roberta?" I fussed, looking her way.

"Don't be mad at me, but it's hidden at your house," she quietly answered.

I stopped my massage to move toward her. "What did you say?" I asked with disbelief.

"I live in a tiny apartment and I knew it would be the first place someone would look for it, so I thought, 'Where's the last place people would think to look for drugs and money?'. I guessed the Sheriff's house. I didn't know where he lived, but knew that you two spent a lot of time together. Your place is pretty famous, and nobody would ever suspect *you'd* have it, so I waited for you to leave for work one day and that's when I hid it," she rambled.

"You hid contraband at *my* house?" I asked through clenched teeth.

"You don't have to get so upset. I knew you had the connections to get out of trouble if you were caught with it. I didn't think it would be an issue if it got discovered at your place," she reasoned.

"Yeah, connections to drop a speeding ticket, maybe, but not for *that*!" I fussed. "Oh, please tell me that you have a warped sense of humor and that this is just a sick joke."

"It's not a joke," she said, shaking her head and looking down at the floor.

"Where at my house?" I demanded as calmly as I could.

"I'm not gonna tell you. You're mad at me. I've said too much already," she said, thrusting her lips into a pout and crossing her arms over her chest.

"Mad doesn't even begin to cover it, Roberta," I said, gripping her lapels to pull her upright. "I might be big and pregnant, but I'll still kick your butt! Talk!"

"Hey! Let me go. I'm not saying anything," she said, trying to pull away.

A sharp pain in my lower abdomen made me release my hold on her and I doubled over.

"What's wrong?" she asked, coming to my side. I took a deep breath and the pain slowly began to subside.

"It might be the stress," I answered, moving to lie on the bed.

"Should I try to get someone to answer the door?" she asked.

"No, the less attention we draw to ourselves, the better. The pain's almost completely gone now," I said. "Have you told them where the stash is?"

"No, I might play dumb, but I know that I'm a goner soon as they don't need me anymore," she answered.

The door suddenly flew open and a stocky man wearing a Mardi Gras mask entered the room.

"Miss Boudreaux, we've never had the pleasure of actually meeting, but I'm quite familiar with you," he said.

"Why hide behind the mask? It's kind of pointless now, isn't it, Donovan?" I asked.

"Ah, so the secret's out? I've heard stories about you. You *are* quite spirited. I like that." He laughed, pulling the mask from his face and casting it aside.

"What do you want with me?" I asked.

"Me? Nothing, though it's nice to know I've got one up on Holden Dautry. Nope, you're the guest of Brad Dautrieve. He'll be the one handling you. She's mine," he said, nodding his head towards Roberta. "Let's go. Time for round two, slut," he said, clenching a fistful of Roberta's hair. She cried out in pain when he forced her to follow him.

"Let go of her! Don't hurt her" I demanded, hanging onto his arm.

He tried shaking me off, but with my added weight, he was getting nowhere. He let go of her to backhand me across the face.

Spencer rushed into the room and came to stand between me and Donovan. "That's it! I've had enough of this. I'm not going to sit back and watch you beat up a pregnant woman."

"Crusher, why did you do this to me? How did you get involved in this mess?" I asked, rubbing my cheek.

"I didn't want to, but I needed the money, Emily. Business hasn't been that great and I was overextended. You two were supposed to be questioned and then set free.

Had I known you'd be fresh meat for a bunch of sadists, I never would've agreed to do it," he directed at Donovan.

"Ewww, I'll only kidnap for you if you promise not to hurt anyone!" Donovan said mockingly. "Give me a break! You're not stupid, Spencer. You knew there wasn't a chance in hell these chicks were getting out of here alive."

"I did not! She's pregnant! You can't tell me that you're so heartless that you'd murder an innocent baby!" Spencer argued.

"She's Brad's problem. I didn't know she was pregnant. I like pregnant chicks—think they're kinda hot. That Dautrieve is one cruel son of a bitch, though. I'm sure the Sonnier guy had to mention that she was knocked up during one of his visits, but Brad still insisted that he wanted the Boudreaux lady," he said.

"Jackson Sonnier?" I asked, trying not to vomit.

"Yeah, Jackson Sonnier. You think it was some big coincidence that you didn't have any run-ins with Brad once he got loose? He went straight to your place to end you, but the Sonnier guy caught him and worked out a deal. Brad would leave you alone as long as Sonnier kept him stocked with drugs. Sonnier even suggested this place as a hideout," Donovan explained.

"You're lying. Why wouldn't Jackson just arrest him?" I asked.

"Because Dautrieve had three other friends ready to finish you off if anything happened to him, and he made sure Jackson knew it, too," Donovan explained. "Then, Dautry resumed command and Sonnier lost unsupervised access to the evidence room. Our last package was delivered a couple of weeks ago when he came by to tell us that the supply had run out and we were on our own."

"Did you hurt him?" I asked.

"I'm done talking about him," Donovan said, boredom in his tone.

"I can't believe this," I said sinking onto the bed. "How much money do you need? My parents will be more than happy to pay anything if you let me go."

"It's too late for the whole ransom thing. Maybe if Holden was still gone, I'd consider it. But, you know as well as I do that he's not about to let me walk away. He'll hunt me down for the rest of his life if need be," Donovan said.

"I could talk to him about that and convince him to let you go," I insisted.

"Nice try, but that's not going to happen."

"Please, anything..." I begged.

"You're barking up the wrong tree with me, sweetheart. It's a good thing Sonnier brought your boy such a big stash to keep him mellow. I'd hate to be you when he sobers up," he said, retightening his grip on Roberta. "Let's go! I have a feeling that I'll be getting what I want from you real soon, Berta."

She began to sob and Spencer closed the gap between them. He sent Donovan reeling to the floor with a good, solid shove.

"I'm done with this. Come with me Emily and Roberta, I'm getting you both out of here," Spencer said.

"Like hell!" Donovan shouted. He drew a snub-nose pistol from an ankle holster and pointed it at Spencer's head.

"You're a lot of things, Donovan, but you're no murderer. This is over. You'll have plenty of time to find a new hideout. Just let us go," Spencer said, holding his arms out and waving his hands to encourage us to join him. The shot rang out before I could take a step. Blood and brain matter sprayed outward and Spencer crumpled to the floor with a horrendous thud. Roberta shrieked and I turned away. There was no saving him.

13

"Spencer underestimated me. Don't make the same mistake, Berta! Get in here you goons!" Donovan Guidry yelled.

Two scraggly looking men entered the room. I recognized one of them as they guy who attacked me in my boat shed. The other person I didn't know.

"Whoa! That's gross! What happened, man?" the unknown guy asked.

"Don't you worry about it! Just get him into the skiff and dump him in the woods across the way. Be sure to use bleach when you hose the boat out. Got it?"

The men argued over who would take Spencer's feet and who should grab his arms. After some debate, they decided each would take an arm and leg. They awkwardly shuffled out of the room, leaving a thick trail of blood behind them. Donovan came over to me.

"You work as a medic so this junk shouldn't bother you. I'll let you two clean up the mess. Ladies, come with me," he ordered, snapping his fingers.

He led us out through a sparsely furnished living room and into a small kitchen. He pulled open the pantry door and took out a bucket, some bleach, and a mop. I glanced around for anything I could use as a weapon. There were no knives on the counter, no fire extinguisher to bash heads, maybe some glass in the fridge? It saved my life the last time I was held hostage.

"Can I get something to drink?" I asked, pointing to the refrigerator. "The stress is making me really thirsty."

I prayed that Donovan would feel some sort of compassion for a huge, pregnant woman. He must've, because he nodded his head while shoving rolls of paper towels into Roberta's arms. Nothing but plastic water bottles, some energy drinks, and some fast food bags. I took a few bottles of water and closed the door.

I scanned again as we walked out of the kitchen, carefully taking note of the floor plan. A small hallway that probably led to another bedroom on the right, a sparsely furnished dining area was behind me. An open door led to a back porch. I didn't get to see much because Donovan quickly ushered me back to the bedroom.

"I guess it's your lucky day. Since I don't feel like cleaning up this mess, you got yourself a few extra hours, Berta. Enjoy them. Now get to work," he said, throwing down the supplies, then slamming the door.

Desperately clutching the paper towels to her chest, Roberta slowly sank to the floor. Her face was extremely pallid and her body trembled violently as she turned to stare out of the window. I was concerned that she was going into shock.

"Roberta, look at me," I said, lightly shaking her, but she continued to stare forward. "Roberta, you can't check out on me. If we're going to get out of here, we need to keep our heads and work together."

"That's gonna be me," she mumbled. "I knew that Donovan was a son of a bitch who liked to rough up women, but I didn't think he was capable of murder. I've never seen a man die before. It was beyond horrible. I can't get the image out of my head," she said, breathing harder and faster.

"Stop!" I held her face so she'd have to look at me. "Now's not the time to fall apart. We have to stay strong if we want to get out of here. You don't need to see this stuff. Go sit in the closet and drink one of the bottles of water. I'll come and get you once I get this cleaned up."

"You can't clean all of that by yourself." She gagged when she looked at the puddle of blood.

"I've got it. Don't look anywhere but straight ahead and go straight to the closet," I demanded, releasing my grip on her. She stumbled into the space near the window and I heard her sit heavily on the floor. The metallic smell of the blood was making me nauseous, so I wrapped a pillowcase around my face and let my mind wander as I worked to scour the mess.

How long have I been here? It's getting dark, so Holden has to realize I'm missing by now. Would anyone report Roberta as missing? What about Spencer Landry? There's no way Holden will ever think to look for me out here. How can I get free, and once I do, then what? I'm in the middle of nowhere. It takes nearly forty-five minutes to get to town by car, how long would it take me if I had to walk it? Maybe I could steal the skiff, but if I do, where do I go? The bayous are full of little cuts and channels. I could run out of gas and never be found. Would Holden reach out to Jackson, and if he did, would Jackson come clean about his involvement? And, that's if he could even find Jackson! He might have a bullet in his head, too.

The floor and walls were finally cleaned and I had no new answers or revelations. I banged on the door. Donovan opened it, taking bites from an apple.

"What?" he asked, smacking in my face.

"It's clean in here," I said, thrusting the buckets out of the door.

"I don't want to touch that! Go put them back where you got them from," he demanded.

I pushed by him to get to the kitchen. "Do you have anything I could eat?" I asked, staring at his apple.

"Dig around and see what you can find. You're so lucky I have a thing for pregnant chicks," he said, slowly looking me up and down. "Where's the snitch bitch hiding?"

"She got sick, so I told her to stay on the other side of the room," I answered, still inwardly cringing from his last comment.

"About right, she never was good for anything but spreading her legs," he said, closing the door behind us.

I put the cleaning supplies back in the pantry, and while in there, I noticed some cans of tuna and ravioli. I took a couple of each and a box of crackers. I started a small pile on the counter. Candy bars from one of the drawers, a keychain-style can opener from another; I still couldn't find a weapon. Some bananas and apples from on top of the fridge and some bottles of water from inside.

"Hey now, it's not like we can just run down to the local food mart and stock back up. I understand you're eating for two, but come on," Donovan commented.

"Sorry," I said, putting the candy bars back. Arms crossed, he continued to stare at me. I put it all back but one apple, one banana, a can of ravioli, and a sleeve of crackers. He seemed okay with this, so I scooped it up and carried it into the room.

"What can I do to convince you to let me go? I'll tell Holden that Brad did this on his own. I won't even mention your name and I'll still get money to you. Just name an amount," I said.

"Nice try. Don't misinterpret my tolerance for stupidity," he said, pushing me through the door.

After emptying the food that was in my arms onto the bed, I checked Roberta. She was curled into a ball on the floor of the closet. I let her sleep.

It wasn't easy opening the can of ravioli with the cheap can opener, so I snacked on the banana while working on it. The sun had long set by the time Roberta finally stumbled out of the closet.

"How long was I asleep?" she asked, stretching her arms overhead.

"A few hours. Here, I got you some food," I said, handing her the apple.

"Did you eat? Maybe you should save this for yourself?" she said.

Damn it, I was starting to like her again.

"I ate. You go ahead," I encouraged. She took several tiny nibbles from the apple before she extended it to me.

"Take it, I can't eat."

"You better make yourself eat. There may come a point in time where we'll have to fight our way out. I won't be able to pack much of a wallop; you need to stay strong."

"You sure seem calm," she said, continuing to nibble on the fruit.

"I've been in situations like this more times than I care to remember, but I'm terrified that this may be the time my luck finally runs out. I have a baby to think about; I can't give up," I answered.

"You're going to be a real good mom," she said with the faintest twinkle in her eye. "Your kid's lucky. My family life wasn't the best."

"Tell me about it," I said, rolling onto my side so I could give her my full attention.

"You already look down upon me. I don't think I should," she said.

"I don't look down upon you, Roberta. I'm not that kind of person. My problem with you is the way you flaunt yourself in front of men, all men, even taken men, *my* men in particular," I said a little more harshly than I'd intended.

"I thought that you didn't like me because your family has all that money and I come from the wrong part of town," she said.

"No," I answered in a much softer tone. "Come on, tell me about it. You might feel better."

"Well, if you insist. I really hope I'm not making a mistake by telling you this," she said with a sigh. "My dad worked offshore and died in an accident when I was five. Mom got tons of money from a lawsuit, but she blew it all by the time I was ten.

Mom never had a job, so the only way she could support us was by sleeping around. One guy would bring groceries; another would pay the electric bill. One really rotten guy got her hooked on drugs, and by the time I was fifteen, she couldn't support her habit anymore.

My body filled out in all the right places and the guys she brought home began paying attention to me, so she took advantage of it. The first time she made me sleep with one of those men she cried and told me how sorry she was. She got over it pretty quickly. Within a couple of weeks, she had so many men lined up that I wasn't allowed to go to school anymore. I couldn't take it, so I ran away.

I bounced from house to house, going to high school during the day and waitressing for money at night. No one was there to see me when I graduated third in my class. Anyway, I'm not telling you this to make you feel sorry for me. I just want you to know that I'm not as stupid as most people think I am," she said.

I was speechless, so she went on.

"I loved going to college, but I was only there a couple of semesters. I mean I had scholarships and all, but it got to be too much. I married this loser contractor who treated me like crap. He used to make me eat last! He expected his food to be on the table at six o'clock on the dot, then he'd eat, then he'd feed the dog, and if anything was left, I got to eat while he watched TV with his nightly

six-pack. I finally worked up the nerve to leave him; I
hitched a ride with a trucker who wrongfully assumed I'd
give *him* a ride. I forced him to stop at the first gas station,
which happened to be Jerry's Gas and More, and told him
to get lost. Mr. Jerry saw the whole thing, asked to hear my
story, and not only gave me a job on the spot, but also paid
for a couple of nights stay in a local motel. I got to eat
from the shelves and take food back with me if I needed it.
Mr. Jerry saw something besides tits and ass when he
looked at me. He was so nice that I decided to stay in
Green Bayou. I'm sorry I'm talking your head off. I'll shut
up," she said, propping her head on her hands.

"No, please keep going," I insisted.

"The bad thing about my working at the Gas and
More was it gave me a chance to see how everyone else was
living. I barely scraped by, living off of bags of fifty cent
potato chips and sunflower seeds, while others came in and
plopped down hundred dollar bills for a pack of gum. I
wanted a better life, and I'm not just talking about being
able to buy things. I saw the way good men treated
women, and I wanted that, too. Before you came to town,
Pete used to be one of the few men who treated me
decently. He asked how I was doing and he'd talk to me
about things going on around town. I looked forward to
his visits. He made me feel so special, and then you came
along. I saw how he looked at you, and I was so jealous.
The same with Holden. I attracted the assholes like
Donovan Guidry while you got the Prince Charmings, and
I resented that. I'm sorry for making passes at Pete and
Holden. If it makes you feel any better, neither of them

returned any of my advances, no matter how hard I tried," she said, lowering her eyes.

I tried to sit up, but a contraction gripped so hard that I had to lie back down. Letting out a grunt, my hands settled on my abdomen. I tried to breathe through the pain.

"Oh, gosh! I made you go into labor! I'm sorry! I didn't mean to! Forget whatever it was that I said that made that happen. I take it back!" she exclaimed.

"It doesn't work that way, Roberta. Once you start labor, it's kind of hard to stop it," I said, taking and releasing a slow, deep breath. "Plus, it's not real labor until the pain comes at a steady rate. I've only had two contractions since we've been here."

Roberta seemed to relax a little and I tried to find a more comfortable position. I desperately longed for rest, but the contractions that were coming every ten minutes made sleeping nearly impossible. The lie I told helped Roberta to rest, but I was in for a long night.

~.~.~.~.~

Even though the sun was shining brightly through the window, I managed to doze between contractions. I woke to find Brad peering down at me. His pasty skin and jet black hair were bad enough, but now his face had a purplish hue and was dotted with acne scars. Greasy hair hung well past his shoulders and his eyes were red and weepy. Involuntary spasms occasionally rocked his emaciated body.

"I got you," he said with a smirk.

"Leave her alone," Roberta said, rising from the bed.

"Ewww-weee! You are one *hot* piece of ass!" he said, turning his attention to her. "I need to convince Donovan that it's okay to share."

"Soon as she tells me what I want to know, she's yours," Donovan said, entering the room. Another contraction came and I tried my best to hide the pain; I couldn't help but pant through it.

"What's wrong with you?" Donovan demanded.

"She's in labor," Roberta offered.

"Labor? Shit, you gotta get her somewhere, Brad," Donovan said.

"She ain't going nowhere. Do you know how long I've waited to get this bitch?"

"You mean to tell me that you're going to off a baby?" Donovan asked.

"I haven't decided yet. I'm going back to bed," he said, scratching his head as he walked away.

"You used to be a paramedic! Shouldn't you be doing something?" Donovan nervously asked.

"I am. I'm going to sleep real well knowing that Mother Nature's giving her more pain than I could ever hope to. Then I'm going to dream of all of the different ways I can get rid of her. I can strangle her, shoot her, burn her, cut her up... Ahhhh, the possibilities are endless," he said, laughing.

"You're a sick bastard," Donovan muttered.

"Takes one to know one. Don't pretend you haven't been having fantasies about what you're going to do with that one," he said. "Hell, I'm gonna take care of a few fantasies I'm having about her right now," he said, suggestively licking his lips as he winked at Roberta. She cringed.

"You're not going to do anything until we come up with a plan about how we're going to handle this situation," I heard Donovan demand before he followed Brad out of the door.

"Can I do anything to help you?" Roberta asked once we were alone.

"Will you help me to stand? I need to walk around," I said, rubbing my back.

Roberta nervously tore at her nails with her teeth while I paced up and down the floor.

"Stop doing that. You're making *me* nervous," I said, holding onto the window sill for support as another contraction came. "I'm guessing that they're about six or seven minutes apart. We still have some time."

"Good, because I have no clue what I should do," she confided.

"Look at it this way, it's going to happen even if you do nothing," I answered.

Trying to focus on something other than the pain, I stared out of the window and counted trees across the bayou. I couldn't make it past fifteen; the contractions made me lose count. I saw the dock. Thoughts of Spencer's lifeless body being hauled away in the skiff gave me the creeps. I looked away.

A large oak tree laden with Spanish moss leaned over the wharf, and an old rope swing gently swayed over the water. I wondered how many people had swung from it, dropping into the bayou while seeking refuge from the scorching Louisiana sun. Maybe I should get Holden to hang a swing from one of the trees at Greenleaf? Thinking of Holden made me want to cry, so I backed away from the window and paced some more.

The pain became so intense that I could no longer breathe or pant my way through it. Slight moans turned into full-fledged groans and sighs turned into loud grunts. Donovan barged into the room and shoved a gun in Roberta's face.

"You have fifteen seconds to tell me where my stash is or I'll pull the trigger. No more playing around, no more chances," he said.

"I…I…" Roberta stumbled on her words.

"Thirteen," Donovan said.

"It's not anywhere near here," Roberta answered.

"If you want to have a chance of surviving, you'll tell me. Ten."

"How do I know you won't shoot me once I tell you?" she hurriedly asked.

"I'm gonna shoot you if you don't. I think it's worth the chance," he answered. "Three, two…"

"It's at Greenleaf Plantation, under the front porch!" she shrieked, throwing her hands in front of her face.

"What! Did you know about this? I thought you two didn't like each other," he said, pointing the gun at me.

"I didn't know anything about it." I panted.

222

"You're either extremely stupid or you're way smarter than I gave you credit for, Berta. I don't have time to mess with you, so here's what's going to happen. I'm leaving to get my stuff. If it's there, then I'll come back and put a bullet in your head, like I did with that Landry character. If it's not, you'll quickly discover all the things I learned about torturing people when I was in prison. Don't think of trying to escape. I might be going, but Brad and his buddy are staying behind," Donovan warned.

Roberta started to weep and I probably would've cried, too, but the pain was making me see double. Donovan slammed the door and Roberta crawled into the corner and started to bawl.

"I'm going to die. Even though I told him what he wanted to know, he's still going to kill me," she wailed.

"Roberta, stop it. It's not over until it's over. I need you to try to stop crying, take a few deep breaths, owww ahhhh…" I waited for the contraction to finish before I completed my sentence, "and let's try to think of something. Brad's here, but I'll bet anything that he's so wasted he couldn't stop us from escaping if he tried. Donovan left in a vehicle, but it's possible that another one might be out there and if not, there's the skiff. I was hoping that we wouldn't have to take it, but if there's no other way, we'll do what we have to. Don't you give up, Roberta! Suck it up!" I said, stooping to give her a solid shaking. She only wailed louder. Lots of violent thoughts raced through my mind, so I moved to the window and took a time out.

Another contraction came on full force and I gripped the window sill to remain upright. *This is not how I want to bring my child into the world! I want a beautiful hospital suite with state of the art equipment and drugs, not a nasty room in an abandoned whore house. I want my obstetrician to deliver my baby, not the sniveling mess rolled into a fetal position.* Exhaustion began to take its toll, as did the lack of food, the pain of labor, and the stress of the situation. I had to rest if I was going to have the strength to push the baby out.

I was about to turn away from the window when a movement caught my eye. Excitedly wiping at the window to clear some of the grime, I saw a skinny, dark-headed teenager swinging from the rope swing. He did a sort of flop off the swing and splashed down into the water before swimming back to the shore and doing it all over again. I rubbed my eyes and realized that it wasn't a kid, it was— Alphonse? But, after the last dunk, he was nowhere to be found. *Oh God, I'm hallucinating about Alphonse!* I silently encouraged myself to keep it together as I called Roberta over to me.

"I don't want to scare you, but I think something's wrong. I'm starting to see things, so you need to help me get to the bed," I said.

Roberta stopped her howling long enough to pull herself upright, gasping and hiccupping her way across the room. She put my arm around her neck, but froze right before she turned away from the window.

"There's a dude out there," she said, sniffling.

"You see him, too?" I asked with surprise, moving so I could peek out again.

"Is that Alphonse Rivet?" she asked, wiping her eyes.

"I'm not hallucinating? Alphonse is really out there?" I asked in a hushed, but excited tone.

"If you're hallucinating, then so am I," she answered. She threw her fist back to bang on the window. I grabbed her arm mid-flight.

"No! Don't make any noise!" I fussed. "They'll hear you! There's got to be another way to get his attention."

"The window's sealed shut," she said, pulling with all her strength to raise it. I quickly searched the room and tossed Roberta a pillowcase.

"Wave this around. Maybe the motion will catch his attention," I said. She did as I suggested while I continued to search the room. "How does Alphonse manage to keep popping up in these situations?" I mumbled to myself. Roberta obviously overheard me.

"His uncle used to bring him out here all the time. The old man knew Alphonse wasn't gonna get laid any other way, so he figured he'd let him get his rocks off out here. It didn't work though. I was talking with some of the other girls and they told me that Alphonse never got any, he mostly just swam around outside while the Sheriff did his thing. They said one of the girls undressed in front of Alphonse, and he giggled so hard, he threw up before she unhooked her bra. After that, he refused to come inside," she explained.

I leaned my head out of the bathroom door and looked at her. "That explains *so* much," I said. "Anything yet? Is he still out there?"

"Yeah, he's sitting on the wharf right now, but no, he doesn't see me yet," she answered.

"I hope I'm right about Brad and his buddy being wasted. If they find him out there, he's good as gone," I said, ducking back into the bathroom.

I rummaged through the drawers—assorted condoms (yuck), some eye liner, a tube of bright red lipstick, several open bottles of massage oil (ewww), dried up body paints (double-ewww), a powder compact. A-ha! Something I could use!

"I've got something!" I said as another contraction sent me to my knees.

"What is it?" Roberta ran to help me. I breathed my way through it, and then apologized to Roberta for nearly breaking her fingers. She helped me to stand so I could walk to the window.

"See how the sun's streaming in? I might be able to use the mirror to signal Alphonse," I explained while trying to get the angle just right. I knew I was getting it done when Alphonse started waving his arms around like he was swatting a mosquito. He stood and darted back and forth down the dock.

"That boy looks like a cat chasing a laser pointer," Roberta commented.

"Come on, look this way, Alphonse," I softly murmured, continuing to move the mirror back and forth. After another few seconds of chasing the reflection around, he stood scratching his head. Staring at the window, he threw his arms across his face when the beam blinded him. "He knows where it's coming from, now will he check it out?"

Alphonse started walking towards the house. He took a few steps and stopped to look around, before cautiously moving closer. He was nearly to the window when Roberta started waving and jumping up and down. Alphonse's face went white and I thought he was going to bolt. "No, don't run away, Alphonse," I said to myself as I shoved Roberta away from the window.

"Hey! What'd you do that for?" She pouted.

"You better hope you didn't scare him off," I fussed. "You know how skittish he is! He probably thinks you're a ghost. Wait, it looks like he's coming back."

Roberta rejoined me at the window. Alphonse raised his hand over his eyes to peer inside. Once he saw us looking back at him, he stumbled backwards, tripped over his feet, and fell to the ground. He quickly shook it off and cautiously re-approached the window.

"Emily Boudreaux? Is dat you? What you doin' in there and who's dat fine lady wit you?" he shouted.

"Shhhh!" I said, as close to the glass as possible. "Can you hear me?"

"I hear ya jus' fine. Why we gotta be quiet?" He pressed his ear to the glass.

"Donovan Guidry, Brad Dautrieve, and some others have kidnapped me and Roberta. We don't have much time. I'm in labor and Donovan will be back soon to kill us. Do you have a cell phone with you?" I asked.

"Yeah, but I don't get no signal out here. I'll have to go down the bayou. What you mean you in labor?"

"The baby's coming, Alphonse. Can you go down the bayou for us? Please call Holden or Bert and let them know what's going on? No one else, okay? And do it fast," I demanded, doubling over again.

"Do you want me to bust in and get you? I watch the Discovery channel. I bet I can deliver your baby for ya," he said excitedly.

"No!" I said in between huffs. "We have someone coming to kill us, Alphonse. Go call Holden or Bert and tell them exactly what I told you."

"Do you want me to…" he started.

"For Pete's sake, Alphonse! Go get help!" I snapped, nearly crying. This time Roberta pushed me away from the window.

"If you get the Sheriff to us in time, I'll let you touch these," she said, raising her shirt and pushing her breasts against the window. "Uh-oh," she said, drawing her hand to her mouth so she could nervously chew on a fingernail. She had an exceedingly guilty look on her face when she moved away from the window.

"What uh-oh? What did you do?" I asked, looking out to see what was wrong.

"I think I killed him," she said, starting to cry. "I thought he'd be motivated to hurry if I flashed him, but instead he grabbed his chest and just fell over."

"Oh, that's just great! Didn't you tell me he had a giggle fit over a bra! What made you think that busting out your double D's would be a good idea?"

"I don't know. Most men really like them. They ask to see them all the time," she whined.

I pushed my head against the glass to check on Alphonse. Though he still clutched his chest, he had a huge grin on his face and the front of his swimming trunks had tented up.

"Relax, you didn't kill him," I said, nodding toward the window. She peeked out and gasped.

"Who knew Alphonse was such a hung son of a gun? Wow," she remarked.

At first, I gave her a sneer, but then curiosity made me lean forward to see for myself. My eyes widened.

"No way. How is that even physically possible?" I breathed.

Alphonse stirred, his hands moving to check different parts of his body. When he got to his shorts, he quickly jerked his hand back and a broad, goofy smile spread across his face. He stood up, shook his head quickly from side to side, and peered back into the window.

"I think that if I was able to see them boobies again, maybe for like a minute or so, it would give me something good to think about and I could get help faster," he said.

"You fainted when you saw them for half a second," I argued.

"That's cause I wasn't expecting 'em," he said.

"I'll go topless from here on out if it gets us out of here," she said. I shushed Roberta.

"A minute's too long. Remember, someone's coming to *kill* us! Five seconds," I negotiated.

"Forty-five. I'll run extra fast," he countered.

"Ten," I said, shooting him a look.

"Thirty," he shot back, wiping his nose with his thumb.

"Really Alphonse! You better hope you can run fast because I'm going to kill *you* when I get out of here. It'll be quicker for her to show them off than for me to

229

keep arguing with you!" I said, backing away from the window.

"And I still get to touch them after you're free, right?" he called. Roberta nodded. "Over the shirt or under the shirt?" he asked.

"Cut it out, Alphonse!" I said through clenched teeth. I pulled Roberta from the window to glare at him, before letting Roberta do her thing.

"Whichever you want," she said raising her top for him.

His body shuddered, his eyes rolled back in his head, and he threw his hands in front of his shorts. Disgusted, I went to lie back on the bed.

"It's okay. He didn't last the thirty seconds, Emily," Roberta said to me. "He's almost to the water. There's a small scooter propped against the tree. I didn't notice that before. He's looking back toward the house. Oh, no! Someone's yelling at him. Come on Alphonse. Go! Go! Greasy haired guy's outside now with that blonde dude. They look like they might chase him. Wait, something's wrong. Alphonse took off, but they aren't going after him. They're coming back toward the house," she said.

"No matter what happens, don't let them know we saw Alphonse," I said, closing my eyes. "Quick, pretend you're sleeping!"

Roberta did as I suggested, barely getting into position before the door opened. I panted through another contraction when Brad entered the room.

"Who was that?" he asked.

"Who was who?" I asked, in between breaths.

"That guy!" he demanded.

"I don't know what you're talking about. I'm in full labor, so I haven't exactly been running around," I said.

"What about you?" he said, poking at Roberta. She jumped up, doing an excellent job of acting confused.

"What's wrong? Don't hurt me," she said, holding her hands in front of her.

"Awww, they didn't see nothing, Earl, but it don't mean he ain't gonna come back. We need to get outta here. Donovan took the gun with him, so lock the bitches in here while I put on the gas. We're gonna make this place go boom," Brad said with a smile.

"No!" Roberta yelled, launching from the bed.

A startled Brad stumbled backwards when Roberta jumped up and latched herself onto his back. Her legs encircled his waist and her fingernails dug deep gouges into his face. He tried throwing her off, but she held on tightly. When Earl tried to pry Roberta off of Brad, she released her leg and kicked him square in the gut. He reeled to the floor. Roberta clawed at Brad's face, and he screamed when she managed to work a fingernail into one of his eyes. He repeatedly rammed her against the wall, after the third hit, she crumpled to the floor.

"You blinded me you bitch!" he yelled, kicking her with such force that her body rolled away from him. Blood marred what vision he had, so the next kick he tried to land completely missed her.

"Get up and find me something to blow this bitch up with!" he demanded of Earl.

"I lost my lighter," Earl answered, still hunched on the ground from Roberta's kick to the ribs.

"Then go see if you can find some fuckin' matches, idiot!" Brad hollered, wiping his face with his shirt. He felt around for the doorway, then slammed the door behind him. I heard the sound of furniture scraping the floor, then the doorknob jiggle. Obviously, he had shoved a chair under the knob. I had to wait for my last contraction to ease up before checking on Roberta. She was out cold.

14

"Roberta, wake up." I used my knuckles to rub the center of her chest. She stirred.

"What happened? Where am I?" she asked, slowly opening her eyes. "Why does my head hurt so bad?"

"Give it a minute and it'll come back to you."

"Oh, I remember now. Did I get him?" she asked hopefully as she sat up.

"I think you blinded him in one eye, but no, he got away. That was a great try, though. What you did was very brave," I said.

"It might have been brave, but it didn't do us any good. What now?" She tried to get her feet under her.

"I don't think there's much more we can do," I said. "I heard a vehicle speeding away from the house. I'm pretty sure they're gone. I doubt it will do any good, but you can try the door."

Roberta pulled, tugged, and beat at it. Nothing happened. She cast aside the now broken, folding metal chair she was using as a battering ram and sank to the floor.

"Roberta, I need you," I said, taking slow, deep breaths. "My contractions are right on top of each another and I don't think it'll be much longer before it's time to push. Can you find some things for me? I need something to wrap the baby in, like a pillowcase. You'll have to tear up the sheets, too. It's going to be really messy. Find something like a shoe lace to tie off the umbilical cord. Oh, this is not how I wanted to bring this baby into the world!"

Roberta, who had torn through the room like a wild woman gathering supplies, was ripping sheets when she stopped to sniff the air.

"I smell gas," she said. "Do you smell it?"

I stopped panting long enough to take a deep breath through my nose. Oh yeah, I smelled it.

"Use that chair to break out the window," I instructed.

It took four strikes before she finally cleared all of the panes from the frame. Using her shoe to move the glass aside, she rattled the bars.

"They're not budging," she said with disappointment. She pushed her face out to gulp some of the fresh air. "Can you make it to the window?"

"I don't think so," I said.

Without fresh air, I would probably die before I could push the baby out. I had held it together as long as I could. There was no more optimism, only thoughts of impending doom. Roberta came to my side.

"Don't cry. Alphonse will be back with help real soon. Come on," she said, trying to lift me from the bed.

"There's no way you'll be able to get me to the window. Maybe I could crawl?" I suggested.

"I'm a lot stronger than I look. Let me try," she said, putting my arm around her neck.

Somehow we managed to make it to the window. I took a few deep breaths of fresh air then a strong contraction sent me to the floor.

"I need you to do something for me, but you're not going to like it" I said, reaching up to tug on her shirt.

"Okay," she said warily.

"You need to look and see if the baby's head is showing." I panted.

"I'm not sure if I'll know what I'm looking at. Maybe I could hold that compact mirror for you?" she asked.

"That won't do any good. Trust me, you'll know if it's the baby's head or not. There's no mistaking it. Wooo, it hurts so bad!" I grunted.

Roberta used her thumbs and index fingers to gently lift the hem of my skirt. She took a peek and lowered it back down just as gently.

"I don't want to have a baby." She rapidly shook her head, looking a little green.

"It must be crowning," I remarked.

"I don't know if it's the gas or what I just saw, but I think I'm going to throw up," she said.

"Get a breath of fresh air," I encouraged.

She stood staring out of the window for a while. "Okay, I've accepted the fact that you can't do this alone. I'll do my best to deliver the baby. Tell me what I need to do, but you're going to have to walk me through this step by step. I can do this," she said assuredly.

"Roberta, I think the gas is starting to get to me. I'm feeling very queasy and it's hard for me to keep my eyes open," I said softly.

"Emily! No, don't you do that! You have to tell me what to do! Stay awake! Here, I'll try to pick you up so you can get some of the fresh air," she said.

"I don't think it'll work," I said drowsily. "I just want to sleep."

She stood behind me, placing her arms under mine, unsuccessfully trying to lift me. I was so weak there was nothing I could do to help her. She was just squatting lower to try again when the door suddenly splintered open.

"Oh, thank God!" Roberta yelled, jumping up and down. "Emily, it's Holden and Bert! They're here to save us!"

"We shut the gas off, but we need to get out of here, now!" Holden said, scooping me into his arms while Bert hooked Roberta around the waist.

"You need to put me down, Holden. The baby's coming," I managed to say once we were outside.

"Now?" he asked.

"Right now!" I answered.

Bert ran full out to his car and returned with Connie.

"Connie! You're here! I need to push," I said, groggily.

She raised the skirt of my dress to take a peek. "Try not to push yet, Emily. Let me get some stuff ready. Bert, bring me the medic bag from your car. Now!"

Holden was behind me, letting me recline against his chest and Roberta was on the side of me, holding my hand when Bert jogged up with the bag. Connie tore through it looking for an OB kit.

"Bert, blankets. Roberta, put this mask on her," she demanded, passing Roberta the portable oxygen tank.

"On it," Bert said, running back to his car.

"Connie, I need to push," I said, removing the mask.

"In just a minute, Emily. Let me finish getting the supplies ready. Put that mask back on and breathe deeply. Are you feeling better since you've gotten some fresh air?"

I nodded, following her instructions.

"It's all I could find," Bert said, tossing some disposable blankets to Connie before kneeling next to Holden.

"I need someone to help me," Connie said, searching through the OB kit for what she needed.

"Roberta can do it," I said through the mask. Everyone's eyes were on me. I pulled it off, unsure if the odd looks were because they couldn't understand me or because of what I had said. "I'm feeling better now. I don't think I need the oxygen anymore. Let Roberta help. She's more than proved herself."

"Okay, come over here," Connie said, a little confused.

Bert gave me his hand to hold when Roberta went to help Connie. Surprise and pain showed on his face when I squeezed.

"I need to push!" I screamed.

"For Pete's sake, let her push! Let her push!" Bert's face contorted with agony as he tried to take his hand back.

"Not yet, Em. Bert, quit being a baby," Connie fussed.

He finally pulled his hand out of mine, raising it in the air to show his now crooked ring finger.

"That's so cool. Are you double jointed or something?" Roberta asked.

"No!" Bert shouted, holding his wrist and waving his hand around. He was suddenly pale and little beads of sweat had formed on his forehead.

"Let me see," Connie said, not missing a beat. She held her palm out to Bert, and before he could place his hand in hers, she snatched his finger and yanked. A *pop* sounded when she set the dislocation.

"What the hell did you do that for! Oh, wait. That feels better," Bert said, slowly testing his finger.

"Good, now move away. Roberta, open these blankets up for me," Connie ordered. She snapped one open and Connie thrust it under my hips. She quickly slid on a pair of sterile gloves. "Okay, Em. Go for it!"

I bore down with everything I had only stopping long enough to take a breath and do it again. I gripped Holden's shirt and reached for Bert's hand.

He started to extend it, but quickly pulled back. "I'm sorry. I love you, but…"

I blindly reached for the first thing I could find. My fingers latched so tightly around his ankle that he let out a garbled rant as he fell to the ground.

"Sorry, Bert!" I yelled between pushes.

"No problem," he groaned, slowly scooting out of my reach.

"Excellent job, Em! The head's out," Connie said, smiling at me.

Holden gave my shoulders a quick squeeze.

"Rest for a second and then we'll do it again," Connie said, suctioning the baby's airway.

"I know I kinda freaked before, but I want to see. Is it okay?" Roberta asked.

"It's fine with me," I said, struggling to find the energy to push again.

"Ready? Let's do this," Connie said. "One, two, three, go, go, go. Shoulders are clear, the chest, and we have a baby! It's a girl, Em! You have a daughter!"

Utterly exhausted, I slumped back onto Holden's chest. The sounds of the baby's cries were like music to my ears. Holden kissed the top of my head then peeked over to see the baby. Connie wiped the baby's face, wrapped her in one of the disposable blankets, and placed her on my abdomen.

"How can something so gross be so beautiful?" Roberta asked with tears in her eyes. "Now, I want a baby."

"You can take her as soon as I cut the cord," Connie said. "Okay, all done."

I lifted the baby from my stomach and into my arms.

"I waited such a long time to see you, little girl," I said, moving the blanket around so I could get a good look at her.

"She's gorgeous, just like her momma," Holden said. "That was amazing. You were so great. I love you, Em."

239

"I love you, too," I said softly.

"What are you going to name her?" Bert asked, testing his ankle before slowly standing.

"We never got a chance to talk about it," I said, glancing back to Holden.

"I don't know if I should be the one to…" Holden started.

"You absolutely should." I cut him off. "Haven't you ever thought about what you'd like to name your children?"

"Out of all my family, I was closest to my dad's mom. I thought it would be nice to name one of my children after her," Holden said.

"That's so sweet! What was her name?" I asked.

"Hortencia Calliope," he answered. All eyes were upon him and he couldn't contain himself anymore. "I'm just kidding," he said with a chuckle, "Her name was Kimberly."

"Kimberly—she looks like a Kimberly," I said, smiling down at the baby. "And, Blair is my Mom's middle name. How does Kimberly Blair sound?"

"Perfect," Holden said.

"I love it," Connie answered.

"Great name," Bert said.

"I don't want a baby anymore," Roberta got out before she hit the ground.

"What's wrong with her?" I asked anxiously.

"Just sit back and relax. She passed out when she saw the placenta being delivered. Bert, go through that bag and see if there's any ammonia… Never mind, she's coming to," Connie said. "Drag her around to your neck of the woods so she won't do that again."

Bert carefully took Roberta's ankles and pulled her away from my nether region. "I don't want to have a baby," she said, trying to sit up.

"Give it some time and you'll change your mind," I remarked.

"So you'll be up to trying for a boy soon?" Holden asked.

"Guess again," I retorted, shooting him a look.

The sound of crunching gravel came from the roadway as an ambulance barreled our way. It came to a stop near us; Chuck and Bridget jumped from the unit.

"I'm sorry it took us a while to get to you! Awww, looks like we missed the action," Bridget said, pulling on a pair of gloves while squatting next to me. "What a beautiful baby!"

"How is everything?" Chuck asked Connie once he gave us a smile.

"Everything went really well with Emily and little Kimberly Blair," Connie answered.

"I'm so glad to hear it," Chuck said, releasing a long sigh. "We would've been here sooner if Alphonse hadn't insisted on guiding us in."

"What do you mean?" Bert asked.

"He met up with us at the intersection right before the turn down the shell road. He was flailing about and yelling gibberish. I tried telling him that we could figure out how to get here on our own, but he insisted on leading the way—on his scooter," Chuck explained. I glanced around looking for Alphonse when I realized that he wasn't in the group.

"He's in the back of the ambulance," Bridget said, answering my unspoken question.

"He kept looking back and waving for us to go faster. He finally lost it somewhere around the fifth or six time," Chuck said.

Roberta threw her hands to her mouth and let out a gasp.

"Oh, don't worry. He got some pretty nasty road rash and is going to be pretty sore, but he's okay. Sorry to say, Em, but you and the little one are gonna have company during your ride to the hospital."

"Give me a minute. I'll check to see how bad off Alphonse really is," Bert said, approaching the ambulance. He quickly looked around, then went inside and closed the doors behind him. Thirty seconds later, a somewhat bloodied and slow-moving Alphonse stumbled out of the ambulance.

"He said that it's not so bad. He's going to ride to the hospital with the rest of us," Bert called, holding a wobbly Alphonse by the scruff of the neck. Alphonse turned his head to look at Bert and wiggled his finger to gesture that he wanted to share a secret. Bert looked confused by what Alphonse was saying at first, and then a slow smile crept over Bert's face. "He's wants to know if he can sit in the back with Roberta."

All eyes were on Roberta.

"He saved my life. I owe him more than that," she said, winking at me before she sashayed towards the car. She wrapped her arms around Alphonse's neck and searched for a spot on his cheek that wasn't bloodied. Finding none, she decided to give him a brief kiss on the lips. The reaction was instantaneous. The tent reemerged, Alphonse spasmed, and we were speechless. Roberta covered her mouth to hide her smile and Bert looked at Alphonse with disgust.

"Dude, you're hosing out my unit when we get back to town," Bert grumbled.

Alphonse stared ahead in a daze, a large grin plastered on his face. Bert opened the back door of his police car, gave Alphonse a quick swat to the back of the head, and nodded that he should crawl in. Once he and Roberta were inside the car, Bert gave an exaggerated shake of the head and threw his arms upwards.

Chuck and Bridget helped me onto the stretcher while Holden followed behind us with the baby. We caravanned to the hospital where Dr. Nelson was waiting.

After everyone left the hospital, Holden slid next to me in the bed and kissed the top of my head. "I'm mad at myself for staying away so long."

"We established that long ago. It's over and done with. You needed to be away from here to get better. And, regardless of how cold and heartless your mother was about our relationship, she made sure you got the best help available. Look at you now. At the time of the accident, I was told that it was doubtful you'd even keep your leg. Now you're walking with barely a limp. You've come such a long way," I remarked.

"I'll never admit it to my mother, but you're right. I'll tell you another regret I have is bringing Jackson into the department," he said. I pulled away to give him a hurt look. "Not because of what happened between you two; but because I assumed he was the same go-getter he was in the past. Being undercover all those years must have changed him. There's no reason those sons of bitches should still be running free after all this time. If he would have done his job and apprehended them, none of this would've happened. I asked around the department and it seems that Jackson didn't put much effort into finding them."

"He didn't have to because he knew where they were," I volunteered.

"What?" Holden asked, sitting straight up.

"I left out that part of the story earlier when giving my statement to Bert. I'm not sure if you want it on record or not, but Jackson supplied Brad with drugs and money from the evidence locker in exchange for my safety. Once you came back to town, he couldn't furnish them anymore, so he cut Brad and Donovan off. I asked what happened to Jackson, but I never got an answer," I said.

"I need some time to think about how I'm going to handle this. Jackson has scheduled two weeks of vacation. It's going to take me at least that long to tolerate looking at him," Holden said.

"Holden, you need to remember that he did it to protect me," I said.

He scowled. "It was a cowardly way of going about it and as you can see, it didn't solve the problem, it just made it worse."

I felt the euphoria that comes with being a new parent slowly leaving me. "Let's not talk about Jackson anymore. Let's talk about something else, okay? Have you gotten in touch with my parents yet?"

His face softened. "No, all calls go straight to voicemail. They're supposed to fly in late tomorrow night, aren't they?"

"They are, but it's not like them to be out of touch," I said.

"They're fine. You, more than anyone else, know how Don and Celeste are. Whatever it is, I'm sure there's a great story behind it."

"You're right," I said with a smile.

A nurse faintly rapped on the door and wheeled Kimberly's bassinet into the room.

"Everything looks great. We have the samples we need from Kimberly and Mr. Dautry. The results will be mailed to your home within the next day or so," she explained. "As for this sweetheart, she's doing just fine. She'll want to eat pretty soon. Other than that, she'll probably sleep. Just give me a buzz if you need anything."

"Thank you, we will," Holden said, closing the door once the nurse left. He leaned down to pick up the baby. "Hi there, sweet Kimberly. Do you want to see Momma?" he asked, gently placing her into my arms. He joined us on the bed.

"That's going to take some getting used to," I said, smiling down at her. "Momma."

He gently stroked Kimberly's arm as I fed her.

"Thank you for letting me share this with you," he said, serenity showing in his eyes.

"I'm glad you were with me."

"I meant what I said earlier today," he said.

"What's that?"

"I love you. I've always loved you, Emily. Even though you infuriate me sometimes, I can't imagine being with anyone but you."

"I love you, too. Thank you for coming back to me, Holden."

He gave me one of the softest, sweetest kisses ever then he carried Kimberly to the recliner across the room where he gently rocked her. After a while, he reclined back with the baby fast asleep on his chest. Happier than I'd been in a very long time, I watched them until I fell into a deep sleep.

15

"Emily! We're home! I sure hope you weren't trying to get in touch with us. Dad forgot the bag with our cell phones in the guest house so we went the entire trip without them. I called the house and left a message on the machine. Why didn't you call our room at the resort?" Mom yelled from the foyer. Holden, Kimberly, and I were snuggled on the sofa in the den.

"I love how your mother has entire conversations without knowing if anyone's even listening," Holden said quietly.

"She has a sixth sense when it comes to that sort of thing. Trust me, she knows I'm here," I whispered.

"Emily Clothilde! Why won't you answer me? I know you're here," she fussed. I arched my eyebrow at Holden to say, "I told you so", and he slowly shook his head.

"I'm in the den! I have a surprise for you guys," I called.

"A surprise for us? What did you do?" Dad asked, walking into the room. "Oh, Celeste! Celeste! Emily! Celeste! Emily!"

"Oh, dear! Is it that bad?" Mom asked, turning the corner. Tears welled in her eyes when she saw us. "Oh, Emily! Holden! I want to hear everything, after I see my... What is it, a boy or a girl?"

"This is your granddaughter," I answered. "Kimberly Blair."

"Oh, Don! Isn't she the most beautiful baby you've ever seen?" she asked excitedly, taking the baby into her arms.

"She's definitely one of the top two," Dad said, kissing my cheek and taking the Kimberly from Mom. "I'm so proud of you, Doodlebug. She's a real sweetheart. How old does she have to be before she can go on vacations with her PeePaw?"

"It'll be a little while, Dad," I answered.

"My turn to hold her," Mom said.

"But, I just got her," Dad fussed.

"Because you took her from me before I was ready to hand her over," she said.

"Emily, tell your mother that she can have the baby later," Dad said.

"Oh, no! I'm staying out of this one," I said.

"I think she has my chin, Celeste. Do you think she has my chin?" Dad asked, turning his head from side to side.

"Not now, Don," Mom said. "How are you feeling, Emily? Did everything go okay?"

"It's a really long story that I'm not sure you want to hear right now," I warned.

"Holden, will I want to know?" Mom asked.

"Eventually, but not right now," he answered.

"Oh, dear." She sighed. "Sometimes, I'm happy that you're my only child. I don't know if I could handle having to deal with more than one of you!"

"Hey, it's not like I asked to be kidnapped," I snapped defensively.

"Kidnapped! I feel a migraine coming on." She closed her eyes and gripped her forehead.

"They both warned you to leave it alone, Celeste," Dad said, making faces at the baby.

"Didn't you hear that your daughter was kidnapped!" she fussed.

"I heard, but everything appears to be fine now. The kids will tell us about it when they're ready," he said.

"I don't understand how you can remain so calm after hearing that snippet, Don."

"It's easy, you just do it."

The bell rang, so an agitated Mom went off to answer it. She returned shortly with the Hebert clan. When Little Andre saw Holden, his face lit up! He chucked the gift he was carrying onto the floor and broke into a full run. He eagerly jumped up and down, begging Holden to pick him up. I sighed loudly. He was my godchild, but whenever Holden was around, I didn't exist.

"Andre Peter! That wasn't very nice," Connie fussed, handing me the gift that Andre had thrown down.

"Oh, he's fine. He missed his Uncle Holden. Let him go," I said, directing my smile at Holden. He leaned down to kiss my cheek, then encouraged Andre to do the same. My heart melted when Andre puckered his little lips.

Connie took a seat next to me, so I pulled the pink bow off of the beautifully wrapped package.

"I hope you like them," Connie said.

"They're beautiful!" I exclaimed, holding up the assortment of newborn dresses.

"Shopping for a little girl is way more fun than shopping for a little boy," Connie said.

"And it takes a lot longer, too," Bert chimed in, laughing while slapping Holden's free hand.

"Cut it out, Bert," Connie warned.

"I'm so sorry that shopping for your goddaughter is such a chore," I teased.

"My goddaughter? Really?" Bert asked.

"If you and Connie accept, yes."

"I got to deliver her and I get to be her godmother! Of course I'll accept! I love it!" Connie exclaimed.

"*You* delivered Kimberly?" Mom asked with disbelief. "Let me guess, I don't want to hear about it right now?"

"You'll hear about it when they're ready to tell you about it," Dad said, passing the baby to Connie. Andre didn't like it, so he slid off of Holden's lap and tried to wedge himself between Connie's knees.

"Looks like we've got a jealous one," Connie directed to Bert.

"I'm on it," Bert said, snatching Andre up. "Come with Daddy; let's see if the fish are jumping today."

"I'll go with you," my dad said.

"Me, too," Holden said.

"Be careful out there. No repeats of Thanksgiving day!" I insisted.

"What happened on Thanksgiving day?" Holden asked.

"Dude, it was insane! Wait until you hear this one!" Bert said as they walked out of the door. Mom excused herself to make a pot of coffee.

"Fill me in. Have you heard anything yet?" Connie whispered.

"About what? Oh, that," I said when I noticed the look she was giving me. "We should know something soon. Just waiting on the letter from the lab," I answered.

"How's Holden been acting? Has he been treating you right?" she asked.

"He's been great. I haven't seen him this way in a long time. He's doing great physically, he's been attentive and caring to me and the baby; it's all I've ever hoped for, except…"

"Except you're worried that it's going to end if the test shows the baby isn't his?" she asked quietly.

"Yes."

"You've talked about that, though. Haven't you?" she asked.

"He says that he's going to be fine with it, no matter the results. They both have. But, once it's there in black and white, I'm not so sure that'll happen. There's so much to consider if Jackson's the father. I don't know how Holden's going to handle Jackson's deal with Brad, not to mention, Jackson's still missing. I've tried calling his cell phone to let him know that Kimberly was born, but he's not answering. I'm worried," I said.

"You still care about him, don't you?"

"Of course I do. We lived together for eight months and he was wonderful to me. If Holden hadn't come back, we eventually would've married. I don't think Jackson's the type to simply hand over drugs and money to criminals, even if it was to guarantee my protection. There has to be more to the story. Maybe it was a sting or something?" I reasoned.

"Wouldn't someone else in the department know about it, though?" Connie asked.

"Not necessarily. Holden totally trusted Bert but he didn't tell him anything about the whole Donovan Guidry scandal. Jackson didn't have that kind of a relationship with anyone in the department. Maybe he was handling things covertly?" I guessed.

"I don't know. It's never simple, is it?" Connie asked.

"You're only just now catching that?" I joked.

"You're right. You'd think I'd know better by now. Change of subject; are you planning to go back to work?"

"I'm not positive, yet. But, I probably will," I answered.

"Oh, really?" Mom asked, carrying in a tray of goodies.

"Why do you say it like that?" I asked.

"I assumed you'd give up that job now that you have a baby. Have you discussed it with Holden?" she asked.

"No, but Holden will stand behind whatever I decide," I said.

"I wouldn't be so sure," Mom mumbled under her breath.

"Do you know something I don't?" I demanded.

"No, you're the one with all of the secrets," she said cattily, setting the tray onto the coffee table.

"Oops, I think the baby might be hungry," Connie interrupted.

"She's sleeping," I said, turning my attention back to Mom. "I'm not keeping secrets from you; I'd prefer to discuss it later, is all. What do you know about the job thing?"

"I don't know anything, except that you and Holden hit a rough patch before. I'm sure that the both of you having careers that force you to deal with less than desirable situations may have had something to do with that," Mom said.

"Whoopsie, someone's diaper needs changing," Connie said.

"So I should forgo using my skills and training to save a seventy year-old diabetic or to rescue a five year-old trauma patient because one day I might have a run-in with a, how did you put it, 'less than desirable' person?" I asked.

"You're not the only individual with the skills and training to help such people, Emily," Mom said.

"Maybe and maybe not. I like what I do and I'm damn good at it! *If* I decide to return to my job, it will be my decision," I said defiantly.

"You know I worry about you, Emily. You've had so many close calls. One day, you're going to find yourself in a situation where luck won't be on your side," Mom warned.

"Really wet diaper here," Connie said, standing.

"Look, I just brought Kimberly home. The point's moot. I know you're concerned about me and I promise you, I'll weigh all of the options before making my decision. We can have a nice long discussion about this in a few weeks, okay?" I placed my hand on her shoulder.

"Oh, dear Lord, something's wrong. You're much too calm about this. You never give up a debate this easily. Are you sure everything went well with the delivery, Connie?"

"Of course the conditions weren't ideal because we were in T-Jack's front yard, but all things considered, the delivery went really well," Connie answered.

"Outside of T-Jack's? Honestly, Emily!" Mom exclaimed.

"I thought you were joking when you said you didn't tell her," Connie whispered.

"No, I wanted to get some alcohol into her first," I whispered back.

"What are you two whispering about? Oh, dear Lord! There's more you're not telling me," she said, rubbing her forehead.

"Mom, it's all over now and I'm fine," I said, kissing her cheek. "I'm going to change the baby. Pour yourself a nice glass of wine and when I come back, you'll know everything."

"A glass of wine? Forget that. Where did your father put the whiskey?" she asked, pulling a rocks glass from under the bar.

"Second shelf, between the dark rum and the tequila," Connie said, gently rocking Kimberly back and forth in her arms. Mom and I stared at her. "What? You think you're the only person who needs a drink when they're around Emily?"

"Oh, great! Just encourage her, why don't you," I said, shaking my head as I walked out of the room with Connie. A knock sounded at the door just as we reached the foyer.

"I'll get her changed, you get the door," Connie said.

"Thanks, Connie," I said as she headed upstairs.

A tiny, stick of a woman in a mail carrier's uniform was at the door. "Good morning! I have a certified letter for Miss Emily Boudreaux. Would you sign for it, please?"

"Sure." When I took the pen she held out for me, my hands were shaking so badly that I could barely sign my name. Noticing my tremor, she looked on with uncertainty then her face slowly began to light up.

"I understand more than anyone the need to turn to recreational pharmaceuticals for a boost, but I think you might want to cut your dosage a tad," she said with a wink.

"Thanks for the advice," I mumbled, closing the door.

I went in search of Holden. Quickly moving down the hall, I spied Mom on the sofa in the den with a pillow over her face and an empty rocks glass dangling from her fingertips. I walked as quietly as I could and joined Holden and Dad on the back patio. Bert and Andre were fishing from the dock.

"What's up?" Holden asked.

"Connie's changing the baby and Mom's getting buzzed because I finally told her everything that happened the other day. Have they caught anything?" I asked, nodding towards the water.

"I don't think so," Holden said. "Want to sit?"

"No, not right now. Dad, can I borrow him for just a minute?" I requested.

"Sure, Doodlebug. I was gonna walk over to see if Bert wanted to take Andre for a ride in the boat."

"Is something wrong?" Holden asked, following me into the house.

"No, everything's fine. Although, you might want to check into why our mail carrier knows so much about recreational pharmaceuticals," I suggested.

"What are you talking about?"

"Just come with me," I quickly said, leading him into the pantry for some privacy. "The letter just arrived and I don't know what to do. Do we open it ourselves or do we wait for Jackson to come back and open it together?"

"Where is it?" Holden asked.

"Right here," I said. My hands started trembling again when I pulled it from my pocket.

"Do you think we should wait until Jackson returns?" he asked.

"Part of me thinks it might be the right thing to do," I said.

"Well, none of me thinks that." He impatiently tore into the envelope.

"Holden Dautry!" I fussed.

He quickly unfolded the letter, his eyes rapidly darting across the page. The expression on his face suddenly changed and I couldn't tell if he was going to cry or be sick. My heart felt as though it stopped beating. The page slowly drifted to the ground and he tightly clenched his fists. Covering his eyes, he turned away from me, and the huge lump in my throat prevented me from speaking. I gently tapped his shoulder, but he shook his head and held up his hand. After what seemed like an eternity, he finally turned to face me. Tears were in his eyes.

"She's mine," he said softly. Holden bear hugged me. "She's mine, she's mine, she's mine. I have a gorgeous baby girl and a gorgeous baby momma and I can't wait to tell the world about it!" He hurriedly put me back down. "Did I hurt you when I hugged you?" he anxiously asked.

"No, you didn't hurt me," I said, laughing.

"We have a baby girl, Emily," he said, taking my face in his hands. "I can't begin to tell you how much I love you." He kissed me in a way that made me wish I wasn't still recovering from delivering a seven pound baby.

The pantry door opened and an embarrassed Connie slammed it shut. "Sorry," she yelled from outside.

Holden bent to pick up the paper and shoved it into his pocket. Cracking the door, I pulled her inside with us.

"Connie, you have to see this," I said, reaching for Holden's pants.

"Wait! Stop! Emily, you know I love both you and Holden tremendously, and I know that I'm always asking you for details about certain things like size and shape, because I'm really curious and you know I'm not a prude when it comes to the whole sex thing, but I'm not sure I'm comfortable with actually seeing it. I mean, Bert's out riding in the boat, and Kimberly's napping and all, but your mom's still in the other room," Connie rambled.

I glanced at Holden, who was staring at Connie and trying very hard not to laugh.

"Not that, Connie!" I said, pulling the letter from his pocket. "This!"

Most people would've been red with embarrassment, but not Connie. Yanking the paper from my fingers, her mouth moved as she read the letter. Her eyes widened and she did her best to contain a squeal. She jumped up and down, her hand over her mouth.

"This is wonderful news," she said, keeping herself as hushed as possible. She threw her arms around Holden's neck and gave him a brief kiss on the lips. "I'm so happy for you!" She ran in place, before slowing it down what would best be described as a high-energy dance.

"I'd be doing the same thing if I could," I laughed, sidling up to Holden.

"And you! My best friend, my honorary sister, you get one, too!" she said, planting a kiss right on my lips. Of course my mother picked that exact time to open the pantry door!

"What's going on in…" she managed to get out before dropping the glass she was holding. Connie was still puckered up, her hands on either side of my face. Holden looked guilty as hell, but I thought quickly enough to stop her from shutting the door on us.

"Mom, it's not what it looks like," I said, carefully stepping over glass shards to chase after her.

"I understand that things are far different than they were when I was your age, but I had secretly hoped that

Constance LeDeaux was exaggerating when she told me about the stripper girl you had a fling with. I'm going to the guest house to take a pill. Hopefully, I won't wake up until tomorrow," she said.

"Mom, I didn't have a fling with the stripper girl! I only kissed her one time! That old woman needs to learn how to keep her big, gossipy mouth shut and to quit tattling on me!" I fussed.

"Are you *trying* to give me a stroke?" Mom asked.

"No! They're all misunderstandings, Mom. Like in the pantry, Connie didn't just kiss me, she kissed Holden, too," I said.

"Mon Dieu! Je ne veux entendre plus!" She practically ran for the door.

"Oh, crap! She's speaking French," Holden said.

"What does that mean?" Connie asked.

"I'm not sure, but it can't be good," he said.

"Mom, stop! You need to listen to this, even though you don't want to," I said, turning her so she would have to face me. She continued to rattle off French phrases.

"Enough with the French, Mom. Connie kissed us because she was happy. We told her some good news and she got really excited. That's all," I explained.

She let out a sigh of relief. "Oh, what news?" Mom inquired.

Damn! I hadn't thought far enough ahead to expect that question! My mind raced for an answer.

"What news, indeed," I said very slowly, trying to buy more time, but I drew a complete blank instead.

"Yes?" she asked.

"The wonderful news is that, uhm, that…Holden and I are getting married," I shot out. Connie's eyes grew large, but not as large as Holden's. Mom started to cry.

"Married! What a wonderful surprise! I'm sorry I misunderstood! You were so right, Connie! If anything calls for a kiss it's this! Congratulations!" she shouted as she gave each of us a smooch. "Where's your father? I can't wait to tell him!"

"I think he's in the boat with Bert and Andre," I said as I massaged my nervous stomach.

"No, they're pulling in right now!" she said, peeking out of the blinds. "Come on! Let's tell them!"

"Whoops, I think I hear Kimberly," I said.

"I should help out. After all, I am her father," Holden said.

"Maybe we should wait until the boaters come inside to tell them," Mom said. "Connie and I can start making wedding plans while you two tend to the baby. Come with me, Connie."

"Uh, okay," Connie said, shrugging her shoulders.

Once we were upstairs, Holden backed me into my bedroom and closed the door behind us. "We're getting married?" he asked, his tone very serious.

"I couldn't think of anything else to say. I'm so sorry, Holden. Oh, what have I done?" I asked, putting my face in my hands.

"I'll tell you what you've done!" He pulled my hands away, forcing me to look at him. "For the second time today, you've made me a very, very happy man," he said, sandwiching me against the wall with his body.

"But we haven't even discussed it," I said.

"What's to discuss?" he asked, nuzzling my neck.

"Holden," I breathed.

"Do you love me?" he asked, moving his lips to the other side.

"Of course I do," I answered.

"Then it's settled. We're doing this."

"We're going to do this?" I asked.

"Yes, we are," he said, his lips lightly grazing mine. "Now give me a date."

"To get married?" I asked with surprise.

"Yes," he said, gently stroking my neckline with his finger.

"I don't know. Did you have something in mind?"

"Next month," he said.

"Next month! Seriously?" I asked.

"The day after your six-week checkup."

"Holden!" I laughed.

"I'm going to give you a honeymoon night you'll never forget and that's a promise," he breathed into my ear.

I felt a zing travel through my body. The feeling intensified when he lowered his lips to mine. His tongue worked its magic on me and I hoped my knees wouldn't buckle. It had been such a long time since we'd shared so intimate a moment that I'd forgotten what an effect his smoldering kisses had on me.

Once I caught my breath, I gently touched my puffy lower lip. "For the second time today, you've made me want you very, very badly."

"I'd ask you to tell me all about it, but…" he stopped speaking to point his finger towards the crying coming from the nursery.

"Something tells me we should get used to that," I said, opening the door.

"I'll get her. You go on down and start planning this thing," he said.

"You're serious?" I asked.

"I've never been more serious in my life," he said. "I'm not letting you get away again."

"I'm not going anywhere." I gave him one final kiss before going downstairs to plan our wedding.

16

With all of the fittings, meetings, appointments, and consultations we had scheduled, the weeks seemed to fly by. Much of it passed in a sleep-deprived blur of color swatches, doctor visits, and cake samples. Luckily, Mom and Connie handled most of the wedding arrangements. Basically, I just showed up when and where they told me to.

Kimberly and I had our follow-up appointments scheduled on the same day. According to her pediatrician, she was not only healthy, but astonishingly alert for her age. Holden joked that it was because she was nosey like her mother. I was not amused.

Once we finished there, Holden took Kimberly home and I went to see Dr. Nelson, and she released me with a clean bill of health. Though I was happy to get the good news, part of me was nervous. Things were wonderful between us, but Holden and I hadn't had sex since before the tornado. I recalled how cold and distant he was that last time.

Since our reconciliation, Holden was acting like he did before Jackson came to town, but part of me was still scared that the past might suddenly come flooding back to him once we were in the midst of lovemaking. I wasn't sure I could bear to see that hurt in his eyes again, especially on our wedding night. As much as I tried to disregard those thoughts, they refused to go away.

Jackson's vacation time had long been over, yet there was still no sign of him. I was concerned, but Holden wasn't worried. He thought that Jackson was avoiding the inevitable confrontation; I didn't think it was that simple. Holden assured me that he was looking into Jackson's disappearance, so I did my best to let it go.

The night before our wedding, after a quick rehearsal at Greenleaf, my parents took the wedding party and some of the out-of-town guests to The Blue Claw for a fried seafood extravaganza. They rented the entire restaurant, so no one felt obligated to keep down the rowdiness. I could easily pick out certain conversations from the cacophony.

Connie was going on about being puffy from eating too much food, and she hoped she'd still fit into her dress the next day. Mom was giving Dad a hard time because he finished his fourth beer, and was about to ask for another. He insisted that she lighten up and ordered two more. When she complained, he handed her one and told her, "Drink up". I quickly walked the other way, pretending not to hear them bickering. I found Holden talking with Bert at a nearby table, so I headed towards them.

Without warning, the restaurant door flew open and it felt as though the room's temperature dropped by thirty degrees. Okay, that's a slight exaggeration, but nonetheless, a hush fell over the room when Luciana Dautry entered.

As usual, her hair and makeup were flawless, and the belted pink sheath she wore accentuated her gorgeous, olive complexion—she was an overwhelmingly beautiful woman. Her head held high, she slowly made her way across the silent room. She stopped in front of me.

"I've heard from a reliable source that I am now a grandmother. I would've preferred hearing it from my son, but due to my recent behavior, I can see why he has neglected to inform me of the event. Holden, I'd like to have a word with you, please." she requested, turning her attention to where he was sitting.

"It's okay, go ahead and talk to her," I whispered to Holden as he stood. All eyes were on him.

"I'll only agree to speak to you if you apologize to Emily and anyone else in this room you may have offended," Holden insisted.

Luciana's jaw set in a way that was familiar to me; just like Holden's when he tried to maintain his calm. Breathing in through her nose, and thrusting her chin higher, she cleared her throat.

"Emily, I apologize if I hurt your feelings. I also offer an apology to anyone else I may have inadvertently offended," she said loudly before looking at Holden.

"It's a start. You'll get a much better apology than that if she wants anything to do with her granddaughter," Holden whispered while wiping his hands on a napkin. "I'll be back in a minute."

The second he was out of the door, Connie edged her seat next to mine.

"Holy cow! What do you think she's doing here?" she asked.

"Maybe she's trying to talk some sense into Holden? You know, most rich boys don't marry their 'whores'," I answered, snidely.

"She's wasting her breath if that's what she's doing. Holden's head over heels, girl! And, so are you," she said, smiling.

"I am," I confirmed.

"I'm so happy for you guys!" She pulled me in for a tight hug.

"Thank you for being here for me, Connie. I was so unsure of things when I moved back to Green Bayou. Then Pete introduced us and we became best friends. Here, I want to give this to you, not just because you're my matron of honor, but because I love you so very much," I said. Connie stared wide-eyed at the small gift box I placed in her hand.

"Awww, you didn't have to do this!"

"I wanted to," I insisted. She tore into the paper, opened the box, and gasped when she saw the charm bracelet. "Each charm represents something we've been through together. I have one, too."

"I love it, Em! Thank you so much!" she said excitedly, putting it on. We reminisced while discussing each of the charms.

After a few minutes, Holden reentered the restaurant, making a path straight to my chair.

"I don't mean to interrupt, but would you mind coming outside with me for a bit?" Holden asked. I looked over at the baby carrier. Kimberly was sleeping.

"Go ahead. I'll keep an eye on her," Connie offered.

"Thanks," I said, pushing out my chair. "I don't think this will take long."

Once we were out of earshot, Holden filled me in. "My mother's still outside and she wants to speak to the both of us, together. She's been warned that I will not tolerate any rudeness, spiteful comments, or otherwise. Are you okay with that?"

"I'm okay with it," I said, taking a deep breath as we went out the door.

My eyes were still trying to adjust to the darkness when Luciana started to speak. "I am a very proud woman, but I am not proud of the way I treated you. Now that you're a mother, I'm sure you can see that there's absolutely nothing you wouldn't do for your daughter. Holden may very well be a grown man, but he's my only living child. I've not made the best decisions where he's concerned, and I don't intend to make the same mistakes with my grandchild. You'll find two gifts when you get home, a gift for the two of you and something for the baby. I hope you'll accept them," she said.

"Thank you," I mentioned, unsure of what else to say.

"And, I hope that after some of the excitement has died down, you'll agree to have lunch with me, Emily. I'd like to get better acquainted with my daughter-in-law," Luciana requested.

"I suppose that would be okay," I said warily. Holden nodded his head.

"I should be going," she said, quickly moving by us.

"Before you go," I said. "Would you like to see the baby?"

She snapped around to look at me. Though her facial expression remained unchanged I caught the slightest trace of a tremble in her lower lip. "I'd love to see her," she said.

"It's still early. Why don't you join us inside?" I suggested.

She looked at Holden, who was still stone-faced. He didn't disagree, so she accepted the invitation.

The largest fake smile I'd ever seen was plastered on my mother's face as we walked by. I quickly motioned with my hands that everything was fine. She took a long pull off her beer while signaling for the waitress to bring her another. Connie was so busy making faces at Kimberly, she didn't realize we had come up behind her. Though shocked at first, she quickly recovered.

"She just woke up a few seconds ago," Connie said, reaching into the carrier to pass the baby to me. I removed Kimberly's blanket, then gently placed her into Luciana's arms.

She gasped. "I never expected her to look so much like you, Holden. Oh, this brings back memories."

Obviously enamored, she sat on the seat that Connie had recently vacated, never taking her eyes off of the baby. Holden placed his hand on her shoulder and her face continued to soften.

"Her name's Kimberly Blair Dautry," he said.

"You always loved your Grandma Kimberly," she commented. "I think it's a fitting name. She's very beautiful," Luciana directed at me.

"Thank you, Mrs. Dautry," I answered. My mother's words about keeping our consciences clear kept repeating in my mind. "Our wedding will take place at my home; six-thirty tomorrow. You're welcome to attend."

Again, Luciana looked at Holden, eagerly searching for permission. He nodded his head and she smiled broadly.

"Thank you for extending an invitation. I'll be there." She rose from her seat. "Thank you for allowing me to visit with my granddaughter. I look forward to tomorrow."

"Good night, Mrs. Dautry," I said when she turned to leave.

"Good night, Emily. Thank you again."

The door had barely closed behind her and Mom and Connie were all over me, demanding to know every last detail. It didn't take long since there really wasn't much to tell. Both commented on how much childbirth had mellowed my disposition. I thought they were full of it.

When we arrived home later that night, a top-of-the-line SUV with a huge, red bow on the hood was parked in the driveway. Through the mail slot were the keys and two envelopes. The first was addressed to "Holden and Emily". The card inside mentioned that the SUV was a gift for our new family because it was supposed to be the safest on the market. I remembered that Holden's brother died in a car accident and suddenly the gift took on new meaning.

The second envelope was addressed to "Baby Dautry" and inside was an antique looking, silver baby rattle.

> *Holden,*
> *This rattle once belonged to your grandfather and it was given to me when I had my children. Now, it's being passed to you for your child. I know you're still angry about what happened after your injury. I regret some of my actions, but I'll never regret the time I spent with you. I've missed you, son. Despite everything, please know that I love you*

and that I am very proud of the man you have become.

Mother

"Wow, that's a very nice letter," I said.

"It's a great letter, but it's totally out of character," Holden remarked.

"You don't think she deserves the benefit of the doubt?" I asked.

"No." Holden folded the letter. "I'll need to keep my eye on her."

"Do you really think she's faking all this?" I asked, convinced that Holden was being harsh.

"There are two things Balladeno's never do: ask for forgiveness and admit that they're wrong. She's done both. Something's up," he said.

"Well, while you're pondering that, I need to get my beauty sleep," I said. "I must insist that you immediately vacate the premises, Mr. Dautry."

"You're going to make me spend the night away from you and Kimberly?" he asked, leaning in and putting his arms around my waist.

"I am. But, I'll see you tomorrow, six-thirty, near the dock," I said, looking into his eyes as he gently ran his fingers through my hair.

"And after that, I'll see you upstairs in that bed." He gave me a slow, passionate kiss.

Mom noisily cleared her throat. "You need to be leaving right now, young man!"

"Oh, let the kids alone, Celeste. It isn't like it's anything new to them," Dad said, pointing to the baby he was holding.

"Dad!" I shouted at the same time my mother shouted, "Don!"

"Don't let your mom fool you, Emily. She acts goodie-goodie, but ask her what she was doing the night before our wedding," Dad said, beaming.

"Don! How could you?" Mom said, turning five different shades of red.

Holden almost fell over he was laughing so hard. Part of me wanted to laugh, but the other part was entirely grossed out.

Dad put his free arm around Mom's shoulders. "Lighten up, Celeste. After tomorrow, our Doodlebug will be a wife and a mother. Did you think this day would come so fast?"

"No, I didn't," she said, wiping a tear.

"Me, either," Dad said. "Well, I'm going to get some sleep. Are Bert and Connie keeping Kimmiepoo tomorrow night?"

"Dad, you aren't going to brand that child, Kimmiepoo!" I fussed.

"What's wrong with it? I like it," he said.

"I'm not even gonna argue about it. Yes, Bert and Connie are going to keep her tomorrow night," I said.

"Good, because Mom and I will be going into DeSoto after the wedding. I'm springing for the spa package. Your mother deserves some pampering," he said, giving her a squeeze.

"How nice! That sounds lovely," she said. "Good night, my sweeties. See you in the morning."

"Good night," Dad said, giving the baby a quick kiss before handing her to me.

"Good night, Dad. And, good night to you too, sir," I directed at Holden.

"Fine, I'll see you tomorrow. I love you, both." He kissed Kimberly's forehead and my cheek, and then he was gone.

~.~.~.~.~.~

Morning began when I woke to the smell of cinnamon rolls and coffee. My contented sigh turned into a shriek when I realized I wasn't alone in my room.

"What in the hell, Connie! You scared the crap out of me!" I fussed.

"We've got so much to do today! Nails, hair, makeup, vow rehearsal, outside setup, inside setup, flowers, cake, food... How can you just lay there like there's nothing going on! Move it!" she demanded.

"Calm down, there's time. The wedding isn't until six-thirty. I have to feed the baby, eat, and have coffee before even thinking about the other stuff." I yawned.

"Emily, I need you to listen to me. You're being way too nonchalant about this. It's your wedding day!" she squealed.

"I know it is!" I shrieked before backing it down to my normal pitch, "And, I also know that I don't have to worry about anything because you worry enough for all of us. Coffee first."

Connie grunted her discontent. "You take the fun out of everything."

"Give me twenty minutes to wake up and you can be as demanding as you want to be," I said.

"Yeah, that's not gonna work," she said, looking at her watch. "I can give you ten minutes, and that's stretching it."

"Ten minutes! I've barely opened my eyes! I still have to feed Kimberly, dress her, dress myself…"

"Stop!" she yelled. "It's all done, except for the dressing yourself part, which you should seriously consider getting a move on. Let's go!"

"Fine, we'll go, but where's my daughter?" I asked, finally getting out of bed.

"Bert took her to Holden's. She's gonna hang with the guys today. They don't have nearly as much on their agenda as we do. They just shower and dress. We've got to handle everything else. She's fine. I just talked to Bert and he said Holden hasn't put Kimberly down since he got her. Isn't that the sweetest thing?"

"Wait, she's where?" I asked, trying to process Connie's rambling.

"She's fine. Here, throw this on. You don't have to look pretty to go to the spa," she said tossing me a pair of gray shorts and a pink t-shirt from my closet.

"Does she have enough diapers? Clothes? Formula? Who packed her bag?" I demanded.

"Listen to me. She is fine. I packed her bag with your mother's help. Bert and Holden are both excellent fathers and your dad's there to boot. We're just a phone call away if they have any questions or if they need anything. She spends most of her time eating and sleeping. I'd be more concerned if she were a toddler running around and getting into everything, like my child," she said.

"Speaking of Andre, where is he?"

"At my mom and dad's. Bert's going to pick him up on his way to the ceremony. Don't worry, your little ring bearer's going to be here on time," Connie answered. "Now, you're down to seven minutes. Get the lead out!"

It did no good to argue with Connie. After sliding on the clothes she handed me, I went downstairs to find that Mom had fixed me a to-go mug of coffee.

"I can't even sit down to eat a cinnamon roll?" I asked.

"Nope," Mom said, pushing the mug into one hand and a paper-towel wrapped pastry in the other. "Let's hit the road so we can get back before the caterer and the florist arrive."

Shoving the cinnamon roll into my mouth so I could lock the front door, I watched as Mom and Connie walked arm in arm toward the car. Neither of them stopped talking long enough to take a breath. Maybe Holden and I should've put some thought into eloping.

17

Even though I gave Connie a hard time about her need to control things, I knew that my wedding day would not have been nearly as special without her help. Just before I was due downstairs, we stood in my bedroom primping and admiring our reflections.

"That gown looks like it was made just for you," Connie said, making sure all buttons were fastened on the ivory, A-line dress.

"And yours could not be more flattering, Madame," I said about the clover-colored, strapless gown she wore.

"We really are some beautiful women, aren't we," she joked.

"Indeed we are," I said, turning to see how everything looked from behind.

"It's almost time to do this thing, but before we go downstairs, I want you to know that I feel blessed that you and Holden came into our lives. We've all been through so much, but every situation we overcame made us grow closer as friends and stronger as individuals. I love you and

I wish you all the happiness in the world, because you deserve it more than anyone I know," Connie said.

"That's not fair! That was such a beautiful thing to say, now I'm going to cry," I said, fanning my face to keep the tears from falling. "You know I'm still hormonal. Oh, geez! I hope I make it through this service without having to test the limits of my waterproof mascara!"

Connie snapped out of mushy mode to become her usual uncensored self. "Oh, you'll do fine. If you get too weepy, just remember that it's been almost a year since you've bumped uglies with that fine ass man out there. The less time you spend sniveling, the more time you'll have to tantalize the... "

I stopped her as soon as she raised her hands in the air to slowly gyrate her hips. "I'm good! I'm not gonna cry. Please, don't finish that sentence!" I laughed.

"You ready to do this?" Connie asked, handing me my bouquet.

"I'm ready," I said, taking a breath.

We found Dad pacing back and forth in the foyer. He looked up when he heard us on the stairs. He didn't have to say a thing, the look in his eyes told the entire story. Connie took her spot in front of us and we began our procession past the twenty or so guests standing on the back lawn.

The sun setting on the bayou served as a backdrop for the large, flower-covered arch near the dock. Holden and Bert, obviously sharing some sort of private joke, turned when Father Robicheaux gently nudged them. The look on Holden's face as he watched me walk down the aisle was something I wanted to remember for the rest of my life. Once everyone was seated, my father gave me away and I became Mrs. Holden Dautry.

~.~.~.~.~.~

Our guests celebrated a good bit of the night away at the reception. Mom wanted servers to walk around with trays of champagne and hors d'oeuvres, but I insisted on a traditional, South Louisiana buffet. Alphonse came out of the dining room with two huge plates piled with food.

"Are you enjoying yourself, Alphonse?" I asked.

"This has been one heck of a wedding, Emily! Thanks for invitin' me and my date. This here is the first wedding I've ever had an actual date for," he said, giggling. "She's gorgeous, too—my date. I don't mean you no disrespect, or anything, being that this is your special day."

"None taken, Alphonse. I hope that you and," I paused when I saw Roberta walking towards us. "Roberta?"

"Yup, she's my date," he said, grinning from ear to ear.

"Hi, Emily. You look beautiful and little Kimberly's gotten so big," she said.

"Thank you. You look very pretty, too," I said sincerely.

Her makeup was soft and the dress that she wore was flattering, but not skin-tight. Her hair was in a chignon with wispy tendrils cascading along her face and neck. She looked like an entirely different person.

"That's nice of you to say. Alphonse, would you mind taking those plates over to the table? I'll be right there. I'd like to talk to Emily for a minute, okay?" she asked.

"You got it," he said, whistling a tune as he walked away. He stopped near one of the older guests. "You see that lady right there in the blue dress? That's *my* date," he said before continuing on to one of the tables across the room. I couldn't help but laugh.

"So, you and Alphonse?" I asked with curiosity.

"I know it seems strange, but he treats me so well. The bad thing is, I can't make contact with him any longer than a couple of minutes without, uh, a repeat of what happened near the police car," she whispered. At first, I was confused, but then I gasped when I realized what she saying.

"The police car? Oh! Oh, goodness. I can see how that could make things—challenging," I said.

"It used to be I could only touch him for thirty seconds or so, but we've been working on it. I figure that within a month, we may actually share a proper kiss," she said.

"I'm not sure what the appropriate response is to that. Best wishes?" I guessed.

"I don't know if there is a proper response. But, I'm fine with going super slow. Who would've ever thought that Alphonse would be the person to make me happy?" she said with a contented smile.

"I never saw it coming, but it's the best news I've heard tonight. I'm so glad that you shared this with me, but maybe you should go check on him?" I suggested, nodding toward Alphonse.

He was pointing Roberta out to all of the people at the surrounding tables. Though most of the guests smiled politely or nodded their head in acknowledgment, I did catch a few rolling their eyes as they turned away.

"Oops, I guess you're right. See ya," she said, hurrying towards their table.

"We don't have time for you to tell me the story right now, but I want to hear all about Alphonse and Roberta later. You come with me. Your groom awaits," Connie said, pushing me towards the parlor.

Though the wedding was small, we honored the most popular traditions. To the delight of the small audience, Holden expertly led me across the dance floor. When the next song played, Dad cut in while Holden danced with his mother. The cake was cut and we fed it to each other, but only after I gave Holden a stern warning about smashing any of it in my face.

Next came the garter toss. By the time the single men had lined up, Alphonse was in such a tizzy to get it that he busted his lip when he pushed Colin and Miranda out of his way. That wasn't Alphonse's only injury; he ended up with a black eye after the bouquet toss. Looking like a skeletal basketball player, he sprang in the midst of a small group of women, stopped the bouquet in mid-air, and sent it wobbling into Roberta's direction. In the process, women were knocked over like a stack of dominos. An extremely embarrassed Roberta didn't know what to do with the smashed up mix of spring flowers that landed in her hands.

The attention on her was short lived, because all eyes went to the pile of women. Most of them shot nasty looks at Alphonse as they straightened their garb, but one very unhappy woman, a sixty-three year old widow, reeled back and dotted Alphonse's right eye. Mom quickly ushered him to the kitchen for an ice pack while Dad did his best to comfort Ms. Arceneaux. Holden and I couldn't hold it in any longer; we took off to the front porch where we howled with laughter.

"Are you about ready to get out of here, Mrs. Dautry?" Holden asked.

"I thought we were staying here tonight," I said.

"Bert, Connie, and Andre are going to stay here tonight with Kimberly. I have something special planned for us," he said, pulling me into his arms.

"Mmmm, I can hardly wait," I sighed.

"Let's go now," he suggested.

"We can't leave yet." I laughed.

"Why not?" he asked, nuzzling my neck.

"You know why not," I said, lightly pushing him away.

"Excuse me. I'm sorry to interrupt, but I'll be leaving soon and there's something I'd like to give you before I go," Luciana said, emerging from the shadows.

"Mrs. Dautry, I didn't realize you were there. The SUV was more than generous. Thank you for thinking of us," I said.

"You're welcome, but this gift is something a little more personal," Luciana said. "Shall we go inside?"

"Sure," I said, holding the door open for her. Holden was right behind us as I ducked in and out of rooms before finally finding privacy in the den.

"When I first met Holden's father, he had no clue who I was or that I came from money. A friend dared me to attend a public high school's football game. I know it seems silly, but we were told that the public high schools were rampant with violence and debauchery and I was the rebellious type, so I didn't hesitate to accept the challenge. In order to win the bet, I had to bring back a ticket stub and a memento from one of the football players," she said.

"I never heard this story. I only knew that you two met in high school," Holden said, sitting across from us.

"Sorry to say son, you get your rebelliousness from me," she admitted.

"Please, go on," I insisted.

"I arrived at the game towards the end of the fourth quarter and was so incredibly nervous that I shook like a leaf while sitting up in the stands. Seriously, stories went around about stabbings and other horrors, so imagine my surprise when nothing happened. Just as I was beginning to relax, the buzzer sounded the end of the game and people started to file out of the stadium. I was in the corner of the bleachers, watching the players leave the field when an argument broke out. I was scared to death and had nowhere to go. A very large man was shoved into me and over the railing I went, right into your father's waiting arms. He gently stood me on the ground, and once he knew that I was okay, he scaled the bleachers and gave both of those men a good earful.

I anxiously bolted for my car, but Stephen chased after me. He encouraged me to wait around until he showered, because he wanted to escort me home. Stephen was such a good looking man, I gladly agreed and waited in my locked car until he rapped on the window. We spent most of the night in the parking lot, reclined on the hood of my car, talking. He said that he knew I was out of my element and wondered why I was there. He had a good laugh when I told him, but he gave me this to take back as my memento." She pulled a chain with a golden football from her purse.

Holden took it from her to get a better look, then he passed it to me.

"I won the bet and six months later, we were married. There are a couple of things I learned from that day. First, rebellion isn't always a bad thing, because great things can be missed if you don't take chances. And second, sometimes the greatest love stories are the unconventional ones. From what I've heard, everything about you two is unconventional. Don't consider the trials that you go through as roadblocks in your relationship, consider any tribulations you may face as testaments of your strength as a couple. All of the money in the world couldn't bring Holden's brother back, heal Stephen, or buy Holden's love, though God knows I tried. Wealth can't buy happiness, but something as simple as this tiny football can," she said.

"Thank you so much for sharing your story," I said, sincerely moved by her words.

"Yes, thank you, Mother," Holden agreed.

"I'm trying to be a better person, son. I was bitter after the car accident took your brother and robbed your father of his quality of life. I was overwhelmed and grief-stricken, and it eventually drove you away. Seeing my granddaughter helped me to put things into perspective. I want to be a part of her life, and I'm not talking about just an occasional visit here and there. I want to do things with her, but this is your wedding day and we can discuss this in greater detail some other time. I should be going," Luciana said.

"Have a safe trip home, Mother," Holden said, rising from the sofa when she stood.

"You'll promise to keep in touch?" she asked, reaching for her purse.

"I will," Holden agreed. Luciana nodded and walked out of the room with her head held high.

"Did you happen to spray her down with holy water when I wasn't looking?" Holden asked, his eyes following his mother's departure. I nearly choked on the champagne I was swallowing.

"No." I giggled.

"I swear to you, that's not my mother," he said, taking the glass from me. "Now, let's go say our goodbyes and kiss our baby goodnight. Be quick about it, because we've got a lot of lost time to make up for."

"Quit teasing me," I groaned, making my way to the parlor.

Fifteen minutes later, we were showered with rose petals while running down the steps of the front porch. We froze when we spied our garishly embellished car.

"Alright, who did this?" I yelled into the crowd. I yanked a blow-up doll free from the handcuffs that held her fastened to the door handle. Holden kicked it across the lawn.

"Hey, Alphonse. The Sheriff just kicked your girlfriend across the yard!" one of the guests shouted from the crowd. A roar of laughter sounded from the group.

"No, I don't need them no more. I done threw all mine away. See, I got me a real girlfriend now, and a perty one at that," he said, pointing to a mortified Roberta. More laughter rang out.

"If she's your girlfriend, prove it! Give her a kiss, Alphonse," the instigator yelled.

"Don't. Not a good idea, trust me. I've been there and it's not something you want to see. Let's go, trouble-maker," Bert said, laughing as he escorted the loud man back into the house.

Holden and I waved to those still remaining outside before driving away.

Once we were on the road Holden asked, "Do you feel any different, yet?"

"I feel lots of things—happy, peaceful, excited, grateful, loved, relieved…"

"All that, huh?"

"All that and so much more. Hey, you didn't mention that we'd be staying at the Holden Hotel," I said, suddenly realizing where we were headed.

"Nothing but the best for my wife," he said.

"It's been a really long time since I visited that place," I said suggestively.

"Do you remember the hotel's policies or do you need a refresher?"

"Please refresh my memory, sir."

"The hotel only accepts cash payments," he said.

"Well, we have a problem, because I don't carry cash."

"Oh, that's not good. I suppose we need to discuss other options," he said, as we arrived at his cabin. He carried me inside the house.

"And what if we can't agree on an acceptable form of payment?"

"Then, you sleep outside," he answered.

"I can't do that. I'm really scared to be out there alone. What will this get me?" I asked, going on tip toe to give him the most passionate kiss I could muster.

"Wow." He cleared his throat. "That gets you a cup of coffee in the morning, but you're still outside."

"Oh, no. I really need to be inside. What about this?" I asked, slowly unzipping my going-away dress to let it slide down my body.

"That gets you a blanket," he said, his eyes dark with lust.

"But I'd like a room with a bed." I carefully unfastened my garters to slowly remove the thigh-high stockings I was wearing.

"Shit, I can't do this anymore, Emily," he said, hugging me tightly as he lifted me from the ground. My legs wrapped around his waist and our lips didn't leave each others' until we were in the bedroom. His fingers worked to unfasten my bustier as quickly as possible.

"I've missed being with you so much," I breathed, wriggling free of the undergarment so Holden could toss it aside.

"I never want us to be apart again," Holden said, kissing my thighs as he slowly slid my panties down.

I cupped his chin and he stood once again.

"Nor do I," I said, sending the buttons of his shirt flying across the room when I ripped it open.

He pushed me onto the bed and my hands couldn't get enough of his strong, sexy body. In a move that surprised him, I switched positions so I could be on top. He moaned as my mouth left his so my tongue could trace a path from his neck, down his solid chest, and across his taut abdomen.

"Oh, Emily," he breathed.

"I'd forgotten how much you turn me on. I want you now," I pleaded.

Holden was once again above me, his fingers laced through mine as he pinned my arms overhead. "You always get what you want, don't you?" he asked, his mouth and tongue leaving my neck to tease and torment my breasts.

"I do and I want you."

"You've got me—forever," Holden said, smiling down at me.

My eyes closed when he entered me and I had to bite my lower lip to keep from yelling out. It felt wonderful and familiar and I realized that I was a fool for ever doubting this man's love for me!

Though incredibly wonderful, the first time didn't last very long for either of us. But, the second and third times more than made up for it! I was exhausted and in complete and total bliss when I finally rested my head on Holden's shoulder. His fingers lightly stroked my upper arm while I played with the light sprinkling of hair on his chest. He moved to sit up.

"Where are you going?" I asked, plopping back onto the pillow.

"Don't you worry about it. I'll be right back." He laughed.

I pulled the covers over my body and waited for him to return. After five minutes passed, I started to worry. I was just about to go looking for him when he came back into the room carrying an armload of wrapped packages.

"What's all that?" I asked eagerly.

"I was supposed to get you a gift, but I couldn't decide on just one, so here you go," he said.

"You didn't have to do that," I said, shaking the package closest to me.

"I wanted to." He took it from me and replaced it with one of the larger boxes. I tore into the paper, anxious to see my present. A beautiful satin robe lay inside.

"I love it!" I said, gently fingering the delicate fabric. After sliding it on, I tore into the next box. Seeing a teeny, little bikini in the box, my mind searched for the right thing to say.

"Do you like it?" Holden asked.

"It's lovely, but you do realize that I just had a baby, right?" I asked.

"It's for our honeymoon. We'll wait until Kimberly's a little older and then we're going to take a proper trip. We're going to waste our days playing on a Hawaiian beach and we'll spend our nights doing other things," he said, moving my hair so he could kiss my neck.

"I can't wait!" I giggled.

"Open this one next," he said, putting a small, red package into my hands. I gasped when I saw the diamond and emerald ring inside. A tear slid down my cheek when I read the inscription inside the band: *05/22 The day I fell in love with another woman.*

"Kimberly's birthday," I said.

"You should've seen the jewelers face when I told him what I wanted the inscription to say," he remarked.

"I can only imagine," I said, sliding the ring onto my finger. "It's so beautiful."

"One more," Holden said, holding up the final box.

"But you've given me so much," I fussed.

"This one's more for me," he said, watching my face closely as I opened it. "What do you think?" he asked.

"We can have lots of fun with the contents of this package." I raised one eyebrow.

"Let's see if you're right," he said, clearing the bed.

~.~.~.~.~

It felt like my eyes had just closed when loud banging woke us up.

"What in the hell?" Holden asked, throwing on a pair of sweatpants. Putting on my robe, I watched as he took his pistol from the nightstand. "Stay here!"

I nodded, but moved closer to the door to hear what was going on. Very few people knew where Holden lived. Who could be at the door?

"It's okay, Em, it's Bert," Holden yelled up the stairs and I was out of the room before Holden could make it to answer the door.

"What's wrong? Is it Kimberly?" I asked in a panic, taking the stairs two at a time.

"No, Kimberly's fine," an exhausted-looking Bert assured us. "I wish I didn't have to do this, but I'm here on official business. I know that technically, I'm supposed to handle things, but there was no other choice in the matter," Bert said, rubbing the back of his neck.

"What is it?" Holden asked.

"We should sit, okay?" Bert suggested.

"Sure, come on in," Holden said.

"Would you like some coffee? I can put on a pot while you two talk," I offered.

"No thanks. You should be here, too," Bert said.

"Bert, you're scaring me," I said, sitting next to Holden.

"You know how you tend to wake up early when you've got kids? Well, Connie was feeding Kimberly in the den around six o'clock this morning. The sun was coming up, so I thought it would be a good time to take Andre fishing. I figured you wouldn't mind if I used the boat, so I went out to the shed to make sure Andre's lifejacket was there before waking him," Bert said.

"Skip ahead to the part that warranted your coming out here and practically beating down my door," Holden insisted. Bert exhaled a long sigh.

"I found two bodies inside the boat shed," Bert said, resting his forehead on his fingers.

"Oh, no! Here we go again," I cried, trying to fight back the tears. I looked at Holden with desperate eyes.

"Give us a few minutes to dress and we'll meet you at Greenleaf," Holden said, taking my hand and leading me upstairs. "Is anyone else from the department out there? Were you able to identify the bodies?" Holden called over the balcony.

"No, I came straight over to get you before calling in the rest, and yes, I know who they are," Bert answered solemnly. "We all know who they are."

<u>The Green Bayou Series</u>

Going Home: A Green Bayou Novel Book One

Awakenings: A Green Bayou Novel Book Two

Déjà Vu: A Green Bayou Novel Book Three

Unforeseen: A Green Bayou Novel Book Four

ABOUT THE AUTHOR

Rhonda Dennis lives in South Louisiana with her husband, Doyle and her son, Sean. She is currently working on the next book in the Green Bayou series. Rhonda would love to hear from you. Visit her website for more information.
www.rhondadennis.net

Or write to her at:

Rhonda Dennis
P.O. Box 2148
Patterson, LA 70392

To like me, follow me, or leave a review:

Facebook: The Green Bayou Novels
Twitter: @Greenbayoubooks
Goodreads Author
WordPress Blog: Green Bayou Novels

Made in the USA
San Bernardino, CA
12 April 2014